THE KNIFE
BEFORE
CHRISTMAS

TITLES BY KATE CARLISLE

BIBLIOPHILE MYSTERIES

FIXER-UPPER MYSTERIES

THE KNIFE
BEFORE
CHRISTMAS

A Fixer-Upper Mystery

Kate Carlisle

BERKLEY PRIME CRIME

NEW YORK

BERKLEY PRIME CRIME
Published by Berkley
An imprint of Penguin Random House LLC
penguinrandomhouse.com

Copyright © 2024 by Kathleen Beaver
Penguin Random House values and supports copyright. Copyright fuels creativity,
encourages diverse voices, promotes free speech, and creates a vibrant culture.
Thank you for buying an authorized edition of this book and for complying with copyright
laws by not reproducing, scanning, or distributing any part of it in any form without
permission. You are supporting writers and allowing Penguin Random House to continue
to publish books for every reader. Please note that no part of this book may be used or
reproduced in any manner for the purpose of training artificial intelligence technologies
or systems.

BERKLEY and the BERKLEY & B colophon are registered trademarks and BERKLEY
PRIME CRIME is a trademark of Penguin Random House LLC.

Library of Congress Cataloging-in-Publication Data

Names: Carlisle, Kate, 1951- author.
Title: The knife before Christmas / Kate Carlisle.
Description: New York : Berkley Prime Crime, 2024. | Series: A Fixer-Upper Mystery
Identifiers: LCCN 2024014166 (print) | LCCN 2024014167 (ebook) |
ISBN 9780593637647 (hardcover) | ISBN 9780593637654 (ebook)
Subjects: LCSH: Christmas stories. | LCGFT: Detective and mystery fiction. | Novels.
Classification: LCC PS3603.A7527 K65 2024 (print) |
LCC PS3603.A7527 (ebook) | DDC 813/.6—dc23/eng/20240329
LC record available at https://lccn.loc.gov/2024014166
LC ebook record available at https://lccn.loc.gov/2024014167

Printed in the United States of America
1st Printing

This book is gratefully dedicated to Shirley Ann Johnson.
Thank you for allowing yourself to play such a significant
role in the story for a very good cause. I appreciate your
kindness, your generosity, and your fun-loving
spirit. Merry Christmas!

THE KNIFE
BEFORE
CHRISTMAS

Chapter One

It was the day after Thanksgiving in my hometown of Lighthouse Cove, California, which meant that suddenly, without any warning, the Christmas season was upon us. It happened the same way every year, so why did I never see it coming? All I knew was that one day we were baking pumpkin pies and discussing the best turkey stuffing recipes, and the next day we were struggling over Christmas gifts and draping our homes in a few gazillion strings of twinkle lights.

Massive blow-up balloon characters were the trend this year. On my street alone, there were at least two dozen huge cartoon faces staring down at me from my neighbors' houses each evening. They reminded me of all those floating creatures in the annual Macy's parade. Unlike Macy's, however, the giant balloon faces on my block were deflated each morning, turning my little neighborhood into something resembling a Salvador Dalí painting. Melting bodies and stretched-out faces were draped across the lawns. It was weird. But 'tis the season.

Despite the oddly surrealistic sight, I whistled a happy tune as I strolled down the street with Robbie, my adorable West Highland terrier. Robbie wore a handsome plaid winter coat, and I wore a big silly smile. I waved hello to my neighbors and managed to chuckle at the sight of their creepy dancing candy canes and awkward singing snowmen. Not even the sight of those withered balloon creatures could snap me out of my cheerful mood. I was riding high.

It hadn't always been this way for me and Christmas. There had been a few seasons when I had resembled Scrooge in all the worst ways. But this year, everything was wonderful. I was in love, engaged to be married to MacKintyre Sullivan, my extremely handsome and very talented writer fiancé. My name is Shannon Hammer, and I'm a building contractor here in Lighthouse Cove, specializing in Victorian architecture. My world was sunny and life was good. The air was filled with the spicy scents of balsam fir and blue spruce, two of our local favorites when it came to Christmas trees.

I wasn't the only one whistling a perky tune in welcoming the season. In Lighthouse Cove, Christmas was everyone's favorite holiday. The shops along Main Street and around the town plaza were gaily decorated, and shoppers were out in force, snatching up all the best holiday deals they could find. The mailman and the various independent shipping services were delivering packages three and four times a day to all the folks who had turned to shopping by mail. My girlfriends were gleefully pulling out their ugliest Christmas sweaters to wear to all the holiday parties. The joyful feeling was contagious.

And as I always advised anyone lucky enough to find themselves in Lighthouse Cove at this time of year, there was no better place to celebrate the season than at the majestic Cliffs Hotel.

The Cliffs Hotel was a Victorian mansion perched along the eastern edge of the rugged Alisal Cliffs overlooking the Cove and the Pacific Ocean beyond. The house was originally four identical mansions constructed by the father of four children. The Cliffs had been beautifully restored, thanks in part to my father and his talented construction crew, who had first taken on the renovation and were steadfast in their efforts to keep the old place in exquisite condition.

There were five stories, and each was accented by classic Victorian turrets and towers and balconies and gorgeous wraparound verandas. There were twenty-two chimneys of every conceivable shape and size, lending the roofline an eccentric charm, which culminated in the delightful widow's walk that topped the south wing.

The surrounding grounds consisted of twenty semi-wooded acres, which offered every possible activity and sport a person could ask for. There were hiking trails and rock climbing for the serious athletes, plus kayaking and stand-up paddleboards for water sport enthusiasts who didn't mind how cold the Cove could get this time of year.

To counter all the sports madness that some visitors craved, the Garrisons had recently renovated their gorgeous luxury spa, adding an indoor pool and a sauna that was serenity and elegance personified.

There were tennis courts, a putting green, and even a pickleball court just a short walk from the hotel steps.

At the opposite end of the property was a half acre devoted to all things kid-friendly, including swings and slides and monkey bars and tunnels and climbing walls. Much of this area was covered in rubber playground tiles that protected the young ones from hurting themselves in case of a fall. There was miniature golf and a batting cage, plus mini go-karts—with adult supervision, of course—and every other kind of fun thing a kid could want to do while staying at the hotel. There was also a clubhouse where indoor activities were offered to the kids, mainly arts and crafts and puzzles and board games for all ages. There were plenty of grown-ups who liked to hang out in the kids' zone, too.

If parents wanted a few hours of kid-free time, the Cliffs provided a staff of bonded loving nannies and childcare professionals, babysitters and supervisors to take care of their little ones. And in case one didn't want to trek all the way across the acreage to check up on the kids, last year the Cliffs had purchased an actual miniature railroad train with three comfy passenger cars and a locomotive that circled the grounds, stopping to pick up guests and deliver them anywhere on the grounds they wanted to go.

Bill and Lilian Garrison were the third generation of Garrisons to own the hotel, and everyone in town knew and loved them. Not only because they were lovable and fun, but also because they were constantly seeking out new and interesting ways to bring Christmas into everyone's lives, both visitors and locals alike. The train had been last year's big surprise, and everyone had fallen in love with it. I knew some folks who had checked into the hotel precisely to take advantage of the train rides. Who didn't want a chance to blow that whistle?

Bill and Lilian had been my parents' best friends before my mother died. After that, my dad remained their close friend and Lilian became a surrogate mother to me and my sister, Chloe. We loved them to pieces.

My dad and his construction crew had always been the Garrisons' go-to company for building and refurbishing the property. Dad's crew had essentially worked to bring the structure into the twenty-first century, and by the time I took over the company, the Cliffs Hotel was considered a world-class property on the level of the Ritz or the Four Seasons.

But more than anything else, the Cliffs Hotel was famous for celebrating Christmas in a big way. It consistently blew the competition out of the water, and this year was no exception. Last year they had bought a train, a real one, for goodness' sake.

This year, Bill had come to me in February with an idea of building an authentic Victorian carnival with at least ten or twelve different booths, each featuring a classic carnival game of chance or skill. Naturally, there would be lots of fun prizes to win, which was basically what a carnival was all about.

"We'll call it the Fun Zone," Bill said to me. "I've picked out a spot well away from the hotel itself and closer to the children's park."

And with that in mind, we began to strategize. First, my team spent several weeks brainstorming with Bill on the best design for the carnival booths. He wanted "big." He wanted "flashy." And he wanted "fun." He wanted something everyone in town would be able to see from a mile away.

We would work on the tent itself later, but we started by grading the land in order to have a flat, solid base and enough drainage outlets to keep the surface dry and smooth. We covered this with several layers of gravel and sand, and then my crew and I poured a six-inch-thick circular slab, eighty feet in diameter, that would be reinforced with both rebar and wire mesh. According to my engineers, this slab would withstand the weight of several thousand pounds' worth of carnival booths, along with the weight of hundreds of adults and children traipsing through the carnival site every night for an entire month.

Once the huge circular cement base was poured, we gave it several weeks to harden. We arranged for road access and plenty of acreage left over to mark out a parking lot.

"I picture a circus tent big enough to be seen from anywhere in town," Bill had said.

I sketched a classic circus tent divided and scooped in twelve sections. It would come to a peak in the center, and it would be covered in Christmas lights.

"It's pretty basic," I explained.

"I'm getting old-fashioned carnival vibes," Lilian said, smiling brilliantly. "I love it. We'll have concession stands scattered here and there, selling popcorn and candy apples. And hot cider."

"Good thinking, Lil," Bill said.

"I'm just loving this whole nostalgia vibe."

"Me too, babe." And that was how it usually went. If it was good enough for Lilian, it was good enough for Bill, who told us to get to work.

As work began on the carnival itself, I happened to run into an old friend, Steve Shore, and asked him to come over to meet Lilian and Bill. I wasn't sure if the Garrisons had considered the Santa Claus element, but since it was Christmas, I was pretty sure they would be excited to include the jolliest Santa Claus of them all. Steve was a member of the Santa Claus Brigade and would definitely have something in common with Lilian and Bill, who were complete Christmas fanatics.

I'd met the entire brigade a few Christmases ago when my construction team and I refurbished a beautiful old mansion, turning it into small apartments for a number of families in need of housing. I was still so proud of that project, even though the grand opening had been marred by murder.

Anyway, I figured since Lilian and Bill were crazy about Christmas, they might enjoy meeting a Santa Claus or two. It was sure to be a match made in holiday heaven.

Now that we had the basic idea for this year's Christmas surprise extravaganza, I shared with Bill Garrison a few conceptual details I'd studied last year when my team and I started construction on Homefront, the veterans' village of tiny homes. At that time I had been looking into dozens of different concepts in modular homes and prefab structures in hopes of giving each tiny home some different space options. Some of the ideas were elaborate, but some were as simple as installing a Murphy bed that could be pulled out and used for sleeping at night and folded up in the morning to provide extra space for an office or a small in-home studio.

I had studied collapsible spaces, folding rooms, sliding walls, car elevators, and lots of other Jet Age house stuff that I found exciting. But we didn't end up using any of those plans for the tiny homes, opting instead to keep things simple. Most of the vets we worked with just wanted a comfortable small space in which to live and hopefully thrive.

But now that we were designing the carnival, it was time to revisit some of those wild ideas. My plan was to build the individual carnival booths with walls that could be folded up accordion-style and layered one on top of the other, then rolled away on special carts to be stored within a space we'd built for that purpose alongside one of the outbuildings. Protected from the elements, the panels would remain tucked away until next year, when we would bring them out again.

I started to explain my ideas to Bill, but he just laughed and held up his hands to stop me. "I love your ideas, but you'd better figure out how to include my newest purchase."

"What are you talking about?" I asked nervously.

Bill never did anything halfway and this was no exception. He pulled out a colorful brochure of the gorgeous antique carousel that was being delivered the following week.

"A carousel?" I said, feeling gobsmacked and not quite believing he had gone out and purchased this adorable carousel.

"It's a beauty," he said. "And we'll have it forever."

I could tell from the pictures in the brochure that the carousel animals were beautifully hand-painted and the choices were inventive. Among the lions and tigers and bears were a dolphin, a dinosaur, an eagle, a gorilla, and a chariot built for two. Also built into the carousel was an ornate calliope that played the most perfect old-fashioned organ music.

"It's small," he explained. "Only twenty-two feet across, but that allows for fourteen pairs of animals. It'll fit right into one half of our design."

It took me some time to calculate just how that would work out, but Bill was right. The carousel, which was indeed a mere twenty-two feet across, would be perfect for our small-town carnival.

The carousel itself would be surrounded by a guardrail and a wide walkway that would open up to all the carnival games. And every inch of what we were calling the Fun Zone would fit under the old-fashioned red-and-white-striped big top, with its scalloped fringe along the high edges.

Strings of Christmas lights would run from the top center down to the edges of the big top. Banners and flags would wave in the wind, and the entire effect would be big, colorful, and fun.

As soon as we got the okay from Bill, my crew and I began to build the game booths. I started with a lightweight wood that we hinged together to create the walls and ceiling of each booth, giving each an old-timey, bandbox effect.

On both sides of each booth, I had attached heavy-duty sailcloth banners that had been silk-screened with pictures of the particular game being played in that booth. The vintage style of the silk screens was charming and fun. I attached the banners to a steel plate using brass grommets spaced about six inches apart. The overall effect was very appealing, according to Lilian and everyone who saw them, and I was proud that my crew made it work so well.

My guys had always referred to me as the Drywall Queen, but these days they'd switched it up to Grommet Girl. It was a silly name and made me chuckle, but the moniker also had a Justice League vibe that I thought was pretty cool. And honestly? I totally loved using grommets. Who didn't?

When we finally unveiled the entire circular complex of booths with their colorful side banners and their vibrant flags flying high and their wonderful games on display, Bill and Lilian were blown away, which made it a really good day for me and my crew.

"The games are perfect because they're simple," Lilian declared. "I remember playing some of them when I was girl. But the design of each of the booths is ingenious, and I know everyone's going to love it."

Early on, we had brainstormed the games and given them old-fashioned names such as Ball-in-a-Bucket, Roly-Poly, Hoopla,

Spray-n-Race, Duck Pond, Put a Ring on It, Walk the Plank, and Blow-Up Bobby.

And finally, since Bill always thought of everything, a full acre had been set aside for temporary parking.

"That should fit about two hundred and forty-some cars," Bill estimated.

I just hoped it would be big enough to hold the crowd that I imagined might start to show up every night of the holiday season.

"Don't worry, Shannon," he said with a big grin. "We can only let in so many cars, and if someone gets turned away one night, we'll give them a couple of game tickets and ask them to come back the next night."

Bill had a much more positive outlook and admittedly more experience with these things than I did.

To add to the craziness, we couldn't forget that besides the folks showing up for the games and carousel rides, there were the hotel guests who used a completely separate parking section closer to the hotel and restaurant. They would be directed to the parking lot located on the other side of the hotel from the carnival area. Luckily, there were directional signs everywhere, and happily, the Garrisons had a dozen more acres to use in case they ran out of space in those two parking lots.

Bill and Lilian had also hired the entire fourth grade class of Lighthouse Cove Grammar School to play elves. They bought a few dozen adorable elf costumes for the kids to wear and gave several training sessions to basically teach them how to be an elf, which included cheering on the players and giving away prizes. I had watched some of the training sessions and had to laugh. The little elf kids were so cute. The entire event was going to be a delight.

The idea of hiring the elves had been Lilian's. Then Bill had called in his lawyers to work out all the paperwork and documentation that came with hiring children. Each kid and their parent were asked to sign contracts and take some safety training so that by the time the kids began their first night of fun, they would all be trained and ready to go. And so would their parents.

It was a family affair in every possible way.

Bill had also hired a whole team of "elf wranglers" to help out. These were all adults who were willing to dress up as elves and actually operate the games. It was remarkable to realize how many adults were excited to dress up as elves. They would be handling the money and such, while the job of the little elves was to share their natural exuberance over the games and the prizes with the rest of the crowd. They would help make it fun for everyone. I couldn't wait to see it all come together two nights from now.

And if I'd thought I would be able to relax once the Christmas holidays were over, I was sorely mistaken. Not that I minded too much, though, because Lilian and Bill had announced a massive new Cliffs Hotel project for my crew and me. They had finally decided to restore and remodel all four floors of the unfinished north wing, including its imposing tower and the dark, dank cellar where, rumor had it, Bill's great-grandfather had died under mysterious circumstances. I couldn't wait to get started on that exciting new job, but I had to get through the Christmas season first.

Thanks to Lilian's generosity, it had become my habit each morning to grab a cup of coffee and a donut from the Garrisons' kitchen and sit out on the steps, where I would make notes and go over my jobs for the day. I was usually joined by a couple of my crew members, who would occasionally bring up an issue or some information connected to an aspect of that day's work. Once in a while, we would slip into a quick gossip session about one of the Garrison kids or their spouses. I tried to keep that to a minimum, mainly because this was their house! But sometimes it couldn't be helped. After all, my sister, Chloe, and I and most of the guys on my crew had gone to school with all of the Garrison kids. It was just one of the many joys of living in a small town.

Other than a few notable exceptions, I considered most of them to be good friends. There was Logan, the oldest of the Garrison kids, who was married to Randi. Then there was Arabella, who preferred to be called by her full name Arabella, *not* Bella. She was married to Franco. The third Garrison child was Stephanie, who was Chloe's best friend. I considered Stephanie the most well adjusted and friendly. She was married to Craig, who was the manager of the hotel's bar.

Chloe and I had both dated Logan Garrison briefly during our teenage years, and back in the day, we'd attended countless slumber parties with Arabella and Stephanie.

All of the Garrison kids and their spouses lived and worked at the hotel in some capacity or other—except for Logan, the oldest son. He had been trained to take over the management of the hotel but decided early on that he wanted to join the navy and serve his country. His parents and his wife, Randi, were nervous about letting him go, but they couldn't exactly refuse him. Instead, they gave him their blessing and prayed for his safe return.

While Logan was out of town and overseas, Randi continued to work for the hotel, starting out in the restaurant kitchen and then moving over to the hotel bar as a cocktail waitress. Randi took full advantage of Logan's absence by convincing his parents that they would all benefit from her taking expensive classes and seminars to improve her knowledge of her chosen field, namely fine wines and champagnes. She did this mainly to improve her own résumé, but I had to wonder if she was biding her time before going out on her own. As long as she remained married to Logan and worked at the Cliffs, she received yearly promotions and generous bonuses and was on her way to becoming a master sommelier, a position that would guarantee an excellent salary if she ever decided to leave Logan.

Everybody loved Logan, but the same couldn't be said of Randi. She was overbearing and obnoxious, and yet she usually got away with her rotten attitude for a couple of reasons. First, because she was drop-dead gorgeous with her statuesque figure, long, thick black hair, and deep blue eyes. And second, because people assumed that she would tell Logan if anyone dared to criticize her. But then, they didn't know Logan.

Stephanie and Arabella were beautiful, too, and for that matter, so was their mother, Lilian. So why did Randi have to be so high and mighty all the time? Maybe she was secretly jealous of the other women. I couldn't figure it out, but I had long ago decided that Randi was simply one of those people who always went to the dark side, always assumed the worst, and always attacked first. Much like my archenemy, Whitney Reid Gallagher.

And that brought up another reason for me to dislike Randi, as if I needed more. Randi was a close friend of Whitney's. Didn't it just figure? The fact was, the two women didn't actually hang out together very often, and I had a theory about that. I thought it might be because they were both so negative that when they got together, they canceled each other out. They could only handle each other in small amounts. It probably didn't make much sense, but that was my theory and I was sticking to it.

Logan made it home to visit his family as often as possible, but it was difficult. Anytime he did come home, his parents and siblings would give him a hero's welcome, hoping against hope that this time he would stay for good. But it didn't happen. The navy still required his presence, and after a week or two of visiting the family, Logan would be shipped off to another destination.

With Logan away, Arabella was offered his management position, but she didn't want it. Too much responsibility, she protested, so Stephanie, Arabella's younger sister, was given the management job, and she excelled at it. Stephanie had a serious drive to succeed but managed to be friendly and normal. To this day, she remains Chloe's best friend. Stephanie was married to another childhood acquaintance, Craig Taylor, who was the manager of the popular hotel bar.

Meanwhile, Arabella had not only turned down the opportunity to work in management but had also fought against working as the head of Housekeeping, mainly because, ugh, housekeeping.

Bill and Lilian had finally acquiesced to Arabella's demands and put her in charge of the new day spa. They reluctantly agreed that this position suited her personality so much more, probably because Arabella enjoyed being pampered more than anything else. We all knew she much preferred being associated with luxury rather than drudgery.

I'd known Arabella since kindergarten, and we'd been close friends until high school, when she traded me in for her new best friend, Whitney Reid Gallagher, the world's most insufferable conniving snob.

Arabella had fallen in love with the delicious Franco Mateo, the

Cliffs' executive chef. Franco was a culinary genius, and on his way to winning his first Michelin star in the next year or so. He was a sweetheart and ridiculously handsome as well. He and Arabella made a gorgeous couple, and rumor had it that they were often seen sneaking off together for a little romance. And who could blame them? They were both so pretty.

Arabella had made a brilliant decision when it came to choosing her husband. But choosing her best friend Whitney? Not so smart. She didn't seem very happy these days, and I blamed Whitney, who was truly a dark cloud in my life. I occasionally wondered what Franco thought of Whitney, but it seemed that he didn't care one way or the other about her. His main passions in life were Arabella and cooking, and that made him even that much more attractive as far as I was concerned.

I supposed there were enough Garrison names and faces to be confusing, but I had known these people forever and didn't have a problem remembering who was who.

I was putting the finishing touches on one of the carnival game booths when I looked up and saw Bill Garrison hurrying down the front steps of the hotel and jogging over to the carnival ring.

He was a tall, handsome man in his sixties and he was still one of my dad's best friends. Dad was retired now, and that was why Bill was always hiring me and my crew to do any work around the hotel. I appreciated it, but I knew that, despite his friendship with Dad, he wouldn't have hired us if we weren't the best in the business.

Now Bill stared at the last booth I was working on and grinned. "Who would've thought to use grommets?"

"Grommets are my thing," I admitted with a smile. "What do you think?"

"It looks great, Shannon."

"Thanks, Bill."

His eyes narrowed as he took in the larger picture of the big top and the carnival games and the carousel. "So, are we going to pull this one off?"

I had to chuckle. "Every year you come up with some fantastic idea, Bill, and you always pull it off. This year is going to be great."

He winked, something he did on a regular basis. It was part of his charm. "You know me, Shannon. I do it for the kids."

I smiled. "Lots of lucky kids in this town."

"I'd say we're all pretty lucky."

"I'd have to agree."

He glanced around again and suddenly looked uneasy. I wondered what he really wanted to say to me, and finally he asked, "Have you seen Arabella out here?"

"I haven't seen her at all today."

He frowned. "I thought I saw her come out here." He blew out a breath. "Well, if you see her, tell her I need to talk to her."

"Of course."

"Thanks, kiddo." He walked away briskly, heading toward the pool and gardens.

It was no secret to anyone that Arabella avoided me at all costs, so Bill's reluctance to ask me about his daughter was understandable. I hated to think that I was the one who made him uncomfortable, but that was on Arabella. And Whitney. Not me.

A few minutes later, my foreman, Wade Chambers, approached and whispered, "Bella alert."

I rolled my eyes, praying that no one had heard him. Since he'd known me forever, he was aware of the age-old situation with me and Arabella. But it was nice that he looked out for me.

"Don't freak out," Wade said.

"I don't freak out." I gave him a look that might've fried a lesser man's circuits. "I've been so over these stupid schoolgirl mind games for years, but Arabella and Whitney are still playing them."

"I know. Sorry about that."

"Not your fault. But thanks for the alert."

Wade gave a quick nod, then walked away as if we'd never spoken. He was nothing if not subtle. I returned to the grommets for one last check of the banners and the booths. They were perfect. I tried to relax, but for some reason, Wade's words must've fried a few of my own circuits, because I realized I was actually a bit nervous. Maybe because Bill had seemed so antsy just now. What was going on around here?

I tried to remind myself that this was my happy place. Grommets, remember? Grommet Girl. Nobody did it better. "You go, Grommet Girl," I whispered, then had to chuckle at my pitiful little pep talk.

I glanced around, expecting to see Arabella, but she hadn't come out this way. I wondered about Wade's "Bella alert," then shook my head, knowing I would stand here and wait until she showed up, only because Bill had asked me to give her a message.

And as much as I loved Bill Garrison, it really bugged me that he'd asked me to watch for Arabella. I knew that as soon as I found her and gave her the message, she wouldn't thank me. I'd still be an outcast in her eyes. She only did it because she thought Whitney would approve. And that was Whitney's fault. Not for the first time, I wondered what it would take to get her out of my life forever.

Chapter Two

Just as I was about to give up and leave for lunch, I heard a *tip-tapping* sound on the steps and looked up to see Arabella standing on the bottom of the front stairs. She was impeccably dressed in a truly darling red-and-white checkered suit with a peplum jacket that emphasized her tiny waist and flounced flirtatiously over a short skirt and bright red heels.

A matching red-and-white checkered hairband held her thick blond hair back from her face. She was impossibly cute, and I wanted to hate her for it, but I couldn't. Mostly I just tried not to grimace as I anticipated her reaction to me.

She noticed me noticing her and muttered to herself. I maintained eye contact and she immediately looked away, clearly wishing she could don an invisibility cloak so I wouldn't see her. But no such luck.

I managed a pleasant tone. "Hi, Arabella. Great outfit."

She blinked. "Oh, uh, have you seen my father?"

"Yeah. He just walked by a few minutes ago and said he was looking for you. He was headed toward the pools."

Her shoulders slumped. "Oh hell." She started to walk in that direction and I almost let her go. But I couldn't do it because I was a nice person, darn it.

"Arabella, wait," I said. "The grass is damp from yesterday's rain, so you'll ruin your shoes if you walk through there. I'll call him."

She made a grunt of annoyance, probably because I was offering to help her.

I ignored her and pulled out my cell phone. When Sean answered, I asked, "Do you see Bill out there?"

"Yeah," Sean said. "He's out by the putting green talking to Oliver."

Oliver was a close friend of Logan's who'd gone to school with all of us. He was a true overachiever, armed with a master's degree in horticulture and urban forestry, as well as a bachelor's degree in enology. With his small team of gardeners and tree trimmers, Oliver managed all the vegetation on all the grounds, including the apple orchard, three acres of grapevines, the forests that surrounded the property, and the shrubbery that lined the steps leading down to the beach below. He specialized in sustainable gardening, green waste reduction, pest management, and water conservation. He was also in charge of the indoor and outdoor pools and the gardens surrounding those pools. And besides all of those amazing qualities, he was a gorgeous hunk of a man, as Chloe would say. Tall and tan, with bright green eyes and brown hair that was bleached and streaked blond from his time working in the sun.

Thinking of hunky Oliver, I almost forgot what I wanted to ask Sean. "Could you tell Bill that Arabella is waiting out here for him? If she walks over to the pool she'll wreck her shoes."

"I'll go get him," Sean said.

"Thanks, Sean."

He hung up and I looked at Arabella. "Your dad will be right here."

She folded her arms tightly across her chest. God forbid she would actually say, "Thank you," but no. Instead she had to simply stand there, obviously feeling awkward. I was okay with that.

A minute later her father came jogging around the corner. "Hey, Belle."

"Daddy." Arabella slipped her arm through her father's and deliberately pulled him away and over toward the hotel steps.

Bill turned around and said, "Thanks, Shannon."

"No problem, Bill."

As they walked away, I just shook my head and breathed deeply. Why did she have to be such a twit? "Let it go, Shannon," I muttered, and packed up my toolbox.

Wade rushed over to see me. "Everything okay?"

"Couldn't be better."

He barked out a laugh. "Yeah, right. You look totally chill."

"I am totally chill," I insisted, then sighed, rubbing my arms from the actual *chill* I'd felt from Arabella. "It never ends. She's so ridiculous."

"Yes, she is." He brushed his dark hair back from his forehead. "And she's been that way since You-Know-Who moved to town."

I grinned at his unnamed reference to Whitney Reid Gallagher. "Appreciate you not saying her name."

He rubbed his arms. "I try never to do anything that might summon her evil spirit."

I had to laugh. "Good one, Wade." Like so many other friends in town, Wade and I had known each other since first grade. He knew the whole ugly history of me and Tommy and Whitney and Arabella and all the psychodrama that had encircled us back then—and still did, apparently.

Now he turned his attention to the banners I'd been working on. "Hey, these look really great."

"Thanks."

He chuckled. "Grommets, huh? Your new raison d'être?"

I shrugged. "Gotta be good at something."

"Well, you're good at everything. I know you're a particular fan of drywall. And now grommets. What next?"

I laughed. "There's always the nail gun."

"Seems to me you mastered that a few years ago."

"I still can't spell my name in nails yet."

"It does take practice," he mused.

"Kind of a waste of nails, though."

"Some things are worth the price," he said, and chuckled as he walked away.

It was a good sound, and it reminded me that life was good. I was *happy*. I had friends. I had love. And Christmas was going to be awesome this year.

On the other hand, it was pretty obvious that Arabella was miserable. She shouldn't have been. She was beautiful and had an awesome family and was married to an absolute dreamboat of a guy. A guy who cooked! But she was emotionally tied to Whitney, and whether she could admit it or not, that had to be depressing.

———

That afternoon I took a break and stood on the veranda staring out at the beach and the ocean beyond. Taking a deep breath, I felt a wave of something like joy. It was so beautiful here. I loved working for Bill and Lilian and most of the family.

"Hello!"

I glanced over and saw my bestie, Jane Hennessey, parking her car, then dashing through the porte cochere and up the steps to the wide veranda where I stood waiting. "Jane! What're you doing here?"

"I got the reservations!" She grabbed me in a big hug. "I'm so psyched!"

"That's fantastic!" I hugged her back. "We're going to have so much fun."

She was referring to another big holiday treat that the Garrison family was responsible for. More than forty years ago, Bill's father had established our very own local Christmas tradition of serving an elegant eight-course dinner in their beautiful hotel dining room every evening from the Monday after Thanksgiving until two days before Christmas Eve. Along with wonderful food, there was entertainment, plenty of music and singing, and even some comedy. And now with Franco in charge of the restaurant and its menu, guests could look forward to an absolutely flawless meal. Without question, it was the most desired reservation in town.

But in order to get that reservation, you had to call on a specific day at a particular time to reserve a table. There were years when the reservations for the entire month were gone by noon. This year, it was Jane's turn to call and reserve a table for our closest friends and boyfriends and husbands. That meant sitting on hold until a phone line opened up and then booking a table for twelve.

"We'll have a blast," Jane said.

"Of course we will. But it's going to be very fancy, so we can't be too rowdy."

She laughed. "Then let's try to get everyone together for pizza and wine sometime after that so we can all get that rowdiness out of our systems."

"You can all bring your rowdiness to my house," I offered.

"Perfect. I'll spread the word."

"Sounds like we're going to eat our way through the entire holiday season."

"You say that like it's a bad thing," Jane said, laughing.

"And by the way, Mac and I have reservations at the Gables for New Year's Eve."

"I know." Her eyes twinkled. "It's going to be very romantic."

The Gables was Jane's beautiful small hotel on a hilltop nearby the old lighthouse north of town. It was located in the recently renovated Gables complex, once known more specifically as the Northern California Asylum for the Insane. Jane had a personal attachment to the asylum, so my crew had worked diligently on the rehab for months. Now it was absolutely lovely, all clean and renovated, with remarkably high ceilings, floor-to-ceiling picture windows, and rounded corners at every edge. Jane promised to make this dining experience unlike anything else, and since this would be the first Christmas season for the Gables, it was sure to be very special.

"Did you just come by to tell me you got the reservation?"

"Of course." She grinned. "It's what we've been waiting for all year."

"I'm excited to hear the news, but somehow I don't believe you'd come all this way over here just for that."

She winked at me. "Well, maybe I also came by to talk to Lilian. She and I have been coming up with ideas for some interactive restaurant events in the New Year."

"That sounds like fun for you."

"I think it'll be great. Lilian is so savvy when it comes to these kinds of innovative ideas."

"She is amazing. But then, so are you."

We both turned at the sound of footsteps and watched Lilian approach. The woman looked like one of her daughters, slim, youthful, blond, and always so cheery and bright; it was hard to be grouchy around her.

"Shannon," Lilian said. "Just the girl I was looking for. And Jane! You're here already! How did I get so lucky?"

Lilian and Jane pressed their cheeks together in greeting.

"You're so sweet," Jane said. "I'm looking forward to hearing all your great ideas."

Lilian smiled. "Likewise. Together we'll come up with an absolutely brilliant event plan."

Then Lilian turned to me. "Now, Shannon, I know you're all tied up with our Christmas Carnival, but if you have any time this week to do a walk-through of the north cellar with me, I'll be able to show you some of those original doors and plasterwork I told you about. And did I mention the gargoyles? You might be interested in seeing them. They make a statement, for sure." She frowned. "I'm trying to think of someplace in the hotel to display them."

Jane laughed. "Shannon loves gargoyles."

"What I love is architectural salvaging," I said, giving Jane the side-eye. To be honest, gargoyles freaked me out and she knew it. But I wasn't going to mention that to Lilian.

Lilian smiled. "Architectural salvaging. That's the perfect term for what we're doing. And the north cellar is a veritable treasure hunt. The gargoyles are awesome. Plus, there's a stack of old tall doors that I would love to put to use somewhere, somehow."

"Tall doors, really?" I said.

"Yes. There was a part of the north wing that was used by Bill's great-grandfather, who was six foot five. After he died, they went through and removed all the doors, but no further construction was done on that part of the hotel, so they're still sitting in a stack down there. And I'm fascinated by them. Honestly, they must be good for something besides, you know, *doors*."

"Tables?" Jane suggested.

I thought for a moment. "Wall hangings? Frames?"

"Mirror backs?" Jane said.

"Ooh, what about a porch swing?" I said.

"That is brilliant, Shannon," Lilian said. "See? You two are already coming up with fantastic ideas. And there are trunks filled with old clothing and all sorts of plaster moldings and, you know, cornices and corbels and wall panels." Her eyes widened. "It really is architectural salvaging, just as you said."

I grinned. "I can't wait." I was intrigued by the plaster pieces and all the other items Lilian had mentioned, too. "Once the carnival starts, I'll trade off evenings with my guys, just to make sure everything's operating well. But during the day, I'm all yours."

"Oh, that's super." Then she laughed self-deprecatingly. "Not sure why it matters since I'll probably be swamped myself from now until New Year's. We've got the carnival and the dinners each night." She sighed, then shook her head. "But still, I might be able to squeeze in some morning time, if you can meet me. And you know, you can always go down there by yourself. I'll give you an extra key."

"Since you've got so much going on, that's probably a better idea."

She nodded, then added a note of caution. "Actually, you might want to take Sean or Wade with you. It's dark and a little creepy down there."

At that comment, Jane met my gaze directly. And I had a sudden wave of shivers. Not that I would admit to needing a man to venture into a scary cellar with me, but it might be nice to ask Sean to tag along. Besides being a big strong guy, he had a good sense of design. "Um, I might do that."

"Great! If I can't go along with you, I'll make sure I get the key to you this afternoon."

"Thanks, Lilian," I said, then added, "See you later, Jane."

Jane turned and gave me a long look, and I knew it meant that we'd be talking very soon. Probably something to do with being careful walking through dark cellars after all the misadventures I'd gotten myself into over the past few years.

Jane followed Lilian up the elegant stairway to the double etched glass doors and disappeared into the hotel. I started to pack up my toolbox after the long day but stopped when I heard a ruckus at the far end of the veranda. I looked over and saw Randi Garrison, Logan's wife, stomping and swearing loudly and angrily.

"Did you see them?" she shouted.

"See who?" I asked, wondering if she was talking about Lilian and Jane.

"Those creepy thieving porch pirates." Outraged, she clenched her fists against her hips. Even angry and swearing, Randi was gorgeous, with long thick black hair and dark blue flashing eyes. She was tall and sexy and she knew it better than anyone, which explained why she was wearing sexy black leggings with knee-high boots and a tight cropped sweater that showed off her amazing abs.

"What are you talking about?" I had actually heard of the porch pirates phenomenon in the past, but I wasn't aware that we'd experienced anything like that right here in Lighthouse Cove. And I certainly hadn't seen any of them this afternoon.

"You haven't heard of them?" she said, gaping at me as if I had three heads. "Those thieves have been stealing things off every porch in town. And you've never heard of them?"

"I've heard of them, Randi. But I didn't know they'd struck in Lighthouse Cove."

She rolled her eyes and I wanted to punch her, but with her teeth bared, she looked like a furious she-wolf.

"Well, they're here," she snarled, "and they just tried to run off with my latest wine delivery."

"They stole your wine?"

"No. I managed to catch them. I saw them lugging a case of Napa Cabernet down the drive and when I went after them, they simply dropped the box and took off running. Too bad."

"So your wine is safe? Nothing broken? They didn't get away with anything?"

"It's all safe. But I still want them arrested."

"Did you open the case? Are you sure nothing was damaged?"

"Yes." She seemed just as angry that there was no damage. "But that doesn't matter. I want to catch those buggers. They're thieves!"

"Did you recognize any of them?"

Frustrated, she pulled her dark, lustrous hair away from her face and growled. "No, which tells me they're new in town."

"Why do you say that?"

"Because I know everyone in town! And I've never seen these evil little brats."

"Brats?" I said. "So, they're young?"

"How should I know? All I know is they're punks."

I took a deep breath and mentally rolled my eyes. I tried again. "How many were there?"

"At least four," Randi said. "Or maybe two. Or . . . I don't know. But they were fast and sneaky."

"Could you tell how old they were?"

"That doesn't matter, Shannon!"

"It matters because if they're little kids, the police might treat them differently. Either way, it would help to give the cops a description." I tried for a calm I didn't really feel because Randi was so annoying.

"Oh, whatever." She blew out a breath. "For all I know, they could be teenagers or younger. Or older. I couldn't tell! They wear scarves and baseball caps so you can't see their hair color or their faces." Her scowl turned to a pout. "They looked sort of skinny."

"You think they might be from the same family?"

"How should I know?" She pounded her fist on the porch railing. "I'm going to call the cops."

"Excellent idea. Call right away while you've still got the information and the picture of them in your head," I said. "Everyone's so distracted around Christmastime, it's easy for thieves to get away with this kind of thing."

"That's a good point." She grimaced as she looked around. "But, hey, do me a favor. Give Chief Jensen a call?"

"Me?" I was taken aback. "Why?"

"It would really save me some time. And besides, you know him better than anyone."

"That doesn't matter," I insisted. And I wasn't concerned about saving her time. "He's not going to want to hear from me because you're the one who saw the thieves. You can give him some kind of description. You know what they tried to take. The police need to hear it from you."

She muttered, "I don't have time for this."

I stared at her. "Well, you need to take the time. If you want to try and stop these guys, you've got to talk to the police."

"Why can't you do it?"

My eyes were going to start bleeding from her idiocy. "Because you're an eyewitness. I didn't even see them. And it was your inventory they tried to take. Just make the call."

She heaved out an impatient breath. "I'm too busy for this."

I was starting to wonder what her real problem was. "Do you want them caught or not?"

"What's that supposed to mean?"

"It means, call the police and report the incident. Nobody's going to do it for you, including me."

She rolled her eyes. "God, Whitney's right about you."

"Don't you even." Angrily I shook my finger at her. "Look, call the police or shut up. It's your choice." I started to walk away, but I could still see her and hear her.

"You're no help at all," she shouted.

I was going to keep walking but realized I had one more thing to say. "I'll be seeing Chief Jensen tonight, and I'll be sure to ask if he's tracked down the porch pirates yet."

"Who are you? My mother?"

"No, I'm someone who doesn't want thieves running wild in my town."

"It's my town, too," she grumbled.

I flashed a feral smile at her. "Then call the damn police."

"You used to be nicer."

"And you never were," I answered.

Just then, Oliver swung the double doors open and walked out. Randi turned and glowered. "Watch where you're walking, hoe-boy."

Hoe-boy? I frowned, trying to figure out that apparent slur. Was it a reference to the fact that Oliver worked in the gardens? With a hoe? Maybe.

Oliver scowled. "Keep your pointy-toed feet out of my vineyards, lady."

"*Your* vineyards? I'm family, dude. You're not. You'd better watch how you talk to me."

"Or what?" he said.

"Or you might just be out of a job."

Not that it mattered, but Oliver had more to do with the success and viability of the Cliffs than Randi ever would.

Oliver began to laugh and it was infectious. He was truly amused by her useless threat, although that laugh had surely earned the wrath of Randi, which was never a good thing.

Oliver jogged away to the parking lot.

Randi turned toward the steps, where an older woman was walking up to the door. "Oh, Shirley Ann. Wait up."

Shirley Ann Johnson turned and greeted Randi, then noticed me over Randi's shoulder and waved. "Yoo-hoo, Shannon!" she cried.

"Hi, Shirley Ann," I said and flashed her a big smile. She was one of the sweetest women I knew and the number one cocktail waitress at the Cliffs bar, where she'd been working for as long as I could re-member. My dad used to say that Shirley Ann never met a stranger, and I hadn't always known what that meant, but I did now. She was friendly to everyone. She was about fifty years old, petite with an amazing hourglass figure, fluffy blond hair, and big blue eyes. She wore tennis shoes and carried a gym bag that held her uniform and fancy shoes.

"How are you, sweetie?" she asked when I came closer.

"I'm doing well," I said. "How about you?"

"Couldn't be better."

She looked ready to chat, but Randi had reached the door and was frowning. "Shirley, you coming or not?"

"Oops, better get going." She winked at me, then rushed up the steps. "Oh, Randi, I want to hear all about these porch pirate people. Do they make a lot of money?"

As the two women walked through the door, Randi turned and gave me the evil eye.

"She's such a cow," I muttered to myself.

That evil eye was Randi's default look. But I worried about Shirley Ann. She was a sweetheart, but she looked tired this afternoon, and I recalled that she'd started picking up part-time work in House-keeping. Was she honestly interested in the porch pirates' scam, or was she just making conversation with Randi? That had to be it.

Although, I remembered a chat about a week ago when Shirley Ann had openly admitted that she needed more money. That was why she was picking up work in Housekeeping. "You know my buddy Joyce Brimley is head of Housekeeping, so she got me some part-time work. We're looking to retire in a year or so," she'd told me.

I'd met Joyce a few times and I liked her. She was lovely, with brown hair streaked blond that she wore in a perfect bob just below her ears.

"You're hardly old enough to think about retiring already," I'd said to Shirley Ann.

"But we've got a plan," she explained. "Going to head for Miami Beach, where we'll sit in the sun until our skin turns to leather, and then we'll nab ourselves a couple of old millionaires with weak hearts. Can't do that on a cocktail waitress's salary."

I had started to laugh until I realized that Shirley Ann was completely serious.

Now I sighed as I watched Randi and Shirley Ann walking down the wide hall with their heads together, chatting animatedly. Were they actually friends? I wondered. It made sense that they were, mainly because they worked together several evenings a week in the hotel bar.

But was Randi actually friends with anyone? She seemed to dislike everyone, but maybe that was just my view. Shirley Ann, on the other hand, was friendly to everyone. She was a fun lady and a kick in the pants, as my father would say. But that description didn't seem to fit into the judgmental world that Randi occupied.

I rolled my eyes inwardly. Apparently I, too, could be pretty judgmental when I set my mind to it.

I stopped dwelling on Randi and closed up my toolbox. It was much more fun to think about Shirley Ann and her bestie Joyce and their plans for Miami Beach. They would have the best time because they both had a great outlook on life.

Joyce had worked hard for years, starting as a housemaid and climbing all the way up to head of Housekeeping. A few years ago, she dated my father for a few months, and they seemed to get along really well. I wasn't sure why the relationship didn't work out, but they were still on friendly terms, so I was glad about that. Like her friend Shirley Ann, Joyce was warm and thoughtful and smart, and she loved talking about her job at the Cliffs. According to her, Lilian and Bill were the best bosses in the world. I had to agree with that assessment.

As head of Housekeeping, Joyce oversaw all the housekeepers and room attendants, as well as the Laundry department: linens, uniforms, tailors, and upholsterers.

It was a vitally important position, even though darling Arabella had turned her father down flat at the very idea that she work in Housekeeping.

Bill had once explained to me that the Housekeeping department and everyone who worked there were absolutely critical to the inner workings of the hotel, and if they failed to operate on all thrusters at all times, the reputation of the hotel could quickly be destroyed.

I assumed he'd given Arabella that same speech, but his words had little effect. She simply wanted nothing to do with Housekeeping, which was a lucky break for Joyce, as well as everyone who worked in Housekeeping under Joyce.

———————

At the end of the day, I picked up my toolbox and walked along the railing that graced the veranda all the way across the front of the property and around to the back stairs that led to the employee parking lot.

We had installed these elegant new balusters last summer once the old spindles began showing signs of deteriorating after twenty years of constant sunshine and ocean breezes.

The veranda stretched from across the front of the hotel all the way back to the private stairway leading to the owners' family kitchen. The veranda was wide enough to accommodate various groupings of patio furniture and colorful umbrellas, where guests could sit and watch the tide roll in and out of the nearby cove. The hotel bar offered cocktail service out here, and a lot of the guests took advantage of that amenity in warmer weather.

As I started down the stairs, I heard Lilian call from the family kitchen. "Oh, Shannon, I'm glad I caught you."

I turned and noticed that the only light coming into the room was from the sun about to dip beneath the horizon. "What's going on? Did you lose another light or two?"

"Or more," she said, standing at the door. "Can you check the circuit breaker switches? We also lost the dishwasher."

My heart sank. Even though the dishwasher was in the private family suite, it was never good to lose power to a dishwasher! But I thought it had been fixed. And just as we were gearing up for the Fun Zone with the carousel and the calliope, both of which would suck up a lot of electricity, the last thing I wanted to deal with to-night was a completely separate electrical problem.

"I'll be right in."

Hearing Lilian's voice reminded me that I hadn't been able to check out the north cellar today. Maybe tomorrow. I really wanted to get a look at those tall doors and all those plaster pieces. I wasn't quite as excited to uncover the gargoyles, but that would stay my little secret.

I left my toolbox out on the veranda but grabbed my flashlight and pushed the kitchen door open.

There was enough ambient light that some of the family members were sitting around the big farm table reading with a flashlight or looking at their phones or simply talking.

We had remodeled this kitchen a few years ago when the Garrison kids started getting married. All three of their spouses had decided to work at the hotel, so everyone was living here. The kitchen had definitely needed to be expanded. Now it had a lovely large area for family meals with a table that seated twelve, a ten-foot-long granite island with five comfy stools, and every state-of-the-art appliance that Lilian could've wished for.

"Hey, guys," I said, "do you know if the lights went out in any other part of the hotel?"

"No," Lilian said. "I've already talked to the front desk and the restaurant, and nobody has called to complain. I think it's just our little corner here."

"Okay. I'll check it out."

"Thanks, sweetie," Lilian said, squeezing my arm. It reminded me that, other than a few outliers, I really did appreciate these people.

"Thought you were on your way home," Stephanie said.

"Almost," I said with a grin. "Gotta check the breakers first." I walked over to the door that led downstairs to the wine cellar.

Stephanie jumped up. "I can check on the breakers, Shannon. You should go on home."

Of all the Garrisons, Stephanie had to be the sweetest. And yet she had the most amazing business acumen of all the kids. Not that the two qualities were mutually exclusive. It was just unusual, I thought. I was glad that she and my sister were still best friends after all these years, and I appreciated her offer to check the breakers herself. But since I was here anyway, and since I considered it part of my job, I decided I'd better check it out for myself.

"No worries, Steph. I've got it." I walked down the wide smooth steps of the private entrance that led to the family side of the wine cellar. Glancing around, I couldn't help but admire the elegant woodwork my crew and I had designed a few years ago.

This renovated cellar was such a beautiful room, much different from the description of the north cellar that Lilian had been talking about earlier. The north cellar was more like a cave beneath a part of the hotel that had never been modernized. According to my father, Bill Garrison's grandfather had died in one of those rooms, and I was pretty sure that was why the family had never been anxious to renovate it.

Until now.

I turned down the hall and found the small closet that held the main breaker box to the left of the staircase before you entered the main wine cellar space.

The Garrisons had converted from their old fuse boxes to a breaker system a few years ago when my dad and his crew were still working here. The hotel had fifty-two guest rooms at the time, along with six family suites, and trying to work off an old-fashioned fuse panel had been ridiculous, as well as dangerous.

I checked each of the circuit breakers until I found the one that had been tripped. I was right about the one kitchen appliance overloading that breaker and reminded myself to talk to the electrician as soon as possible to reroute a couple of the appliances to a different breaker.

For now, I reset the switch and closed the box. From upstairs, I heard a muffled cheer, so I assumed that reset had fixed it.

I started to climb the stairs back to the kitchen, taking it slowly, again checking out the wine cellar from every level, just to make sure things were in working order. Even though the wine cellar was used by the restaurant bartender, sommelier, and waiters, this staircase was considered private. No guests were allowed up here, only members of the Garrison family and any other authorized personnel.

Once in a while, one of the Garrisons would come down here to find a special bottle of wine or champagne for an event. And every so often, a few of them would sit down here and enjoy a glass of wine or an impromptu wine tasting. The family had their own entrance off the kitchen through the door I had used, while the hotel bar manager could access their wine cellar door around the corner from the main bar.

Thinking of wine, my mind flashed on that porch pirate incident earlier in the day, and I thought about Randi. She was so angry, and I knew it had something to do with the porch pirates and a case of wine she'd received. But somehow she'd redirected her anger from the thieves to me, simply because I'd insisted that she report the near-miss crime. Had I challenged her too directly? Even though the porch pirates hadn't managed to steal the wine, she knew she absolutely should report it to the police. Now I wondered if she'd made the call.

It was just weird. Did she realize how lucky she was to have escaped the theft? She could've lost hundreds of dollars in wine. Maybe I really would check in with Eric Jensen when I got home.

I really hated having all these uncharitable thoughts about anyone.

The truth was, I rarely had to deal with Randi one on one, and I thanked my lucky stars for that.

Halfway up the stairs, I noticed that the kitchen door was cracked open a few inches, so I could tell that all the lights were working now. I would just have to double-check that each of the appliances was back in working order. I wanted all the wiring to be perfect before the carnival began tomorrow night. But since the family was in for the evening, I would take care of that tomorrow.

I jogged up the remaining stairs and returned to the kitchen— just in time to hear Lilian scream bloody murder!

Chapter Three

I charged into the kitchen in time to see a man standing behind Lilian and squeezing her like a big bear. The guy was tall and wide-shouldered and . . . familiar. It only took me another second to realize that everyone else in the family was watching, wearing big smiles on their faces.

"Logan," I said with relief. I'd been prepared to defend Lilian from some pillaging marauder, so I had to take a few seconds to regroup. In my defense, I hadn't seen Logan in at least ten months, but somehow he looked so much larger and more muscular than I remembered. Maybe it was the peacoat he was wearing. It probably added another ten or fifteen pounds or more.

But now I could see Lilian's face, and she was laughing and crying with pure joy. I felt my own throat tighten at the sight of Logan holding his mom as if he were breathing new life into her.

Another door, the one that led to the stairs going up to the family suites was flung open, and Arabella ran in. "Logan!"

"Hey, kiddo," Logan murmured, and Arabella simply stopped and began to cry. "Come here, sweetheart." He pulled her into his arms and held on.

Within seconds, the other family members were laughing and shouting, slapping Logan's back and hugging him.

Franco walked in and gave Logan another bear hug. "Is good to see you," he said in his charmingly accented English. "You are well?"

"I'm great," Logan said. "You're looking healthy and happy."

"I am excellent. My wife, she makes me so. Ah, here you are, *cara mia*." He reached out and wrapped his arm around Arabella's waist and pulled her close. In turn, she wrapped her arms around him, and I had to admit, it was sweet to see her react with love. I rarely got to see that side of her.

"That's nice to hear," Logan murmured.

I didn't see Stephanie here and wondered if she had gone upstairs or back to work. I thought about sneaking out, not wanting to impose on this tender family moment. But then Logan's gaze met mine, and he let loose a slow smile. "Shannon Hammer, how're you doing?"

"I'm good, Logan. It's really great to see you."

"I've got to say the same." He kept his arm wrapped around his mom. "I hear you're getting married."

"I am." I smiled. "We haven't set a date yet, but sometime in the next six months or so."

"Fantastic. He's a great guy."

He winked at me, and I figured he must've developed the habit of winking from his father. It certainly worked like a charm for Logan, just as it always had with Bill.

Then Stephanie walked into the kitchen, and her mouth fell open. Suddenly, she was shouting, "Logan!" and wrapping her arms around her big brother and hugging him like a koala bear clinging to a eu-calyptus branch. "You're home! You're home."

"I'm here."

"I'm so glad."

"Me too, Sis," he said quietly.

"How long can you stay?"

The sound of their father's pounding footsteps interrupted his response, and we were all silent as Bill stepped into the kitchen. He stopped and stared at his oldest son, then grinned. "Would you look what the cat dragged in," Bill said, his voice filled with emotion.

"Hey, Dad," Logan said, smiling.

Stephanie stepped back to make room for her father, who simply wrapped his big arms around his oldest son and held on to him. It was a long moment before anyone said anything. I felt my eyes tear-ing up again, and I doubted I was the only one.

Finally, Bill spoke the question on everybody's mind. "How long can you stay?"

"I'd like to talk about it when everyone's here, if you don't mind."

"Well then, let's get them all in here."

It took a few minutes of wrangling, and I should've taken that as a sign that it was time for me to leave, but I was dying to know his answer to the question. And besides, Logan was a friend of Mac's and Eric's, though I didn't know when or where they had met, so it made sense for me to stay long enough to find out what was going on. So I could pass the news on to them, right? Plus, I admit, I'm the nosy type. So I stayed put.

Stephanie's husband, Craig, was the hotel bar manager, so he was still working in the busy restaurant bar. Despite his absence, their private kitchen was crowded with siblings and in-laws, and the atmosphere was festive. Lilian brought wineglasses down from the cupboard, and Bill quickly opened two bottles, and Stephanie poured small amounts of wine into each glass and everyone helped themselves.

"Okay, sweetie pie," Lilian said, patting her older son's arm, "tell us your news. I don't think I can wait any longer."

Logan glanced around the room, making sure everyone was here. But he was frowning. "Not yet, Mom."

I knew why. Randi was missing. Logan's wife hadn't made her appearance yet.

"So? Did you get promoted?" Bill asked.

"Where are they sending you?" Arabella demanded.

Stephanie grinned. "I'll bet it's Washington, DC. Some big government office. Am I right?"

"I was going to guess North Carolina," said Bill. "Lot of military bases down there."

"Maybe you go to Italy?" Franco said, his charming Italian accent warming every woman's insides, including mine.

"No more guessing," Lilian said, holding up both palms in protest. "I hate that you're going to leave us again. So just tell us." And her eyes filled with tears again.

"Okay, Mom." Logan pulled his mother closer, gave the room one more scan, then shrugged. "Here's the news. I wanted to wait to share it with all of you."

That was when Randi finally walked in.

"I've been honorably discharged," Logan revealed. "I'm not going anywhere. I've come home to stay."

The news was followed by several seconds of complete and utter silence.

Then Lilian shouted, "Oh, hallelujah!"

Arabella and Stephanie laughed and hugged each other.

Bill pulled Lilian into his arms and held on to her as she wept happy tears.

Randi hadn't said a word, but maybe she was keeping it all inside. Or maybe she already knew. I couldn't imagine Logan would keep that news from her.

As I studied her, I realized that with her mouth literally hanging open, she appeared dumbstruck. Not a particularly attractive look on anyone, but Randi managed to turn it to her advantage. "You could've let me know before you just showed up," she said.

It was such a snotty thing to say, but it was completely in character for Randi. She was obviously the one person that Logan had been waiting for, and it just figured she'd make him wait. I was kind of surprised that he hadn't told her before tonight.

Logan shrugged, his smile tightening. "And you could've answered your phone. I called. Numerous times."

Randi's eyes narrowed. "I always answer my phone."

"Not when I called last night and several times today. I was thinking you saw my number and decided not to answer."

"That's BS."

He chuckled. "There's that foul mouth I've been missing so much." Looking around, he grinned. "That's insane, right?"

Stephanie rolled her eyes. "*Insane* is a good word for whatever's going on with you two."

That comment earned her a dirty look from Randi and a quick laugh from Logan. Stephanie laughed, too, obviously used to getting the stink eye from her sister-in-law, Randi.

At that moment, Stephanie's husband, Craig, pushed his way

through the kitchen door. "Hey, I just heard—" Craig froze when he spied Logan.

"Buddy!" Logan said jovially, and grabbed Craig in a loose head-lock. "How about a noogie for old times' sake?" He scraped his knuckles against Craig's scalp.

"Knock it off, you big ass," Craig said, laughing as he pushed Logan away. "You're still such a loser."

Logan laughed. "And you've missed me."

"Yeah, right."

Logan gave Craig a quick, tight hug, then stepped back. The two men stared at each other. They were the same age and had been friends all through school. When Craig married Logan's sister Stephanie, Logan was his best man.

"Welcome home, man," Craig said.

Logan grinned. "Thanks, man."

They were both close to six feet tall, but Craig was stockier while Logan had classic broad shoulders and slender hips.

I wondered, did anyone like getting noogies? And what a dumb word, right? Studying Craig, I thought he looked pained. I couldn't blame him. Noogies could hurt.

Having grown up with a younger sister, I'd never been a victim of the random noogie attack. It seemed to be a mild form of torture that mainly boys and men used on each other, further verifying the age-old theory that boys were weird.

Randi watched the two men for another few seconds and shook her head. Then she took a quick look at her wristwatch. "I've got to go check on the bar. Craig, you stay and chat with Logan."

Stephanie gave Randi an incredulous look. "What is wrong with you?" She turned to her husband and grabbed his arm. "Craig, honey, can you cover for Randi for a few minutes so she can visit with Logan?"

"Of course," Craig said, obviously in agreement. Then he looked at Randi. "You stay as long as you want. I'll handle the bar." Glancing at Logan, he said, "See you later, man. Glad you're home."

"Thanks, man."

Randi rolled her eyes. "Fine. Whatever."

Glancing at Randi over his shoulder, Craig's eyes were narrowed on her. Did he disapprove of the way she'd dissed her husband? I couldn't quite figure out Randi's brain, even on a good day. Craig seemed to have the same problem, as he shook his head, then left the room.

Logan patted his chest. "I'm definitely feeling the love."

Randi had to know she was being a witch, but she couldn't seem to help herself. "Oh, shut up, Logan."

"There's my sweet girl," Logan said, grabbing his wife around the waist. Laughing, he added, "I'm not sure why I've missed that crabby attitude of yours, but there it is."

Randi's cheeks turned pink with embarrassment, and all of a sudden, she was hugging him as though she really cared. Logan had been gone for almost ten months, and she hadn't touched him until this moment. I thought maybe the only reason she did was because he had embarrassed her.

What was wrong with her? I wondered. But it really wasn't any of my business. I watched her body language, and except for that one hug, she clearly seemed to be avoiding the man. And he certainly didn't seem to have much in the way of love or tenderness for her.

I knew she wasn't shy about expressing her feelings, good or bad. I just didn't get her attitude. First of all, Logan was a certifiable hunk of a man. Gorgeous and smart and funny as well. But that didn't mean that he was nice to her in private. They'd known each other forever, and maybe he had begun to treat her badly. Or maybe she was the one treating him badly. And why was it any business of mine?

But I cared about Logan and his parents. And in case it wasn't clear, I was not a big fan of Randi's.

Still, even if Randi was mad at Logan for a perfectly understandable reason, she'd have to be stupid to behave so badly in front of his family, especially his mom and dad. They wanted their son to be happy, and since Randi was his wife, they had given her an excellent job with wonderful benefits.

I sighed. Again, I wasn't being fair. I had no idea what it was like to live here in this hotel with her husband's family while he was away for six to eight months at a time.

Maybe she was so good at her job, the Garrisons would gladly keep her on staff no matter how badly she treated their son Logan. But I doubted it.

Whatever the situation was, I still thought that Logan deserved a nicer wife than Randi.

And with that thought, and the realization that I'd been short-tempered half the day because of a few of the snarky women around here, I acknowledged that it was definitely time to go.

"I've got to get home," I said softly to Lilian.

"Will we see you tomorrow?" she asked.

"Absolutely," I said. "It's the last time we'll check everything before the crowds show up tomorrow night."

"It's going to be great," Lilian said. "And again, if you have any spare time, let's go check out the north cellar."

"I'd love to." I mentally surveyed my schedule. "It should only take twenty minutes to test Booth Number Ten and then I'll have a few hours free."

"Great. Track me down and we'll take a run over to the north tower," Lilian said.

"I'll do it," I said.

"Can't wait to see Booth Number Ten in action," Bill said, and winked at me. Booth Number Ten was the code name for Santa Claus's booth. We hadn't revealed to anyone in town the news that Santa Claus was going to be a nightly feature at the Fun Zone. Which was why Bill couldn't help winking whenever we talked about it.

"It's going to be fun." I was looking forward to seeing everyone's reaction tomorrow night. I was confident that it would all work perfectly.

"See you then, Shannon," Stephanie said.

"I'll be here." I turned and flashed Logan another big smile. "Welcome home, Logan."

"Thanks, babe," he said, lowering his voice. "Say hi to Mac. Tell him I'll give him a call."

"Sure, I'll tell him." I waved goodbye before walking out the door.

———————

Pulling into my driveway, I parked my truck next to Mac's SUV. I recognized Eric Jensen's car parked out on the street—it was hard to miss the police chief's big black SUV—and wondered what was going on. I slid down from my truck, shut the door, and locked it. Immediately, I could smell something wonderful and hoped it was coming from my house.

I could hear Robbie barking before I reached for the doorknob. As I stepped inside, he came running and I grabbed him up in a big hug. "Hi, cutie pie." I squeezed the little Westie lightly and fluffed his fur, then set him down on the kitchen floor.

"What about me?" Mac asked, pulling me into his arms for a warm kiss. "Am I a cutie pie?"

I laughed and he kissed me again. Oh, mercy, was he ever. His dark brown hair was ruffled, probably from running his hands through it in frustration while writing some key scene in his latest bestselling thriller. His beautiful blue eyes sparkled with wit and intelligence, and I was completely in love with him. Teasing, I fluffed his hair. "You are the most handsome sweetie cutie pie I have ever seen in my entire life."

"Thank you," he said, doing his finest Elvis impression. "Thank you very much."

"Thank *you*," I said, laughing.

"No, thank you," he repeated softly, and gave me another kiss, this time long and deep and soulful and . . . whew. "I'm glad you're home."

When I could speak, I whispered, "Me too."

Tiger, my orange-striped cat, and Luke, Mac's black devil cat, both took turns winding their lithe bodies around my ankles. I leaned over and gave each of them some light scratches behind their ears. "Hello, my beauties."

Robbie was back at my feet demanding my attention, so I picked him up and carried him over to the kitchen table, where I sat down and gave him a brisk belly rub.

"Since your hands are busy, Red," Mac said, "I'll get you a glass of wine."

Mac had a couple of nicknames for me, both of which were

connected to my long, thick, curly red hair. The most obvious one was "Red." But he also called me "Irish" on occasion when it suited him. I'd always had an ongoing battle with my hair. Cut it? Don't cut it? But once I met Mac, he convinced me to keep it as it was, with only the occasional trim to keep me from turning into Scary Rapunzel.

When he brought the wineglass over to the table, I took a quick sip of a really excellent red wine. "I think I'm drinking the good stuff."

"You are," he said. "Because I'm cooking the good stuff."

"Is that what I'm smelling?"

"Yes."

"Smells wonderful." Robbie jumped down and settled in his little bed, but the two cats weren't quite ready to relax so they continued to prowl.

Mac grinned. "Can you guess what it is?"

I took a few more sniffs. "It smells like an amazingly rich tomato sauce. With some kind of delectable savory something-or-other tossed in for good measure."

"That's a good guess. The savory something is *Ibérico* pork sausage."

"You've got to be kidding. You put it in the pasta sauce?"

"Yeah." He grinned. "I know I'm overdoing it, but damn, I can't get enough of it."

I could barely contain my excitement. "I'm not complaining."

Mac and I had recently spent a week in New York, where we discovered a fabulous Portuguese restaurant that served an *Ibérico* pork dish that melted in your mouth. Mac was so enamored with the meal that when we got home, he ordered two pounds of various cuts of *Ibérico* pork, to be sent to us by overnight mail.

All I could think was, thank goodness we hadn't been hit by the porch pirates. If we had been, they might've had to change their name to the *pork* pirates.

I started to laugh at my own silly joke. Mac crossed the room and gave me a kiss. "What are you laughing about?"

"I made a little joke."

"Let me hear it."

"It's really stupid."

"That's the best kind."

So I told him about the porch pirates and then I told him my joke. And he laughed.

"That's a pity laugh," I insisted. "But that's okay, because I shouldn't be laughing about it."

He pulled me closer. I rested my head on his shoulder and said, "I love you."

He kissed my cheek. "Because I laughed at your joke?"

"Maybe a few other reasons."

"Ditto, baby." He rubbed my neck and studied my expression. "You look a little drained. Hard day?"

"Yeah," I admitted. "Mostly having to deal with crabby personalities." I reached for my wineglass and took a sip. "That reminds me. Logan Garrison said to say hello and to let you know that he would give you a call."

"Good. Thanks."

I frowned. "When did you guys meet?"

He reached for the big spoon and stirred the sauce as he talked.

"I met him at Homefront a few times when he was here on leave. Eric introduced us and suggested that we both think about volunteering. We did, then we were both recruited to join the advisory board. And here we are."

"How did I not know that?"

"I think around that time you were involved in renovating the insane asylum."

"Oh yeah." I thought about it. "That job kept me distracted for quite a while." I changed the subject. "Should I make a salad?"

He shrugged. "I pulled a few greens and veggies from the garden, chopped them up, and threw them into the big bowl."

"That sounds like the definition of a salad to me."

"That's what I was thinking."

I gazed up at him. "Are we having company? I thought I saw Eric's car outside."

"You did. He and Chloe took a walk to the pier. They'll be back in a few minutes."

The Lighthouse Cove Pier was a block away down Main Street. There were a half dozen seafood restaurants, a burger joint, and another dozen gift and novelty shops. Among that last category was a fairly decent shop that sold quality beach towels, bathing suits, T-shirts, caps, and other beach wear.

"What are they doing on the pier?" I wondered.

"They decided to pick up some fried clams for an appetizer."

My eyes widened in pleasure. "That sounds yummy."

"I thought so, too, although I would never choose to use the word 'yummy' in a sentence."

I laughed. "Of course not."

"They should be back any minute," he said. "But in the mean-time." He pulled me close again and kissed my neck, tickling me. It made me giggle like a schoolgirl.

"Stop that," I said, not really protesting. "I sound ridiculous."

"Nope. You sound sexy." And he kissed me again, just as Chloe and Eric walked into the kitchen.

"Oops, we seem to be interrupting." Chloe started to back out of the room.

Mac just laughed. "Come back, you guys."

"Is it safe?" Chloe asked.

I gave her a look. "Get in here."

She held up a big white takeout bag. "Okay. Because otherwise, we'll have to eat these yummy deep-fried clams all by ourselves."

I glanced at Mac. "See? Yummy."

"Must be a girl thing." He went to the cupboard and pulled down a plate and a small matching bowl.

Chloe carefully shook the fried clams onto the plate, then spooned the tartar sauce into the bowl. I reached for four small forks so we could pretend we were in polite society.

"Thanks for picking up the clams. They look delicious." I pulled a bottle of Pinot Noir from the wine cabinet, and Mac took four glasses out of the cupboard. I opened the bottle and poured the wine. "This is the same wine I was drinking earlier. You're really going to like it."

Chloe took a sip and nodded appreciatively. "Mm, it's great."

We all started nibbling as we chatted about the latest news around town. A few minutes later, Mac filled our biggest pot with water to heat the pasta.

As always, the four of us laughed and talked as we prepped the meal, then sat and enjoyed the fresh salad and the rich chunks of *Ibérico* sausage cooked right into the thick pasta sauce.

I told them about the Garrisons' Christmas Fun Zone and how amazing it was going to be. Mac talked about the very fun stuff the Homefront veterans were planning as a Christmas fundraiser. It all sounded wonderful.

"Oh, Eric," I said, "I meant to ask you. Have you heard of any porch pirate gangs operating in town?"

He immediately straightened up and his eyes narrowed. "Why do you ask?"

I almost laughed because he was suddenly so suspicious. "Because Randi insists that porch pirates tried to steal a case of wine from the hotel. She saw the guys and chased after them. They dropped the box and ran away."

"Why didn't she call the police?" he asked.

I shook my head in disgust. "I told her to call you, but I guess she was just too busy. She wanted me to call you instead."

He frowned. "Why?"

"Because she likes to pretend she's important and I'm the hired help," I said. "I blew her off."

"Good," Chloe said. "She's got a lot of nerve."

"Anyway," I said, turning back to Eric. "Because of the holidays, are you seeing a lot of porch pirate activity?"

He hesitated, and I thought he'd refuse to tell me anything. But finally he said, "Actually, we just arrested three guys today who call themselves pirates. They managed to get away with quite a lot of booty before we caught up to them."

Chloe grinned and elbowed Eric lightly. "I get it. Pirate booty."

His smile was smug. "I still got it."

Our laughter was interrupted when the doorbell rang. Robbie began to bark and raced to the front door.

I looked at Mac. "Are you expecting someone?"

"It's probably Logan," Eric said, staring at his phone. "I just got a text from him."

I frowned. "But he just got home, like, less than two hours ago. His parents might want him to stick around tonight after being away for ten months."

Instead of responding to me, Mac held up his phone. "I got a text, too."

"What's going on?" I asked.

Mac wrapped his arm around my shoulders as we walked to the front door. "We have some business to discuss with Logan."

"Really?" I looked at Chloe. "Did you know about this?"

She gave Eric a sideways glance. "No, but I'm going to find out."

"It's not subterfuge," Eric said, walking to the front door. "All will be revealed in a minute."

Robbie let out another quick bark as Mac reached the front door.

Chloe quickly cleared the plates off the table and placed everything on the kitchen counter next to the sink.

"Thanks," I said to her. "I'll do the dishes after Logan leaves. I don't want to miss anything."

"Right there with you, Sis."

As Eric and Mac greeted Logan at the front door, my sister whispered, "Do you think everything's okay at the Garrisons' house?"

"His family was absolutely thrilled to see him." I lowered my voice. "Except for Randi. I don't know what's wrong with her. She was downright hostile. Maybe they had a fight over the phone before he arrived." I shrugged. "Or maybe they're just fed up with each other."

"That would not surprise me," Chloe whispered. "Logan is so mild-mannered, but Randi has been irritable since the day she started first grade. It figures she would decide to be prickly just as Logan comes home."

"I have a feeling there's more to tell," I said quietly. "But we'll have to talk about it later."

"True," she murmured. "The guys won't want to hear any gossip, but I will."

Seconds later, Mac walked into the kitchen with Logan, followed by Eric. "Look who's here."

"Logan!" Chloe said, embracing him in a big hug. "Welcome home. It's so good to see you."

"You too, Chloe," he said. "It's really good to be home." He glanced around. "Have I interrupted your dinner?"

"We just finished," I assured him. "But there's plenty left over if you're hungry."

He grinned. "No, thanks. Mom fed me well."

"Glad to hear it. Mac, can you get some drinks for everyone? We can sit in the living room."

"You bet," he said.

"I'm going to finish clearing the dishes. It'll only take a minute."

Mac offered Logan a beer and he accepted. Eric settled for a cup of coffee instead.

"I'll bring your coffee," Chloe said.

"Thanks, love," Eric said.

Mac got two bottles of beer from the fridge and joined the guys in the living room.

Chloe knew how to operate our mini coffee machine with the recyclable pods, so in less than a minute, she was carrying a mug of steaming hot coffee out to Eric.

"Go ahead and join them," I told her. "I'll be right out."

It only took another minute to load the dishes into the dishwasher, all the while wondering what Logan was doing here. Not that I wasn't delighted to see him even though I'd seen him an hour or two earlier. I wondered again about his marriage. Was he happy? I grabbed my half-full wineglass and joined the others.

I sat down on the carpet and set my glass on the coffee table. "So what's going on?"

Mac grinned. "We're talking about Logan's new job."

I stared at Logan. "You have a new job at the hotel?"

Mac glanced at him. "I haven't told Shannon your news yet."

"You have news?" I frowned. "Is everything okay at the Cliffs?"

"Everything is just great," Logan said, visibly relaxing in his chair. "For the most part, I loved the navy. But I can't tell you how great it is to finally be home for good."

I smiled. "Your family was obviously thrilled to have you back."

His mouth twisted with sarcasm. "Some more than others."

"Well, *we* love that you're here to stay," Chloe said loyally.

"Thanks, Chloe. I appreciate it."

"So, what's the big news?" I demanded.

Logan was hesitant. "That's kind of why I'm here."

"Okay, I'm intrigued," Chloe said.

Logan chuckled. "You guys may think I'm a complete idiot, but I haven't told my family about the new job yet."

"What new job?" I asked again.

"Yeah, what's the big secret?" Chloe said.

Logan looked at me, then Chloe. "Well, I've really enjoyed being on their advisory board, and now I have the opportunity to go to work for Homefront as their community director."

"What does that mean in English?" Chloe asked.

Eric chuckled. "He's the guy in charge."

I stared at Mac. "Why didn't you say so?"

He shrugged and explained, "It really wasn't my news to share."

"Okay." I turned to Logan. "But you haven't told your folks yet? Do you need a little help with that?"

He gave a tired laugh. "No. I didn't tell them tonight because everyone was freaking out over the news that I'm home for good. And I knew that if I told them the rest of it, there would be trauma and tears. I just didn't want to deal with it tonight. Tomorrow will be soon enough."

Mac laughed. "It better be, since you'll be leaving the house right after breakfast to go to your new job."

"Stephanie doesn't even know?" Chloe asked. "Why didn't you tell her?"

"I wasn't ready to tell anyone until I got here."

"I think you should tell her tonight," Chloe said.

Logan frowned. "You're probably right. I really haven't thought this all the way through."

I chuckled. "You've been in the military too long."

"You say that jokingly, but it's true. I haven't had to make these strategic family decisions for years."

"Well, you're a good guy, so I think the decisions you make will be good for everyone."

"Hey," Eric said, "how about if we all show up tomorrow morning to help you give them the good news."

Logan took a slow sip of beer. "That's not such a bad idea."

"Seriously?" Mac said.

"Yeah. Mainly because I'm not sure they'll take it as the good news that it is, if it just comes from me. But if you guys are there, your presence will signal something happy, and it'll keep the tears and drama to a minimum."

"I'll be happy to explain to your parents exactly how we recruited you," Eric said.

"Explain it to me," Logan said with a grin. "I want to make sure it'll go over with the folks."

Eric laughed. "Okay. I spoke to your commanding officers to find out if you had the temperament, the intelligence, and the courage and determination to deal with people who've suffered emotional trauma and who have brought a lot of baggage with them. I found it interesting to hear many of your commanders say that they found your sense of humor to be the key feature that would see you through the worst times in this job."

"Yeah? Well, I do tend to use laughter to get through some diffi-cult situations. But that was my key feature? Interesting."

"Let me assure you that they also raved about your smarts and your clever ideas and your technical prowess and blah blah blah."

We all laughed.

But I was still wondering about the idea that his parents would actually cry over what I considered great news. Or maybe he was referring to someone else. His sister? His wife? Probably.

"Let's do it," Chloe said. "And maybe we can give Stephanie a heads-up since she was probably thrilled to see you but is now freaking out, thinking that you're about to kick her out of her be-loved CEO desk and take over."

Logan ran his hands through his hair in frustration. "I should've told her first thing, but I didn't. She's probably wondering what in the world she's going to do for a job now that I'm home."

"She won't have to worry much longer," I said.

"So, you're okay with us coming over in the morning?" Mac asked.

Logan thought for another few seconds. "I don't want to come across as a total wimp, but I would love to see you guys show up."

"Then we'll show up," Eric said. "Is seven too early?"

"No, that's perfect. And we've always got coffee and donuts in the kitchen."

"Hey, just like Homefront," Eric said.

Logan chuckled. "That's kind of what cinched the deal."

A few minutes later, Logan left, and Mac and I finished cleaning up the kitchen. Chloe and Eric helped.

I finally said, "I can't imagine tears or trauma coming from Lilian or Bill."

"Oh, heck no," Chloe said. "That'll all be coming from Randi."

Of course she was right. Logan's wife was the ultimate mean drama queen.

"Come on, babe," Eric said. "You can't know that for sure."

"I've known the woman my whole life," Chloe said. "She's always been a drama queen; right up there with her good pal Whitney." She looked at me. "Am I right?"

"One hundred percent," I said. "Not even Arabella comes near her level of vitriol."

Chloe laughed. "Arabella is a sweet little piker compared to her."

A few minutes later, just as Eric and Chloe were slipping into their coats, I said, "So tell us about Logan's new job."

"'Community director' sounds fancy," Chloe said.

"Very fancy," I agreed. "What will he be doing?"

Mac nodded. "Essentially he's taking over for Vince."

I felt my mouth drop open. "Vince is leaving? Where's he going?"

"I'll miss him," Chloe said.

"We all will," Eric said. "But he's still with the company. He's moving to Denver to open up a new Homefront."

I thought about it. "That's actually what he does best."

"That's why the timing couldn't be better," Mac said. "Vince is a really good project manager, working with the city planners and construction crews and starting up the whole project."

"And now he'll be doing that in Colorado," I said. "Hey, isn't he from Boulder?"

"Yes," Mac said. "Another reason why he's happy to be moving."

"Then that works out well," Chloe said.

"Logan will have more of a true executive administrative role," Eric explained. "He'll be in charge of long-term strategic planning, overseeing daily operations, managing personnel, delegating tasks to staff."

"I'm impressed," I said.

"I was, too," Eric said. "His commanding officers really did rave about him. He's got strong leadership and supervisory skills, excellent organizational and time management skills."

Chloe chuckled. "Nice to know he wasn't chosen just because he's a pretty face."

"Even though he is," I added.

"Look at the time," Eric said, grinning as he escorted Chloe to the front door. "Better get you home."

Chloe and I were still laughing as Mac and I walked them to their car.

Chapter Four

The next morning Mac drove his car and followed me to the Cliffs Hotel, where I planned to work with Bill and my crew that morning. If the rollout of Booth Number Ten went well, as I knew it would, I would have most of the afternoon to explore the north cellar.

Mac would only be here long enough to help spill the beans to Logan's family about his new job. After that, Mac would go back home to continue working on his latest Jake Slater novel, while I would stick around the Fun Zone to make sure that everything worked like a charm. Technically, the Santa Claus reveal would be tricky because of everything that had gone into creating Booth Number Ten. I was certain that we had worked out all the kinks and couldn't wait to see the looks on the faces of the kids when they saw Santa Claus revealed.

But the biggest surprise of the night would happen when everyone walked into the Fun Zone and saw Bill's beautiful new carousel for the first time. That was truly something the entire town would enjoy for years to come.

I parked in my usual spot and Mac pulled in right behind me. He jumped out of his car and came over to open my door.

I smiled. "Thanks."

"And here's Eric," Mac said as the police chief parked his SUV next to my truck. I was glad to see Chloe, who slid down from the passenger seat.

"Perfect timing," I said. "Let's get this over with."

"You sound a little nervous," Mac said. "You okay?"

"I had a few odd thoughts during the night," I admitted.

"What does that mean?"

"Just weird dreams that don't mean anything." I pushed an errant curl back from my forehead. "I can't see Bill and Lilian giving Logan any grief about the new job."

"I can't, either, so just keep good thoughts."

"I will. Thanks."

Chloe slipped her arm through mine and squeezed. "You really are nervous."

"Why do you say that?"

"You're shaking." She laughed. "Chill, girl."

"I'm a little anxious about the big Fun Zone opening tonight."

She squeezed my arm a little tighter. "It'll be great."

"As long as everything's working properly."

"Okay, starting now, we won't think about anything but happy stuff."

"Happy stuff. Got it."

"This won't take long," Eric said with complete confidence. "Logan's folks are cool."

THE KNIFE BEFORE CHRISTMAS

Chloe beamed at him. "Absolutely."

Mac wrapped his arm around me. "No worries."

I nodded firmly. "No worries."

The "no worries" mantra lasted until I climbed the steps leading up to the Garrisons' kitchen. Then I started wondering. Was there someone in there who'd give Logan a hard time about this?

But why would anyone in the family ever argue against Logan taking the job at Homefront? It was a wonderful place for veterans to live, and it represented hope and friendship and community. But I'd seen for myself that not everyone in town thought so. I guess we'd have to see what the Garrisons thought of the place.

I was arguing with myself and not coming up with any clear answer. I finally told myself to shut up and wait for the final family verdict.

Bill and Lilian were so open and honest, and everyone loved Logan. There wouldn't be any disagreements, and we would all leave here feeling perfectly happy about the decision Logan had made. Fingers crossed.

And then I thought of Randi. She was a wild card. She could be super antagonistic or just plain ornery sometimes. It often felt like she was making a scene only to bring attention to herself. But even if she pulled that number, she wasn't going to change Logan's mind about working for Homefront.

Deep breaths, I thought just as Mac took hold of my hand.

"No worries, remember?"

"I'm trying."

He smiled at me, and I felt calmer as we stepped up to the kitchen door. Before we could knock, Logan opened it and shook his head. "This is so dumb. You guys are great, but I'm sorry I made you all come here this morning."

"You didn't make us," Mac said. "We wanted to be here."

"And I'm already scheduled to be here anyway," I said. "I'm working with your dad, so don't worry about me."

"Are your parents around?" Eric asked as Logan led the way into the big family kitchen.

He hesitated. "Yeah."

At that very moment, Bill walked into the kitchen.

"Shannon?" he said. "You're here early."

I waved. "Good morning, Bill."

Then he spied Mac and Eric. "You guys are here, too. What's going on?"

Eric glanced at Logan. "Let's do this."

Obviously nervous, Logan rolled his shoulders and shook out his arms. "Okay."

"Do you have a minute, Bill?" Eric asked. "We'd like to talk to you."

"Sure. You want to sit down?" He pointed to the big kitchen table. "Grab a cup of coffee and a donut if you're hungry."

Lilian walked in and beamed. "Well, this is a nice surprise."

"Come sit down, Lil," Bill said. "The kids want to talk to us."

Kids, I thought with a smile.

Lilian's smile was radiant. "Isn't this wonderful? Anybody want coffee?"

"I'm good," Eric said.

"I've already got a cup," Bill said, sharing a curious look with Lilian.

"There's donuts, too," Lilian added.

"I'll take a donut," Mac said, and grinned at me before he jumped up from the table. He wasn't used to having donuts around and was determined to take advantage of it.

Lilian finally took a good look at all of us. "Are you all here to welcome Logan home?"

I smiled. "We're really glad he's home."

"Me too." But she scanned our faces and spent a few extra seconds staring at Eric. Then she frowned at Logan. "Sweetie, are you in trouble with the law?"

"Oh, jeez." Logan rolled his eyes. "No, Mom. Eric's just visiting."

I could hear Mac squelching a laugh.

"Well, what the hell is going on?" Bill finally demanded, raising his voice. "My nerves of steel are starting to fizzle and freak out."

"Okay, here's the deal," Logan said. "Mom and Dad, I've been offered the position of community director for Homefront. And I've accepted the job."

There was complete silence.

Bill and Lilian stared at their son, then turned to each other. After a long moment, Bill said, "That title sounds impressive."

Lilian asked, "But what does it mean?"

"It means I took another job," Logan explained quietly. "I'll be running Homefront, the veterans' community just down the road."

"Yes, we know all about Homefront," Bill said.

"It's a marvelous place," Lilian added.

Logan nodded. "I agree. I'll be working there in an administrative capacity, overseeing daily operations and finances, managing personnel, and fundraising. But I'll also work with the vets themselves, and that's what I'm really excited about. I'm hoping I can make a real difference in their lives. And I hope I have your support."

Lilian sucked in a breath. "Good heavens. Of course you do. Always."

He continued quickly. "I love you guys, and if it's okay, I'll still be living here with you. And my wife, of course. But instead of working in the hotel, I'll have another job just down the street at Homefront. And the thing is, Stephanie's doing a great job, and we all know she loves it. I don't think I could do it any better than she does. So that's what I wanted to tell you."

"I'm not sure what to say," Lilian whispered.

"It was never my plan to work anywhere else but here," Logan hurried to explain. "I always thought I'd come back and work with you at the Cliffs. But when I was offered the Homefront job, I realized it was the perfect fit for me. So I hope you're not disappointed. All I really want is for all of us to be happy."

He blew out a hefty breath and sagged back in his chair as though he'd just run a marathon.

"Was that so hard?" Bill asked, lightly squeezing his shoulder.

"It was torture!" Logan said. "You guys have worked really hard to make a place for all of us kids to thrive. And, well, I never wanted to disappoint you."

"Disappoint us?" Lilian said. Her eyes welled up and she slipped a tissue from her pocket. "No, sweetie. Never."

Bill blinked. Reluctantly he pulled out a handkerchief and wiped his eyes. "Mom's right. You could never disappoint us. We're so proud of you."

"And you promise you'll still live here?" Lilian asked, her voice wavering with emotion.

"Of course. I mean, if it's okay with you and Dad."

Bill stood. "Come here." He pulled his son into his arms. "I love you, son."

Lilian hurried over to her husband's side and patted Logan's back. Then Bill grabbed her and hugged her. Then Logan was hugging her and the three of them were hugging one another.

Mac grinned. "That's a whole lot of love right there."

"Looks like our work here is done," Eric said, slipping on a pair of sunglasses.

"You two cynics," I said, shaking my head. "You can't fool me. I saw tears in both your eyes."

"That's a damn lie," Eric said, making Mac laugh.

At that moment I noticed Sean and Wade pulling up in their trucks.

"I'd better get going," I said. "My guys are here."

And then Stephanie walked into the kitchen. The first person she noticed was her best friend, my sister. "Chloe? What're you doing here?" She looked around more closely. "Mom, are you okay? Are you crying? Logan, what's going on?"

"Come here, Sis," Logan said, holding his arm out.

She whipped around. "What's wrong? Mom is crying. Are you sick?" She grabbed her brother.

"They're happy tears," Lilian said through her sobs.

Stephanie looked at Logan. "I don't get it. What happened?"

"I've taken an administrative job at Homefront. You're going to stay here and be the permanent company administrator. The CEO, right, Dad?"

She blinked and looked at her father. "Dad?"

"That's right, honey. You're the boss."

Stephanie couldn't quite fathom how everything had changed overnight and turned back to Logan. "So, wait. You're not working here anymore? But you're not leaving town, right? You promise?"

"I'm going to live here with you all, so I'll still be able to give you grief on a regular basis."

"Don't kid around," she said, and wrapped her arms around him. "Are you serious?"

"You're too good at the job, Sis. I can't compete with you."

"Very funny." She rolled her eyes, then stared at her best friend. "Chloe, did you know about this?"

"Not until last night."

"Why didn't you call me?"

Chloe laughed. "It was really late last night."

"Really late," I corroborated.

Stephanie took a deep breath. "Okay."

And suddenly Lilian was hugging her and Bill, and they were all crying and laughing.

"Seriously, we're done here," Mac murmured, slowly walking backward.

"Yeah, I've got to get going." Eric shoved his cap onto his head. "Logan, you're due at work in about a half hour."

"You don't want to be late your first day," Chloe said.

"No, ma'am."

I caught Bill's glance and pointed toward the carnival site. "I'll be out working on Booth Number Ten."

"I'll join you in five minutes," Bill said.

Lilian caught me before I made it to stairs. "I'm having a meeting with my kids at around three thirty, and I'd like you and Wade to be there, too. Can you make it?"

"Sure. What's it all about?"

"I'm still working out the details, but basically, I'm going to give each couple an assignment for the new building. I want them to design something. Anything really. A bedroom suite or an entryway or even a speakeasy in the basement. I'd love to see them use their imagination. Take charge. Have fun with it."

"That's a great idea," I said, then smiled. "Is this your way of getting them more involved in ultimately running the property?" Lilian had discussed this in the past with my father and me.

"Baby steps," she said, chuckling. "They've never done much in this area, and that's my fault. Mine and Bill's. I'd like them to start taking responsibility for the place, and this is one way to get them involved, don't you think? And we'd like to award the couple with the best idea some sort of monetary amount. What do you think? Maybe a check for ten thousand dollars?"

"Wow, that's generous."

She frowned. "Guess I'd better finalize that amount with Bill."

I grinned. "Okay. I think it's a really smart plan, and it'll get them involved in the actual nuts and bolts of the hotel property."

"That's right."

"Do you have anything in particular you'd like me to say at the meeting?"

"Good question." She chuckled. "You're the central figure in my plan."

"Me?"

"Yes. I'd like each couple to come up with a design for one of those areas I just mentioned, and I want them to work with you and Wade to make it happen. So it's not just an idea. It'll be a real project with a contractor and carpenters and electricians and, well, obstacles. You get the idea."

"I do. And I'm happy to do it. Will there be some limits in terms of costs and so on?"

"Yes, of course, but that won't be included in this preliminary phase."

"Okay. And if it's okay with you, I might even come up with a few thoughts on the subject myself."

She grabbed my hand and squeezed. "That's what I'm counting on."

Steve Shore drove up just as I was walking over to the carnival area. He parked nearby and jogged over to give me a big hug.

It was always remarkable to get a hug from someone who was as close as it came to the personification of Santa Claus. Except at this moment, he was wearing blue jeans, a thick flannel shirt, and boots.

I gestured toward his clothes. "I hardly recognize you in your civvies."

"Ho ho ho!" His belly actually shook as he laughed, so he held on with both hands. It was amazing that no matter what he was wearing, his laugh was always the classic *Ho ho ho* of Santa Claus. "I considered wearing my full Santa regalia," he said. "But I didn't want to give away any surprises."

"I'm glad you didn't. We've been trying to keep your first appearance on the down-low until everyone sees you tonight."

With a wide grin, he promised, "Nobody will hear the truth from me."

I stared at his casual outfit, topped by a San Francisco Giants baseball cap. As down-to-earth normal as his clothing appeared, it couldn't hide the fact that the man was the spitting image of Santa Claus with the aforementioned big belly, full white beard, and pink cheeks. He was jolly, too, of course, with twinkling eyes and a laugh that was infectious.

"You won't have to hold on to the secret much longer," I said.

"I'm glad," he said, his eyes twinkling. "Because I'm itching to tell everyone! Ho ho ho!"

I couldn't help but grin, then noticed the group walking toward the Fun Zone. "Oh, here comes Bill."

He was accompanied by Wade and Sean, thank goodness, because if the booth electronics didn't kick in right away, it would take several strong men to get it working.

Bill and Steve greeted each other like old friends, even though they'd just met once before. Santa Steve had that friendly effect on everyone.

Wade pushed the lever that operated the ceiling of the booth, and we watched it rise up over the elegant velvet-tufted chair inside. Then Wade and I got Steve settled on what looked more like a throne, which suited him perfectly.

"Fits like a mitten," he said with a grin.

And once he donned his complete Santa garb, it would fit even better, I thought.

"Let's make sure this thing works," Wade muttered so that only I could hear him.

I smiled at Wade. "It's going to work because I insist on it."

He grinned. "It's going to work because we've tried it three dozen times already, and it's perfect every time."

Believe it or not, it had taken some heavy-duty engineering and some timing issues to get the Santa Claus booth to work correctly. At a certain time of the evening, the calliope music would change tempo, and all the lights would fade out. Then thousands of tiny lights would illuminate the booth itself, and that was when the audience would see the sides slowly part, and the ceiling would rise up almost to the top of the big tent, then slowly slide backward, and all three pieces would disappear behind the back wall.

The music would hit a crescendo, and big spotlights would flash on, and thousands of twinkle lights would fill the space. And that's when everyone would see what they had hoped to see all evening: Santa Claus!

I had watched it work perfectly more than a few dozen times, and it never failed to tickle me. Mainly because I knew that every kid in the audience, and most of the adults, too, would be thrilled at the sight. Then several dozen elves would enter, carrying stanchion poles that they would place along the sides of the red carpet so any kid wanting to see Santa would be invited to line up on the red carpet and wait for their turn to talk to the jolly old elf.

It would all be wonderful and easy, as long as the timing of the lights worked. I wanted perfection, not only for Bill and Lilian but especially for Santa Steve.

"I'd call that perfect," Bill announced when the demonstration was finished.

"I would, too," Steve said. "It's a very tasteful Santa Claus reveal."

"We wanted it classic," I said. "Because the rest of it, the carnival and the carousel and the music, is as classic and charming as it gets. Bill and Lilian don't do anything simple."

Bill grinned. "No, we don't go in for *simple* much."

I had to laugh.

"It's pretty much guaranteed," Wade said. "The crowd is going to go wild."

"That's the plan," Bill said. "As far as timing goes, we'll move you into position through the back hallway about ten minutes to eight. Then we'll start the light change at eight, and you'll be revealed a minute later. You'll have kids lined up until nine thirty, when Santa will say goodnight to everyone. That's the official end of the evening. But we'll actually shut down the park at ten p.m."

Steve gave him a thumbs-up. "I'll have my phone alarm set on vibrate, so I'll know when to say goodnight." He glanced up at Wade. "I'm assuming I'll be miked."

"Absolutely," Wade said, opening his magic audio briefcase and handing Steve a wireless lavalier microphone. "You probably know how to use one of these."

Steve grinned. "Sure do."

"Let's test it right now."

Steve clipped the small microphone to his lapel and tucked the transmitter into the back pocket of his trousers. He flipped on the switch and began making several clicking sounds. "Testing, testing," he said.

"We hear you loud and clear," Sean called from the other side of the base.

"This is nice," Steve said, "but will anyone be able to hear me over the calliope music?"

"When the lights go off," Wade explained, "we'll fade out the music. You'll be in complete darkness for maybe thirty seconds. Then there will be an automated drumroll as the lights flash back on and the booth opens completely. All lights are on you and you'll be good to go."

Steve grinned. "Perfect. I already read through the script you sent."

"It's pretty basic," Bill said. "And it'll mostly be you ad-libbing your Santa Claus stuff."

"I'm pretty familiar with that jazz," Steve said, and everybody joined him laughing.

"Once you're introduced, we'll bring the music up a little because the carousel and the carnival will still be operating. But at that point, it'll mostly be you and one kid at a time. We'll have a few grown-up elves watching the line of kids and the time. We want each kid to have their time with Santa."

"I usually give them less than two minutes," Steve explained. "That's really plenty for most kids. You'll want to tell the elves, or I can do it."

"We've tested the music a few dozen times, but if by chance it gets too loud," Wade said, "we'll be on it. And if we need to modulate your voice, we will. But you're a pro, Steve, so we probably won't have to do too much of that."

"I appreciate that," Steve said modestly. "As long as the kids can hear me, it'll be good."

Bill indicated the red carpet that stretched from Santa's chair and ended at the wide pathway that wound around the carousel. "They'll be lined up right here."

"Good," Steve said. "In my experience, the kids usually hush each other up as soon as I start to speak."

"Kids are smart," Bill said.

Steve grinned. "You know it. And they don't want to get caught being naughty in front of Santa Claus."

We all laughed, then Wade said, "You'll be out here with the kids for about an hour and a half. You said that length of time was good for you."

"It's fine."

"Good," Wade continued. "I hate to repeat myself, but I'll go ahead and say that the red carpet is already laid out, but the elves will walk out carrying stanchions with red velvet rope that they'll set up along both sides of the carpet to keep everyone in line."

"Got it," Steve said.

"Then more elves will be out here, handing out candies and little toys and goodies for the kids while they wait, and then again after they're done talking to you."

"At nine thirty," Bill said, "one of the grown-up elves will whisper in your ear that it's time to shut it down."

"Is that what the elf is going to say?" Wade asked.

"No." Bill chuckled. "He's going to check his watch and whisper, very loudly, 'Santa, it's time for bed.'"

Steve grinned. "I like that. I assume he'll say it loud enough for everyone to hear it through my microphone."

"That's the plan."

"So that's when I start to say goodnight to the kids and the crowd," Steve said. "And as I said, I'll have my watch set to vibrate. And I'll wave and laugh until you close up the booth and the kids and their parents have begun to move out of the carnival space."

Wade grinned. "Sounds like you've done this before."

"Once or twice," Steve said. "Ho ho ho."

"The grown-up elves will direct people away from the Fun Zone and toward the parking lot," Bill said. "We have lighting in the parking areas, and the elves will have flashlights to help with directing folks."

"Meanwhile, once we've got you back inside the booth," I continued, "a half dozen grown-up elves will join you in there.

They'll help you out of your chair and then escort you out to the parking lot."

"That's good," Steve said, "because that chair is pretty cushy. I might wind up taking a nap if I'm sitting there for too long."

"I promise we'll get you out of there within ten minutes. Are you okay with that?" I asked.

"Of course." He patted my arm to assure me. "I can always check my messages and scroll through social media while I wait."

I had to smile at his casual words. It was amazing to work with such a professional.

"And then tomorrow," Bill said, "we'll meet back here and do it all over again."

"It'll be even more fun the next time," Steve said.

Everyone grinned and Bill said, "Good job, Shannon. Wade."

"Thanks, Bill," I added, then turned. "Thanks, Steve."

Steve nodded. "I'm really impressed with everything you and your team have done to pull this whole thing together."

"It's going to be wonderful," Lilian said to Steve. "I want to thank you so much for being here."

"It's always my pleasure."

"Just warning you," Bill added. "Once everyone finds out that Santa Claus is here, you could start to get mobbed."

"That's what the adult elves are here for," I said quickly. "They're your bodyguards."

Steve smiled softly. "I never worry about children tracking me down. They're always respectful when I'm in my Santa duds. I generally just give them a 'ho ho ho' and remind them to be nice."

"As opposed to naughty?" Wade asked.

Steve grinned. "That's right."

Bill checked his watch. "Okay, call time this afternoon is four thirty, at which time we'll have dinner served here on the veranda, right outside our kitchen door."

"That's awfully nice of you," Steve said.

"We all have to eat." Bill winked at me. "And food ensures that everyone gets here on time."

There was more laughter, and then Steve turned toward the parking lot. "I'm off to a local hospital where Santa Claus has promised to show up for the kids."

"That's so generous of you," Lilian said, slipping her arm through his.

"I'd like to say I do it for the kids," Steve said as they strolled, "but honestly, I think it brings me more joy than anyone else."

My crew and I had done everything we could to make sure that both the carousel and Santa Steve's booth, aka Booth Number Ten, worked perfectly. They were both doubly important because they would be providing the big surprises of the night. Nobody yet knew about the carousel, and we hadn't divulged the presence of Santa Claus, either.

I checked my watch and decided to make my way up to the Garrisons' kitchen, where Lilian planned to present her kids with another big surprise.

On the way, I stopped in the main lobby to pick up a hotel brochure for reference. I thought it might help me get through Lilian's meeting.

I walked into the family kitchen and immediately realized that

Lilian, her kids, and their spouses were all seated at the table, including Logan. Bill was missing, along with Wade and Sean, but I knew they were still testing the lighting on Santa's booth.

"Ciao, *dolcezza*," Franco said, making me smile.

"Ciao, Franco," I said in return.

"Hey, Shannon," Stephanie said. "Ready for the big night?"

I grinned. "Yeah, I'm excited."

"I hear your crew did a fantastic job," Logan said.

"I happen to think so," I said, with a big smile. "I hope you all enjoy it."

That's when I noticed Randi roll her eyes in contempt. What had I ever done to her? She was truly impossible! Then I realized that Logan and I had been chatting just like friends did. That's why she was cranky. She didn't like that.

I exchanged smiles of greeting with most of the others, and then I turned my attention to a huge tray of sandwiches set along one of the long counters. A few of the sandwiches were gone, but there were still enough left for a small army. A big bowl of potato salad and another of coleslaw sat nearby. The counter was also lined with cans of soda and juices, and there was a pitcher of iced tea, too.

Lilian waved me in. "Grab a sandwich, Shannon. I want to wait for Bill, so it'll be a few minutes before we start."

I gave her a thumbs-up, then reached for a thick tuna sandwich with lettuce and tomatoes, placed it on a heavy-duty paper plate, and added a scoop each of coleslaw and potato salad. I grabbed a handful of paper napkins and walked to the end of the counter farthest from the table. When I saw Wade and Sean walking with Bill toward the kitchen, I took my first bite.

Even though I'd known everyone at the table for years, I was instantly more comfortable seeing my guys approach.

Stephanie caught my eye and grinned.

"How's it going?" I asked. I had almost added "Ms. CEO" but thought better of it. Who knew what might be bubbling inside some of these family members? Jealousy? Anger? Suspicion? After all, Stephanie had essentially just become their boss!

Bill led the way into the kitchen, and Wade and Sean followed. There was plenty of commotion as they all grabbed sandwiches and salads and found places to sit. Wade and Sean joined me at the counter, and maybe it was silly, but I felt more secure having my guys close by.

Bill took a few bites of his sandwich and chewed thoughtfully. Then he and Lilian exchanged a quick glance, and he gave a slight nod.

Lilian smiled and said, "I'm glad you could all make it to this meeting. It's important that you all hear what we have in mind. I think you'll like it, and I promise to keep it short."

"Sounds ominous," Craig said.

"Nothing scary, I promise you," Lilian said lightly, although I couldn't help feeling that she was annoyed by the comment.

"As you know," she continued, "after the New Year, we'll be starting to renovate the fourth tower building, and it should take us six months. As you can imagine, it'll be quite a production." Then she flashed a perky smile and said, "This is where you all come in."

"I knew I should've had a drink first," Craig muttered.

"That's enough," Stephanie whispered firmly.

Craig crossed his eyes and made a face.

Randi giggled.

"These people are like six-year-olds," Wade murmured.

"And twice as annoying," Sean said under his breath.

I met Lilian's gaze and smiled encouragingly. It felt as if she could use some support.

"So, here's the plan," Lilian said. "I want each of you, as a couple, to come up with a design idea for the soon-to-be-renovated building. Pick a location. There are nooks and crannies everywhere. You can choose a hotel room or a landing or part of a stairway. You can design the interior of an elevator. There's an old sundeck on the top floor. The hotel rooms are a bit bland, but they won't be when you're finished with them, right? Are you getting the idea?"

"Yeah," Stephanie said, with some enthusiasm.

"Good," Lilian said. "Mainly, I want each of you to start taking an interest in this property. Dad and I won't be here forever, and at some point in time, it will all be left to you. We've held off giving you too much responsibility, but we both agree that it's time for you all to start taking an active interest in everything that goes on here. So this is our first hands-on assignment. It's an easy one. There will be more."

"You say you want us to build this thing with our hands?" Franco asked.

"No, dear," Lilian hastened to explain. "It's more of an idea I'd like you to come up with."

"Ah. I see," he said.

"Great." She smiled. "And as I said, you'll be working as a couple with Shannon and her crew as advisers. They'll be able to give you all sorts of guidance with your ideas. You don't actually have to hang curtains and move furniture around. An extensive drawing with samples of materials or an elaborate explanation of your idea will suffice. Does that make sense? Are there more questions?"

"Yeah, Mom," Logan said. "When would you like us to start working on this thing?"

"Oh, dear. Not right away. We'll start after Christmas. We're all too busy to do anything before the New Year. And between now and then, we'll be sure to have some more criteria for you all to follow."

"So, wait a minute," Stephanie said, staring at her notepad. "You're saying I could take one of the elevators and redesign the interior?"

"Or, what about a hallway?" Craig said.

"Or one of the hotel rooms?" Arabella whispered.

"Or a public bathroom?" Randi suggested.

There were a few laughs, and Lilian said, "Yes, exactly! As I said, we'd like you to work as a couple, and you'll run your ideas by Shannon and her two crew members. They've been instructed to keep you from going too far over the edge."

Logan grinned. "Thank goodness for that."

"And again, feel free to start thinking about it, but no work will start until after the New Year," she said. "Oh, and I should mention that at the end of this . . . this, hmm, this exercise, we'll all vote on the design we like the best. And the winner will receive . . ."

She stared at Bill, who shrugged.

She shrugged as well, then said, "How does ten thousand dollars sound?"

The room erupted in happy screams and laughter.

Before they could start asking questions about money, Lilian said, "That's all for now, darlings. But whenever you have a question, just ask me. Or Shannon. For now, we'd all better get back to work."

She walked to the kitchen door, then turned and looked at me. "Shannon, can you meet me outside for a minute?"

"Of course."

I found her leaning casually against the railing, staring out at the Cove, and when she turned, I saw that she wore a big, sappy grin. I knew she was energized by her kids getting into the decorating idea. That was nice.

"Did you want to ask me something?"

"Yes. I want to ask if you're ready to go exploring in the north cellar."

I had to laugh. "Yes. Let's go."

Chapter Five

Lilian started down the steps to the walk lane that led to the other buildings and immediately began to shiver. "I didn't realize it was getting so cold."

"Do you want to go back and get something warm?" I zipped up my puffer vest.

"Definitely. I'm going to go get a jacket. I'll just be a minute."

"No problem. I'll wait here."

She took off running back through the kitchen. After she was gone, I could hear some grumbling from the kids. I moved closer to the window to hear what was going on. I hated to miss anything. I could see in, too, though I thought I was obscured from view by the plants on the windowsill.

"It's not fair," Randi said, sounding more resentful than angry.

"What part isn't fair?" Stephanie asked. "It's not like Mom is forcing anyone to decorate a room. She just wants us to claim some ownership in this extremely prosperous business. We're all benefiting from it, so why not participate in its growth? And what the heck? You might win some big bucks."

"I don't consider that we're necessarily benefiting from it," Randi countered. "I work hard, and they benefit from that, so why should I give even more?"

"That's so shortsighted," Arabella said quietly. "Mom's bending over backward to get us involved in the business. I think it's important. And exciting."

I was surprised to hear Arabella arguing with Randi. She always went out of her way not to offend Randi, knowing how the woman could turn on you. And it didn't help that their mutual friend Whitney could turn on either one of them at the drop of a hat.

They probably weren't worried about Whitney, but I was. Always. I knew how destructive she could be to anyone who got close to her.

"It's not fair," Randi grumbled again.

"I don't even know what you're talking about," Stephanie said, shaking her head.

"Well, look at it from my perspective. I mean, Logan's been gone for months."

"I'm standing right here," Logan drawled.

"Yes, he's right here," Stephanie said, glancing at her brother, then turning back to Randi. "And now he's living here permanently. So no excuses, Randi." She clapped her hands together like a disciplinarian. "You need to get busy."

"And you need to shut your mouth," Randi said through clenched teeth.

Stephanie grinned saucily. "Why would I want to do that?"

"Because you don't know what you're talking about."

"Shut up, Randi." Logan sounded exhausted.

I had to admit I was shocked to hear Logan talk to his wife that way.

"Me?" Randi gasped. "How dare you! What about her? You haven't been around here for ten months, and now you're going to tell me to shut up? You don't have a clue about what's going on here, either."

"Well, I do have a clue," Steph said, glaring down at Randi. "And I'm perfectly happy to tell you to shut your piehole."

Her husband, Craig, grabbed her arm. "Come on, babe. Let's not fight."

Steph looked up at her husband. "I'm not fighting, Craig. I'm just sick to death of her attitude, and I *do* have a clue about what's going on around here."

I couldn't see Craig's face, but I could imagine the look of shock. Steph wasn't exactly shy, but she didn't usually respond with that kind of in-your-face bravado. Not to Randi, and not to her husband. But good for her, I thought. Maybe her new position in the company had given her an extra dose of audacity. Definitely a good thing.

"Why are you suddenly picking on me?" Randi had the nerve to sound hurt.

"Because sometimes you're just thoughtless," Stephanie murmured. "And since we all live together and work together, some of us notice. And I've decided that you need to be called out when you behave badly."

"What's that supposed to mean?"

"It means exactly what I said," Steph said. "You're rude, and you go off on people who don't deserve it."

Randi tossed her shoulder forward in defiance. "Sometimes they do."

"My mother never deserves your bad attitude," Logan interjected.

Randi snorted a laugh. "Well, I don't care."

He stared at her for a long moment, then murmured, "Well, that just says it all." Without another word, Logan turned and walked out of the room.

There was silence for a long moment, then Arabella took a deep breath and spoke, clearly desperate to lower the temperature and change the subject. "Well, I for one am excited to get started on this project and make Mom's dream come true." She ran her fingers up Franco's arm. "I think we can win."

Randi huffed in disgust. "Oh, great. Knowing you two, you'll probably decide to decorate an elevator like a bordello."

"Excuse me?" Arabella said, sounding confused. After all, she and Randi were supposedly friends, and that definitely sounded like a dig. I almost felt sorry for Arabella because, in reality, Randi wasn't a friend to anyone. "What does that mean?"

"You're starting to sound jealous, Randi," Stephanie said.

I couldn't help myself. I took a chance and peeked in the window to see Randi staring daggers at Stephanie.

Stephanie stared back defiantly and finally said, "You look like you have something to say."

Randi glanced around the room at the faces that were staring back at her. Stephanie's husband, Craig, was staring at the floor, shaking his head. He didn't seem willing to stick his neck out during this conversation. I couldn't blame him.

It was Randi's turn to suck in a deep breath. "I have nothing to say to any of you." And she walked out of the kitchen.

It was kind of a shock to see Randi backing down. Her style was so much more confrontational than the rest of the group's. Stephanie's words must've stunned the heck out of her, but in my humble opinion, Randi needed to be taken down a peg or two once in a while.

Lilian entered the kitchen wearing a bright blue puffer vest. She ignored her kids, who still sat at the table, and rushed out the door to meet me. I scooted away from the window in the nick of time as she pushed her way through the back door. "Ready to go?"

"I sure am," I said.

At that moment, Bill called from farther down along the veranda. "There she is! Lil, honey. We have a minor problem. Can you come down here for a minute?"

She buried her face in her hands and emitted a tiny scream. "Why can't I catch a break?" She sighed and turned to me. "I'd better see what the problem is. Sorry, Shannon. I was hoping we could escape for just a few minutes."

"I can wait if you think it won't take much time."

"I never know, and I've already kept you waiting too long." She gave me a tight smile. "Look, why don't you take the key and go check out the cellar for yourself? Then you can tell me what you think, and maybe we'll do a longer tour later in the week."

I smiled. "That works for me."

She solemnly handed me a thick medieval-looking church key attached by a chain to a regular-sized modern door key. She explained that, unlike the cellar doors in the newer buildings, the north cellar door was on the outside under the stairs that led up to the old veranda. "Please be careful."

"I will." And away I went, leaving her to deal with her lovely husband and her squabbling children.

It took me less than five minutes to walk to the hotel's north wing at the opposite end of the property. Of the four wings of the hotel, this building was the farthest away from the cliff and the steep steps that led down to the beach. It didn't matter, though, because the winter day was icy cold, and nobody was heading for the beach. I knew that this time of year, most of the hotel guests would be doing their Christmas shopping in town or taking advantage of the spa facilities. There was some activity over at the children's park, of course, but the rest of the hotel grounds were virtually deserted. However, that did nothing to diminish the grandeur of the old hotel.

I knew as much about this hotel as I knew about the entire town itself and many of the buildings within. I had personally worked on dozens of them with my father and with my own crew, and since I'd grown up here, I knew the history and folklore of the town as well as anyone.

This four-story Victorian mansion had been built by Stanfield Garrison, Bill's great-grandfather, in 1875 during a building boom that began in 1867, when a prosperous dairy farmer named Henry Clausen decided to build a summer home for his burgeoning family in the grand style of the Gilded Age.

Many of the earliest and most impressive mansions were built by other wealthy dairy farmers whose elaborate homes were referred to as butterfat palaces.

Garrison didn't stop with one mansion but soon built another in the same style to suit his wife's sister and her family. Both homes were set along the Alisal Cliffs overlooking Lighthouse Cove.

Stanfield's son eventually built two more homes on the same coastal property. And the next generation of Garrisons turned those four mansions into one truly grand hotel known as the Cliffs.

Bill was the fourth generation of Garrisons to own the Cliffs Hotel, and his contribution had less to do with the architecture and more to do with recreation and visitor enjoyment. On his watch, he had built the miniature golf course, the batting cages, the train, and many updates to both the children's park and the fabulous luxury spa. And now he and Lilian would also be updating the entire north wing and the cellar, which they had talked about turning into a British-style pub.

I found that same cellar door and stared at the hinges in surprise. They looked practically new and very shiny, even though the rest of the thick old oak door was battered and splintered and looked its age, which had to be at least 150 years old. Nevertheless, the key slipped easily into the lock. Again, I had expected corrosion all over the interior mechanism, but when I heard the click and the darn thing almost flew open, I blinked in surprise.

I decided that Lilian must've recently begun to oil the hinges and the lock in anticipation of coming down here to start work in the next few weeks.

I stepped inside the cellar and the door surprised me once again with well-oiled hinges that caused it to close rapidly behind me. There were no windows down here, and with the door closed, the space was so dark that I couldn't see my hand in front of my face. I groped along the wall until I finally found a light switch. And again, to my utter surprise, the switch worked, lighting up the space nicely.

The brick walls were dark gray, and they looked much thicker and older than those in the other cellar. The ceiling was vaulted, and I realized that at its highest, it appeared to be at least eight feet up. Then I recalled that Bill's great-grandfather was six foot five inches tall, and I wondered if some of their other ancestors had been as tall as he was.

Once this space was renovated, I thought, it would make a fabulous cozy pub.

The air in the room was cold, but not as stuffy as I'd expected it
to be. I also caught the scent of something pleasant in the air. Were
they storing Christmas decorations in here? The scent had a definite
Christmas vibe, which usually meant some combination of cloves
and maybe cinnamon or ginger or peppermint or pine. Right now I
was picking up on both cinnamon and clove scents.

I moved farther into the room, which wasn't easy because there
was furniture everywhere, although it was neatly arranged, like a
jigsaw puzzle. There were two long sofas, several chairs, a dining
table, as well as a few cabinets and hutches. Stacked on top of the
furniture were piles of old linens, including towels, sheets, table-
cloths, napkins, runners. I had to wonder why the hotel held on to
all of this old stuff. Maybe they would be using some of it in the new
wing, although I couldn't imagine the Garrisons finding a use for
such old pieces. Antiques were one thing, but some of this stuff was
simply shabby. Maybe Lilian was planning to sell all these items at
some point. The owners of some of the antique shops in town would
love to see this stuff.

At one end of the longest sofa sat a crate filled with plaster pieces,
just as Lilian had mentioned. I recognized many items, even the
smaller chunks, since I'd been working with these types of pieces
for as long as I'd been involved with Victorian home construction.
There were a number of whole pieces, including corbels, which were
a type of wall bracket. There were some lengths of crown molding
along with an elaborate cornice, which I generally considered a more
ornamental type of crown molding. And there was one delicately
designed ceiling rose, completely intact. A ceiling rose was often

used to encase the wiring of a lighting fixture attached there. Historically, these pieces were made of plaster or occasionally wood, but in modern times, you could find a plastic or PVC version that worked just as well.

Now I wished I'd called Sean to come along with me. He could usually pick out the most beautiful secondhand plasterwork, and we often ended up using some of the pieces when refurbishing the Victorian homes in the area. But that wasn't the only reason I wanted Sean here. Frankly, there was a level of creepiness in here that he would find intriguing, while it mostly just spooked me. And even though the lights worked just fine, they cast disturbing shadows along the thick gray walls.

I shook off the feeling and told myself to soldier on. I was still wearing my tool belt, so I wasn't completely unarmed. I could surely protect myself if anything came for me.

"You're an idiot," I muttered, and could just picture myself attacking a prowler with my industrial-sized measuring tape and pliers.

I sighed. There was nothing down here that was going to hurt me—except for my wild imagination. There was mostly just a lot of old furniture and furnishings that were neatly arranged to fit into every nook and cranny of these two rooms.

Along with all of those were dozens of sets of old glassware in every shape and size, some of them delicately etched. These were all tidily arranged on every flat surface. More linens were piled in this second room, and I supposed it made sense that an old hotel would go through hundreds of sheets and pillowcases in a year. But once they were yellow with age, why would you keep them? I knew Lilian well enough to know she couldn't possibly be a hoarder. So why didn't she give all this stuff away to some worthy charitable organization?

I suppose she could be looking at a thrifty way to save money by turning the sheets into pillow liners or napkins or drop cloths.

"Huh, drop cloths," I thought aloud. "Good idea." I could actually use some new ones. I would have to remember to talk to Lilian about that.

I was pretty certain I'd seen all there was to see down here.

And that's when I spied something I hadn't noticed before. Tucked behind an ornate walnut hutch was a desk. An absolutely spectacular burl cylinder desk. I had to admire any craftsman who could carve something out of burl wood that was as unique and graceful as this piece of furniture.

I had a thing about burl. Maybe I loved it because it was generally considered a deformity. Burl grew like a wart out of a tree trunk or branch. As it grew, it folded into itself over and over again and ended up containing knots and ropelike tangles that resulted in a very hard piece of wood. When it was sanded and smoothed and carved, it became a unique and dramatic piece of furniture, very beautiful and very expensive.

I made my way across the room to get a closer look at the desk. It was perched between the walnut hutch and an antique armoire.

It was even more beautiful up close. *A unique piece of art,* I thought. It felt masculine, not just because of the natural color but because of the fascinating texture of the wood. It would be the perfect gift for Mac. I doubted he would use the desk for writing his books because his writing process was fairly unshakable. He always sat in a particular chair and used a particular desk, and that rarely changed. He even lined up his pencils and pens in a particular order. It was a writer thing. But he might consider using this one to pay bills or write letters. Or we could simply display it as an intriguing piece of furniture art, because that's exactly what it was.

They called it a cylinder desk because the main part was rounded, much like a rolltop desk. Except that this rolltop was one piece of wood that was rolled back to reveal the many compartments and shelves and drawers and nooks and crannies under the cylinder. Searching more closely, I found two hidden side drawers and a pull-out pad that gave me the shivers, in a good way. I knew Mac would go crazy for it.

Even if Mac didn't love the desk as much as I thought he might, we could always move it over to the lighthouse mansion, which Mac was currently renting out as a very successful writers' retreat space. The desk would get some use there, I thought. But that was silly. He would love it!

Would Lilian ever give up a piece of art like this? I doubted it. But it wouldn't hurt to ask.

It was probably silly of me to spend any more time mooning over it. If Lilian wasn't willing to sell it to me, I would have to let it go. But as they say, everyone has a price. So again, it wouldn't hurt to ask.

I whipped out my phone and took a few pictures, then slid it back into my pocket and started toward the door. And that's when I smelled that oddly fresh scent again. *Cloves, definitely,* I thought. But also something herbal. Thyme? Bay leaf? I wondered. And . . . citrus. Orange peel, maybe?

It suddenly occurred to me that Lilian must've assigned some of her housekeeping staff to keep this cellar clean and tidy. Maybe there was something in the cleanser they used that left that trace odor.

My crew would be disappointed that I couldn't discern the exact notes of fresh spicy holiday scent. It was sort of silly, but they considered my sense of smell to be one of my superpowers since I could invariably name almost any tree by the scent it left behind. That was especially true when we were working with newly sawed lumber because that's when the wood's essential oils emitted the strongest scent. On the off chance that my guys weren't familiar with a type of wood we were working with, I could often guess it just from the scent. Even with older pieces of lumber, if I sliced off a thin chunk with my pocketknife, I could sniff it and usually identify the wood.

It was a gift. What could I say?

Wade occasionally commented that I had a more powerful sniffer than a bloodhound. Strangely enough, I considered that a compliment since we worked in construction and had to be aware of all sorts of odd smells and sounds that might indicate a problem. Gas leaks, water leaks, different types of mold, smoke. Anything could lead to disaster if we didn't catch it immediately.

As I approached the door, I realized how much my mind had wandered. I glanced up at the ceiling—and screamed!

"Oh God!"

I stood shuddering for several long seconds. There were gargoyles dangling from the ceiling! Not one or two, but dozens. They were hanging on the walls, too. Who in the world hung gargoyles from the ceiling? Was I hallucinating? Was this Lilian's little joke on me?

Why had I not seen them before? I remembered glancing at the ceiling earlier and thinking how high it was. But I'd been looking at a different part of it.

"Time to go," I muttered, and rubbed my arms, now convinced that I was developing permanent shivers and chills.

As I got closer to the door, I wondered if Lilian actually had plans for all these gargoyles. Did she intend to put one in every hotel room? That would be weird, but Victorian hotels could get weird sometimes. And just look at all of these creatures! There were so many of them. Some with long tongues and others with pointed ears; some with wings, some with horns. Some looked like animals and others like humans. To me, they all had a touch of devilishness. I was usually not so wishy-washy, but damn, they gave me the willies!

I knew I was being ridiculous. There was no rhyme or reason for the fact that the little stone creatures freaked me out, but they did. I didn't even want to look at them, but how could I not? The one closest to me had pointy ears and a long tongue that curled up and aimed itself right at me, clearly mocking me. I shuddered.

"Ridiculous," I muttered. Next time I'd be sure to bring Sean along. He was the one who got a kick out of gargoyles. Not me.

As I skirted a solid oak table holding more of the lovely etched glassware, I checked my watch. I was shocked to realize that I had been down in this cellar for over an hour.

I had to leave now to give myself time to drive home, shower and change clothes, then drive back here before the carnival officially opened. I made it to the door and opened it easily. Stepping outside, I locked the door behind me and jogged to my truck. Just as I reached the tailgate, there was a shout.

"Hey!"

I barely managed to hold back the shriek as footsteps pounded behind me.

"Shannon!"

I almost collapsed with relief as I recognized Sean's voice. "Good grief," I muttered. All those stupid gargoyles must've freaked me out worse than I thought.

"Sorry if I scared you," Sean said, frowning.

"You didn't scare me," I insisted. "I . . . just . . . It's nothing. My mind was elsewhere." But I couldn't make eye contact with him. He would be able to tell immediately that I was completely full of nonsense.

"Okay." He studied me for another second, then shrugged. "Well, I'm glad I caught you."

"What's up? What're you still doing here?"

"My crappy old drywall blade broke. If I can borrow yours, I can finish spreading the mud and taping tonight. Then tomorrow it'll be ready for sanding. I really want to be finished with this project by the weekend."

"That would be great. And I don't blame you for wanting to finish it."

"Aw, come on," he said. "Randi isn't so bad."

"Oh, really?" I chuckled.

He shrugged. "At least she's hot."

I rolled my eyes. "You are such a guy."

He grinned. "What can I say?"

Rolling my eyes, I unlatched the tailgate of my truck, opened my toolbox, and pulled out the second shelf. I considered this shelf my repository for all things drywall, including a double-sided drywall cutter, a couple of foldable jab saws, one full set of drywall knives along with various others, and numerous taping knives in different lengths.

"Take your pick," I said.

He stared at the tools, then gazed up at me, looking vaguely queasy. "Jeez, Shannon. Everything's pink."

I frowned at him. "Do you even know me?"

He laughed. "I know all about your pink tools fetish, but I don't think I've ever seen so much pink in one place in my entire life."

My people knew that I bought quality pink tools made by top manufacturers. My crew rarely borrowed them and certainly never kept them for long.

"Is this pink thing going to be a problem?" I asked.

"Nope." He was still grinning as he reached for a medium width six-inch drywall knife. "I'll take this one." He held it closer and studied the blade. Then, frowning, he gazed at me. "Have you even used this one? It's in perfect condition. Looks brand-new."

I smiled sweetly. "That's because I take very good care of my tools."

"I'm impressed."

"Thank you. Are you sure you don't want the twelve-inch blade? You'll get faster results."

"Yeah, but I prefer the control I get with the smaller blade."

"That makes sense. Do you need any help?"

"I'm good. I'll be done in an hour, and then I'll see you later at the carnival."

"Okay. Call me if you have any problems, with the job or with . . . you know, people."

He chuckled. "Yeah, I get you. But, Shannon, Randi really doesn't bother me."

"You are one of the rare lucky ones."

Now he grinned. "You know I am."

I had to roll my eyes again. "I love you, Sean, but . . ."

"You don't have to say it." He was still grinning. "I know I'm a dog."

"Yes, I'm afraid you are. But you're a good dog."

Now we were both laughing. "Thanks for the knife."

"You're welcome. See you later."

As I started my engine, I was still thinking about Sean. We were both kidding about referring to him as a "dog." He had always been completely professional around any client we had ever worked with. And he'd saved the day by agreeing to work with Randi despite her crappy moods and vitriol. We both knew I never would've been able to put up with her bad temper on a day-to-day basis. And worse, so much worse, was that it made my skin crawl to realize that every word I said to her would've been reported back to Whitney. Eventually, I might've been tempted to punch her out, which would be highly unprofessional, to say the least. So I was thrilled when Sean agreed to supervise the construction of the sommelier's office. Recently, Randi had demanded that Bill hire someone to build her an office in the wine cellar. Despite our busy schedule, I had agreed because I knew it would shut Randi up. And privately, I agreed with her. It made sense to have the sommelier's office down here. And with Sean on the job, the project wouldn't take more than a week to complete. He was cool and mild-mannered as well as being a superior craftsman. And apparently, he didn't mind having Randi around.

"Whatever gets the job done," I said to myself, silently giving thanks before turning on the radio to catch the latest news.

As I drove past the Garrisons' private kitchen entrance, I noticed Stephanie sitting on the steps, gazing up at Oliver, who stood on the cobblestone walkway chatting with her. Her smile lit up her face and she looked so happy, it made me wonder for just a moment if something was going on there. But, no, Stephanie was happily married to Craig, the bar manager. And then I remembered the snotty comments Randi had made to Oliver the other day, and I just had to shake my head. Everybody loved Oliver, and he was obviously a good friend of Stephanie's, so Randi wasn't doing herself any favors. But what did I know? People could be so confusing.

The sun was getting close to hitting the horizon when I pulled into the driveway and parked next to Mac's SUV.

I grabbed my bag, headed for the kitchen door, and dashed inside. After some hugs and a quick rubdown for Robbie and some soft strokes and ear scratches for Tiger and Luke, I turned to Mac, who was shaking his head.

"I'm always last in line."

I laughed. "I love you so much," I said, and scratched his ears.

"That really makes up for it." His tone was borderline sarcastic.

"I promise I'll be ready in thirty seconds," I said, and raced for the stairs.

He laughed. "Hold on, love." He grabbed my arms and pulled me close to touch his lips to mine. "You've got plenty of time."

"Do I? It feels like I'm running behind." Relieved, I collapsed against his warm rugged chest.

"That's better," he said, holding me.

"You feel so good," I murmured.

"So do you, but you've obviously had a long day."

"You could say that." I pulled off my puffy vest. "Long and weird."

"Weird, really? You know how much I love weird."

I laughed. "Yes, I know."

"Go take your shower," he said. "I'll have a glass of wine and a little something to snack on when you get out."

"Oh, bless you." I kissed him.

"And then you can tell me the weird parts." He kissed me back.

"You know I will."

When I came downstairs forty-five minutes later dressed casually for the evening in a thick black sweater, black jeans, and my favorite chunky Chelsea boots, Mac handed me a glass of red wine. "We still have a few minutes before we have to leave."

"Wonderful." I took a sip, then grabbed a piece of cheese, set it on a cracker, and bit into it.

"So, tell me about your weird day," he said.

I sipped my wine and did just that. "It started with this incredibly smart and savvy idea that Lilian came up with and then, afterward, having to listen to Randi gripe and moan about that same smart idea." I explained Lilian's genius decorating idea, and finished by mentioning that the best design would get ten thousand dollars.

"Wow," he said, shaking his head. "That girl's got problems."

"Yes, she does. I would blame it on Whitney, but I think Randi may outdo her when it comes to plain old mean stupidity."

He winced. "That is a problem."

"Yup." I bit into a cracker, then took a quick sip of wine. "Maybe I'm just jealous."

"You and I both know that that's completely bogus."

"You say that because you've only heard the story from my point of view."

"No." He held up his finger to stop my train of thought. "Maybe you didn't know that I've heard Logan's side, too. And I've also seen and heard firsthand the whining and the lies and disloyalty that pour from her mouth. I don't trust her as far as I can throw her."

"I appreciate that," I said, beaming at him. "But I'm not sure Lilian and Bill see it the same way."

Mac grabbed another cracker and handed it to me with a slice of cheese on top. "You know they do."

"You're right. But if I complained to Lilian about her, Randi might tell Lilian that I'm jealous of her, and that's why I say mean things about her, blah blah blah."

"That's a bunch of crap, but I get your point."

"Let's stop talking about her."

"Best idea yet," Mac said. "Let's go."

As we climbed into his SUV and headed for the Fun Zone, Mac asked, "How did the final run-through go this morning?"

"It's going to be spectacular," I said with a happy smile.

"Can't wait to see it." He turned onto Cliffside Drive. "So, what else happened today?"

"Oh! I almost forget to tell you about the gargoyles."

His eyes widened. "Say what?"

"You heard me."

"I did, and I'm intrigued."

"It's so bizarre. Lilian has literally hundreds of gargoyles stored in the north cellar. They're hanging from the ceiling and climbing the walls. It's just freaking weird."

At a stoplight near the top of the hill, he reached over and smoothed a thick strand of curly hair away from my face. "You've had yourself quite a day."

"You could say so." I took the opportunity to burrow into his shoulder. "I just hope everything goes well tonight. I don't need any more shock waves."

The light turned green and Mac drove on in silence. After a moment, he said, "Holy cow, Shannon. It looks amazing."

"What?" While I'd been worrying about tonight, I hadn't paid attention to where we were.

I turned and gazed at the Fun Zone. "It looks so pretty."

"It looks spectacular."

He was staring at the Cliffs Hotel, which was covered in a million tiny lights and had taken on the appearance of a hugely elegant fairy palace.

Across the field from the hotel was the Fun Zone, with its big brightly striped red-and-white circus tent hovering over the entire zone. And it, too, was covered in sparkling lights.

Mac followed the signs to the parking lot that had been designated "special guest" parking.

"It looks enchanted," I whispered. "Like magic."

"It's beautiful," Mac said.

Dozens of light strings streamed down from the center of the big top tent and spilled over the sides like glistening waterfalls.

Mac leaned over and kissed me. "You did good, kiddo."

"Thanks." I grinned. "I had a little help from my crew. And Bill and Lilian, of course."

"They all deserve praise because it looks amazing," he said.

"Okay, but we should make sure everything's in working order before I take any bows."

"You have a point," he agreed. "So let's go check it out up close." He grabbed his heavy jacket from the back seat and opened his door. "Ready?"

"For the big show? I think so." I slipped into my own jacket. "Even though I've been working on it for weeks, it's a real thrill to see it up and running in all its opening night glory."

We both stepped out of the car, grabbed each other's hands, and hurried over to the Fun Zone.

Chapter Six

"There are already hundreds of people out here," Mac marveled as we surveyed the crowd. "The Garrisons have done it again."

"It's exciting, isn't it?"

"Yeah, it is." He gave me a light squeeze. "And you did a fantastic job constructing this thing."

"I had a little help," I said, but his words warmed me.

"Of course. But the carousel alone is like a glittering gem. And then you managed to make it all fit together with the games and seating areas and mini concession stands under this perfect little jewel of a big top."

"Jewel of a big top. I like that." I pressed a kiss to his cheek. "Thank you."

"Okay, that's enough praise. I've got to go wage a battle between the forces of good and evil."

"I take that to mean you want to play your first round of Whac-A-Mole."

"Yeah, except I notice you guys changed the name to Bonk the Christmas Bunny. Very soft and sweet and politically correct."

"Hey, it's Christmas," I said, laughing. "And it's for little kids. They tend to like bunnies more than moles."

"Either way works for me." He pulled me in for another kiss. "But no matter how you sugarcoat it, they're still going to be bonking bunnies, so it could turn into a bloody battle. Even for the little kids."

"They're not real bunnies. But okay, big guy. After you bonk a few bunnies, I want to ride the carousel."

"You got it. Even though that carousel's for girls."

"Them's fighting words, dude," I said, scowling. But a few seconds later, I began to bat my eyelashes. "I'm willing to demonstrate why guys like the carousel, too."

"I believe you." He laughed and kissed me again.

"Hey, you two."

We both turned and saw Logan Garrison standing nearby.

"Logan, how are you?" I gave him a quick hug and then noticed that he was holding the hand of a little boy who looked about five or six years old. That little guy was likewise holding the hand of a slightly bigger boy who had to be his brother. A third boy stood on the other side of Logan, eyeing the Bonk the Bunny game with longing. The three boys were clearly brothers with their shaggy white-blond hair, matching black sweatshirts, jeans, and blacktop tennis shoes.

"The game's all yours if you want it," Mac said, holding out his mallet to the oldest brother.

"Yeah!" he said, then quickly looked at Logan. "Can I?"

"Sure. Do you know how to play it?"

"Gosh, yeah!" He grabbed the mallet and pushed the start button.

The two younger boys stood on either side of their brother and egged him on, trying to figure out when the mole—the *bunny*—would pop up.

Logan grinned. "Good job, Rowan." Then he turned to me and Mac. "This old guy here is Rowan, and these are his brothers, Phineas and Hudson."

"My name is Phineas, but you should call me Finn," the middle boy insisted.

"Yes, he's Finn," Logan said with a grin, tousling his unruly hair. "Sorry, bud."

"I'm Hudson," the youngest said. "You can call me Hudson."

I grinned. "Okay, Hudson. That's a cool name."

"I know."

"How old are you, Hudson?"

"I'm five years old. I'll be in first grade next year. My mom couldn't come tonight because she's sick. But I promised to bring her a prize and also some popcorn and a candy bar."

"That's very thoughtful of you," I said, noting that Hudson was a talker. "I'll bet she's really going to like that."

"Their dad was killed in Afghanistan two years ago," Logan murmured in my ear. He needn't have worried that the boys might overhear him; they were totally tuned in to bonking the bunnies. Plus, the crowd was noisy and energetic. "And their mom, Aurora, was recently diagnosed with stage two breast cancer. She's undergoing chemotherapy, so some of us at Homefront have taken the boys under our wings."

"Oh dear," I said. "Those poor little boys. And their poor mother. I'm so sorry."

"It's rough," he agreed. "Aurora had to quit her job as a hairdresser because she just can't keep up with the physical demands. She took a leave of absence, and she had to give up the apartment they were living in."

"That's a shame," I said. "Is there anything we can do to help?"

The emotion and gratitude I saw in his expression was almost overwhelming. "Thanks, Shannon. We were able to get her and all the boys into one of the family houses at Homefront, just until she's well enough to go back to work and afford a place of their own again."

"I'm so sorry," I said. "And she just lost her husband a few years ago, too."

"And those boys lost their father," Mac said.

"That's really terrible."

"Yeah," Logan said. "But she's a real trooper. So are the kids."

"Sounds like it. Her name is Aurora?"

"Yeah. Pretty, huh?"

"I love it," I said. "Sounds like you've known her for a while."

"I feel like we've known each other for most of our lives."

"She must really appreciate you being around."

"I'm glad to be here for her."

We were silent for a moment. Then Hudson interrupted with a less-than-subtle yanking on his jacket. "Hey, Logan. Can I play the Bonk the Christmas Bunny game now?"

"Sure, bud," he said. "Do you still have some of your green tickets left?"

"Oh yeah!" The green tickets could be bought for pennies, and then red tickets accrued with any of the games. Later, the red tickets could be turned into prizes. Any money left over would be donated to charity.

Hudson dug into his pocket, pulled out a string of eight or ten green tickets, and handed them to Logan. "Here!"

"Well, isn't this a cozy little gathering."

I felt an instant chill as we all turned to find Randi staring at Logan through haughty eyes. What was her problem now?

"Hey, Randi," Logan said, his tone casual. "I didn't think you'd make it out here tonight."

"Oh really?" she said wryly.

"Yeah." He turned to the boys. "Boys," Logan said, getting their attention, "this is my wife. Her name is Randi Garrison." He said it slowly. Then to Randi he said, "This is Rowan, Finn, and Hudson." As he introduced each boy, he gave their shoulders a squeeze. It was a clear sign of affection and Randi picked up on it immediately. She seemed to grow more annoyed as each boy was introduced.

Hudson stared up at her, awestruck. "You're pretty."

She stared down at Hudson, then blinked. Finally she looked at Logan, unsure what to say. She couldn't seem to handle the compliment, as if she hadn't expected anyone to say something so flattering to her.

"Hello, Randi," I said, deliberately diverting her attention away from Logan and the little boys. "It's nice that you could take a break and come out for a while."

"Oh yeah," she said cynically. "My employers are just so generous."

"They really are," I said. "You're so lucky to work here."

She stared at me as if I'd lost half my brain, but I didn't care. She was such a dark cloud. She looked at all the boys, then finally, she glared back at me. "I'd say the Garrisons are the lucky ones to have me on their staff."

I had to suppress a groan. She was so condescending I could barely keep from laughing in her face. But I knew she would only make life miserable for everyone connected to me and that wouldn't be fair to anyone. I turned away, vowing to have nothing more to say to this twit.

"Well," she finally said to Logan, "I'd love to stick around and play with you and your little friends, but I've got a job to go to. Some of us do work for a living."

"Guess you'd better get back to it then," Logan said, not bothering to hide his contempt.

She didn't acknowledge the boys, just flipped her hair away from her face and walked purposefully back to the hotel.

She actually sounded jealous! Of those three darling boys? Who could figure her out?

"Is that lady really your wife?" Hudson asked, sounding doubtful. "She looked mad."

"She had to go back to work," Logan said easily.

To distract them all, I asked, "Did you guys ride the carousel yet?"

"Yeah!" Finn said excitedly. "I got the camel! He's the tallest one in the whole carousel."

"I got to ride the shark!" Hudson shouted.

"That's the one I want to ride," I said.

"It's a good one," he said, nodding rapidly.

"I played Ball-in-a-Bucket," Finn said, "and I won a stuffed tiger for my mom."

"That is a wonderful gift," I said.

He shrugged self-consciously. "I know. She likes tigers."

I smiled at him. "Me too."

When the boys began to talk among themselves, Logan murmured, "Thanks, Shannon."

"Of course. They're good boys."

"Yeah, they are."

I turned to Mac. "Are you ready to ride the carousel?"

"Yes, I am." He slipped his arm through mine. "Let's go."

I gave Logan a hug, then said to the boys, "You guys have fun, okay?"

"Okay!" Hudson said, punching his fist in the air.

While waiting in line with Mac, I said, "Pretty sure Logan didn't expect Randi to show up tonight."

"He looked bummed out that she showed up," Mac said. "But he hid it well. Do you think she'll give him more grief than usual for hanging out with those kids?"

"They're just little kids," I said. "But I'm sure she'll make him pay for it."

"But why?" Mac wondered.

"Because he wasn't paying enough attention to her."

He shook his head in disgust. "Of course."

"She's jealous of anyone or anything that takes attention away from her."

"That's a hard way to live."

"Yes, it is," I agreed. "Did you notice she didn't say one word to those boys?"

"I noticed." Mac shook his head. "She's a scary woman."

"You won't get an argument from me." Strangely enough, Mac and I had never discussed Randi before. But we tended to agree on certain subjects, and apparently Randi was one of them. It helped that Logan was our good friend, and it was obvious that Randi did not treat him very well.

I checked my watch. "It's almost time for Santa Claus."

His eyes narrowed. "You're not thinking of sitting on his lap, are you?"

"Would that be a problem?" I asked dryly.

"Absolutely not," he said with a laugh. "But seriously, what do you have to do for Santa?"

"I've got to make sure the Booth Number Ten mechanisms are working well and the lighting is perfect. Then, once he's out and talking with the kids, we can wander around, ride the carousel, play some games, or maybe take a ride on the train. Or—what the heck?—we could stop for a drink in the bar. I just need to be back here at nine thirty when Santa Claus shuts down."

"Will you be doing that every night until Christmas?"

"Oh no!" I grimaced. "I'm just realizing that I didn't go over the schedule with you."

"No worries. Give me a quick rundown."

"Okay. I'll be doing this same thing maybe once a week. My entire crew will be taking turns, switching places each night, plus Wade and Carla will fill in where necessary."

"Sounds like you'll have plenty of people to take care of Santa."

"Yes, we'll have him covered."

Mac grinned. "So once Santa shows up, let's start with another few rounds of Bonk the Bunny."

I slipped my arm through his. "I'll cheer you on."

We both watched as the lights flickered and then began a chasing pattern all around the top of the tent several times before the music rose to a grand crescendo. Then slowly but surely, the top of the special booth began to rise up and the sides slowly slid down. The lights continued to chase in different colors until the booth was completely open and the man inside stood up and waved. And laughed. "Ho ho ho!"

The audience went wild. "Santa Claus!"

"Wow," Mac said. "Very impressive."

"Amazing." I laughed in delight. "It worked."

The elves entered quickly with their stanchions, and all the kids raced to get in line.

And all we could hear was the screams and shouts for "Santa Claus!"

"Let's move a little farther down the way," Mac said.

"Good idea." I stopped to set the alarm on my phone and then kept walking. It was only slightly quieter at the far side of the Fun Zone.

"This is wild," Mac said. "Do you want some popcorn?"

"I'll share some with you."

"Great." We got in a short line at the popcorn booth and watched the crowds until we got our popcorn and stepped to the side.

"I know it's crazy," Mac said, "but I love this kind of stuff. The noise and the kids and the carousel and Santa Claus. It brings back memories of all sorts of good times."

I hugged him. "I'm glad."

I glanced up when I heard my name called and turned to see Shirley Ann waving at me. She was with her friend Joyce, who was head of Housekeeping.

"Hi, Shirley Ann," I said. "And, Joyce, hi. Have you both met Mac Sullivan?"

Shirley took Mac's hand. "Oh, it's a real pleasure, Mr. Sullivan. I hope you don't mind my telling you, I love your books."

"Thank you, Shirley Ann. Believe me, I never get tired of hearing that."

"Are you two having fun?" I asked.

Joyce squeezed my arm affectionately. "We always manage to have fun no matter where we are or what we're doing."

"That's a good policy," I said. "We're about to play one of the games. Would you like to join us?"

"Thank you," Shirley Ann said. "But we were looking forward to taking a ride on that gorgeous carousel."

"It really is lovely, isn't it?" I agreed.

"It reminds me of a precious jewel box," Joyce said. "All those shiny golden mirrors along the top edge reflecting all the pretty colors."

"And the music is so charming and old-fashioned," Shirley Ann said.

"It's starting to get crowded, so we should get in line," Shirley Ann said. "But, Shannon, I'm dying to ask, who were those adorable children you were talking to a few minutes ago?"

She could only be referring to the three boys that Logan had been watching. I explained to Shirley Ann who everyone was and mentioned that their mother was ill. "So Logan was taking care of them tonight for her. They're all living at Homefront temporarily."

Shirley Ann explained to Joyce, "Logan is Randi's husband."

"Yes, of course," Joyce said, then wiggled her eyebrows. "He's a handsome one, isn't he?"

"Yes, and as sweet as can be," Shirley Ann added.

"I hope the boys' mother isn't too seriously ill," Joyce said.

"I'm not sure," I said, unwilling to say too much about a person I didn't even know.

"Well, I thought I'd seen those little boys around here before. They're so darn cute, aren't they?"

I smiled. "They really are."

Joyce grabbed hold of Shirley Ann's arm. "Girlfriend! Let's go!"

"Yay!" Shirley Ann cried. "We're off to the carousel."

"Have fun," I said, and walked away with Mac. When we were far enough away, I turned to Mac. "Was that awkward?"

"You mean, them asking about the boys? Or you trying to avoid talking about their mother? Or why they've seen the boys around here before?"

I sighed. "So, it was awkward."

"Only because you never answered either of their questions."

I straightened my shoulders. "That's because I can be discreet."

He grinned. "Of course you can."

I frowned. "I'm not even sure why I felt like I had to be discreet. Shirley Ann and Joyce are both wonderful, but they're both good friends of Randi's. I couldn't help but feel protective of the little boys."

"I get that," he said. "And it's a good thing to be protective of kids, no matter who's asking the questions." He kissed me. "But I have noticed that you have a very suspicious mind."

"I guess I do."

"I find that extremely attractive."

I let loose with a short laugh. "You are quite insane."

"Agreed." Mac grabbed my hand. "Let's go bonk something."

———

After six more rounds of Bonk the Bunny, Mac relented, and we took a nice, easy ride on the carousel. After that, we still had another forty-five minutes to kill before I had to be back for the "Goodnight Santa" session, so we walked into the hotel and went straight back to the bar. It was a lovely room with soft lighting and quiet Christmas jazz playing in the background. I was relieved to see Stephanie's husband, Craig, tending the bar because I didn't think I could handle another five minutes of Randi's hostile vibe. I knew she often worked as sommelier for the dinner crowd and then switched to work the bar later in the evening. And that made me wonder how she got along with her customers. She had to be more pleasant to them than she was to me and all the others she treated with her usual level of contempt. Otherwise, how could she keep her job?

But then again, she was married to the owners' son. That probably counted for something.

"Hi, Craig," I said as I pulled out a barstool and took a seat. Mac chose to stand next to me.

"Hey, you two," Craig said jovially. "What sounds good tonight?"

"Do you have anything festive?" I asked.

He grinned. "I'm serving a Winter White Cosmo that's fantastic. Starts with premium vodka, white cranberry juice, a splash of orange liqueur, and garnished with an orange curl, a cluster of sugar-coated cranberries, and a sprig of rosemary."

"My goodness, it sounds wonderful," I said. "I'll have one."

Mac ordered a shot of whiskey. No frou-frou sugarcoated cocktails for my guy!

Craig set out two small bowls of nuts in front of us, and as he fixed my drink, he asked if we'd been out to the Money Pit yet.

"The Money Pit?" I asked, confused.

His grin had a cynical edge. "I mean the Fun Zone."

"Oh." *Wow, bad attitude,* I thought, but tried to keep smiling. "It's really fun," I said with emphasis. "It sounds corny and old-fashioned, but we're having a blast."

"I agree." Mac wrapped his arm around my waist. "The carousel itself is a classic, shiny and beautiful. And some of those games are so much fun, I didn't want to stop."

"Huh," he said. "Guess I'll take some time to check it out tomorrow." Then he placed our drinks in front of us on the bar and said, "Cheers."

Mac held up his glass and I clicked mine against his. We both said, "Cheers."

After my first sip, I said, "Wow, this is delicious."

"Glad you like it," Craig said. "And it's good to hear your thoughts about the carnival. It's getting high marks with a lot of people." He sighed. "Sounds like another win for Bill."

"Nothing wrong with that," Mac said lightly.

"Absolutely not. When Bill wins, we all win."

But Craig's expression wasn't quite as cheerful as his words indicated. Again he sounded almost cynical, and I wondered why but didn't ask. Instead, I flashed a brilliant smile. "Well, I intend to report that the Christmas cocktail served in the hotel bar is simply delicious."

Now Craig grinned. "I appreciate it."

Two new customers walked into the bar, and Craig moved over to take care of them after bidding us a good evening.

Ten minutes later we finished our drinks and waved to Craig as we walked out of the bar. Mac wrapped his arm around my shoulders. "I really hope they hold on to the Whack-the-Bunny after Christmas is over."

I tried to be stern. "Get it straight, Mac. It's Whac-A-*Mole* or Bonk the *Bunny*. You can't have it both ways."

He leaned his forehead against mine. "I saw you giggling when I called it Whack-the-Bunny."

I'd been catching myself giggling all night. "Maybe I did," I admitted. "It's mainly funny because of the way you say it."

He pulled me close and whispered, "I just love to hear you laugh."

"And I just plain love you all over, Mac."

On the veranda, we held on to each other and stared out at the cliffs. The moon was reflected on the surface of the Cove, and I could've stayed here like this for hours.

But a few minutes later, my watch vibrated. "Sorry. Santa Claus is going to be closing up shop in ten minutes. We'd better move it."

We set off walking across the parking lot. "Santa Steve sure keeps busy, doesn't he?" Mac murmured.

"He does. I mean, there are a lot more Santas in the brigade this year, and they're all pretty good. But Steve is the best. The Garrisons were lucky to get him."

"I'm going to guess you had something to do with it."

I smiled coyly. "It's possible."

The lights of the carousel and the Fun Zone began to flicker gently, just as our lighting director had designed it. We were about fifty yards away and I could see Santa stand up and wave goodnight. "Goodnight, children! Dream happy thoughts and always remember to *be nice*!"

The kids repeated after him, "Be nice!" Then they waved and shouted, "Goodnight, Santa Claus! Goodbye, Santa Claus!"

Still waving, Santa sat down in his chair. "And we'll be back for more fun tomorrow night! Goodnight! Goodnight!"

He continued to wave to the children as the music rose to a crescendo, and the roof of Santa's clamshell box lowered slowly, finally closing up completely.

The kids screamed and applauded and shouted, "Goodnight, Santa! Goodnight!"

As the lights throughout the Fun Zone began to dim, we heard Santa call out one more "Ho, ho, ho!" Then his voice faded as the lights continued to dim. Finally, everyone got the hint that the show was over and applauded one last time.

The lights went out altogether for two seconds. Then they rose slightly, and the announcer—our own Bill Garrison—thanked everyone for coming. "Santa Claus wants everyone to spread the word," Bill said. "He'll be here every night until Christmas Eve! Goodnight now! Have a safe trip home!"

There was thunderous applause, and lots of little kids screamed happily until the lights dimmed one last time and the show was over.

Backstage, I knew a few of the elves were escorting Santa Steve down the back corridor and out to the priority parking lot. Other elves were directing people to their different parking areas.

A few minutes later, Mac and I slipped around the back of the Fun Zone toward the same priority parking lot.

"That was an amazing light show," Mac said with a grin. "Was that all Buck's design?"

"Pretty much," I said. "I'm awfully glad he moved up here to work with us."

"He's a great guy." He draped his arm around my shoulders. "Did you have fun?"

I leaned against him. "I did. It was old-fashioned and kind of sweet. What did you think?"

"I had a good time," he said. "Of course, I was with you, so naturally, it was fun."

"Aww," I said. "I had a good time, too."

"Hey," Mac said, pointing. "There's Wade and Sean."

We all waved at each other from a few dozen yards away. There was no way they could hear me, so I would text them when I got home. All I wanted to say was "Talk to you tomorrow."

In the priority parking lot, we caught up with Santa Steve and stopped to talk.

He greeted us both and shook Mac's hand. "How are you, Mac?"

"Doing well, Santa."

"Ho ho ho," Steve laughed. "You know you can call me Steve."

"Not when you're dressed like that, I can't."

He laughed again. "Ho ho ho."

His laugh was so infectious, we both joined in.

"So, how was your first night, Santa?" I asked.

"The kids are great, as always," he said with enthusiasm. He really was a wonderful Santa Claus. "They love the carousel, by the way. It's getting high marks."

"It's a beauty," I said.

"And the Fun Zone was even better than anyone thought it would be."

"I agree," I said. "It's a fun way to spend a few hours."

"And by the way," Steve said, "a few of the elves snuck into the line to ask me for hints on how to win those games you've set up."

"Did you give them any?"

He winked. "Of course. Gotta help out my homies."

That made me laugh. And it reminded me that many of those

young elves were only nine or ten years old. They still qualified for a visit with Santa.

"You heading home, Santa?" I asked.

"I've got one more stop for a holiday party at a nearby retirement home."

"Isn't it kind of late?" I asked.

"Oh, no." He shook his head. "This time of year, Santa's work is never done."

Chapter Seven

The next morning I joined Wade, Sean, and Buck for a meeting in Bill and Lilian's private living room upstairs. A bit more formal than their usual kitchen table meeting, it was to be a postgame discussion, as Bill liked to call it, and I didn't know quite what to expect.

On a sideboard were donuts and lots of coffee, which gave me some hope that the conversation would be a happy one. Bill wouldn't hand out bad news with his donuts, would he?

We didn't have to wait long. After he took a bite of his chocolate-dipped cruller, Bill got the ball rolling. "In case any of you were thinking I might want to complain about last night, let me ease your mind. I thought it all ran like clockwork, and I can't say enough good things about every aspect of the work you all did."

"I agree, everything was wonderful," Lilian chimed in. "Especially the lighting. I've never seen the hotel and grounds looking so magical. Honestly, I'm so impressed."

"That's your cue, Buck," I said, leaning over to make eye contact with my superstar lighting guy. "Take a bow."

I was delighted to see his cheeks turning pink.

"Thanks, everybody," Buck said. "But Wade did most of the heavy lifting."

"I just followed your directions," Wade insisted. "You're the artist."

"Agreed," Bill said, then moved to the next item on his checklist. "And Santa Claus. Wow, Shannon. Thank you for introducing us to Steve. What a fantastic Santa Claus."

"How did you meet him?" Lilian asked.

"He's an old friend of my father's," I said. "And you should see what happens when the entire Santa Brigade gets together. It's pretty wild. But Steve is the best, isn't he? Truly jolly."

"He transcends jolly," Lilian enthused. "He made the world come alive for every kid out there last night."

I smiled at Lilian. "That's such a nice way to put it. And the parents love him, too. He's pretty special."

"Okay. Next on my list," Bill said, consulting a clipboard. "I have to say that I was very impressed and appreciative that you and some of your crew stayed through to the end of the evening."

I smiled at his kind words and didn't bother to remind him that I'd given him a crew schedule last week. "That's part of our service, Bill. And just to remind you, we'll have a couple of crew members here each night, just in case we have an emergency or something needs a quick fix."

"That is greatly appreciated," he said.

"Just part of the service," I said again. "And besides, we all want to take a turn around the Fun Zone at least once or twice this month."

"I hear that." Bill grinned. "So far, it's all working really well. I want to thank you and your entire team. I'm grateful and happy this morning."

"Me too," Lilian said.

"Then I'm happy, too," I said.

After the meeting, I walked out of the Cliffs Hotel with Buck, Wade, and Sean. "Okay, guys. You know I'll be at that dinner tonight while you're working the carnival, so I just want to double-check which two of you will be covering the gig for me."

Sean checked the calendar screen on his phone, just to be sure. "It's me and Carla tonight, and Wade and Buck tomorrow night."

"Right," Wade said. "And we'll have a meeting with everyone on Thursday to confirm the schedule for the rest of the month. Besides us, we've got Todd, Johnny, Amanda, and Douglas joining as well."

"Meeting at the pub, right?"

Sean grinned. "Of course."

I nodded. "Good. So, change of subject. Do you have time to show me Randi's new office?"

Sean grinned. "Let's go."

It took us less than thirty seconds to jog downstairs to the wine cellar. We crossed the beautiful parquet wood floor and stopped.

"The floor inside the office isn't ready to stand on yet," Sean explained as he opened the door. "But you can see the walls and the built-ins."

I stared inside the small office and nodded my approval. "This lighting really works."

"Yeah, you were right about the fixtures. They've got a combination art deco mid-century modern vibe that's pretty nice."

Wade moved in closer to study the pattern on the panels. "I dig that raw finish on the wood."

"Yeah, me too," Sean said. "The wood isn't actually raw, just rough-hewn with a really thin coating of varnish to finish it off. Pretty cool, huh?"

"It's a great look. Not at all feminine, but it's kind of sexy. If that makes any sense at all."

"Totally!" Buck agreed.

"I really like the way you made up for the lack of windows by adding these panels," Wade said.

"That was Shannon's idea," Sean said.

Wade nodded at me. "Nice going, boss."

"And Buck picked out this very cool light feature," Sean said.

"The man's a lighting genius," Wade said.

Buck beamed a smile.

"I hope Randi let you know how much she appreciated all this hard work."

Sean shrugged. "She said she was okay with it."

"Wow, high praise," Wade said.

We were lucky to get that one comment, I thought. "For Randi, it's as close as you'll get to gushing."

"I noticed she doesn't say much when she likes something," Sean said. "But she really lets you have it when she doesn't."

I frowned, wondering if Randi had "let him have it" during his time on this job. I wasn't sure he'd tell me if she did, so I didn't ask.

I took one last look around, then nodded. "It's really beautiful, and even if she never says so, you did a fantastic job."

Sean grinned. "Your opinion is all that matters, boss."

"Oh really?" said a voice from the stairway. "Her opinion is all that matters?"

Sean's eyes widened and we all turned to see Randi glaring at us.

Wade muttered an expletive.

"Hey, Randi," I said, keeping my voice level. "We were just checking out your new office. Looks fantastic."

She rolled her eyes and moved to step inside the office itself. Sean quickly held up his hand.

"You can't walk in here yet," Sean said. "Floors will be dry tomorrow."

Her eyes narrowed. "What are you all doing here?"

"I was showing my boss what a beautiful job we did."

"It does look great," I said in agreement. "I hope you're happy with the result." As soon as I said the words, I wondered what snarky comment she would come back with. I glanced at Sean and Wade. "We've got to get going."

"I'll have some notes for you later, Sean," Randi said officiously. "I'm not altogether thrilled with the result."

"We'll change it if it's absolutely necessary," I said. "But nobody can go inside the office until tomorrow. Those heels you're wearing could ruin the finish."

She stared at me, hands fisted on her hips. "In that case, Sean will just have to redo it."

I gave her a hard look. "And I'll have to charge your in-laws for that unnecessary work."

She tossed her hair back. "What do I care?"

"Really?" I gave her one last serious glare, then turned and jogged upstairs.

Wade and Sean quickly followed.

Once outside, I gritted my teeth. "She's such a twit."

"I don't know, Shannon," Sean said easily. "I think she's starting to like me."

Wade barked out a laugh, and we chuckled all the way to the parking lot. But then I started worrying again and grabbed Wade's arm. "If she gets me fired, you'll take over supervising."

"Get real, Shannon," he said. "Your family's been friends with the Garrisons for as long as you've all been alive. They're not going to fire you because of something that witch said."

"But she's a member of the family, after all."

"So what?" Sean said. "They all hate her."

"Arabella doesn't hate her," I said. "Although they had a little dustup yesterday. Anyway, Craig doesn't hate her. They work together every day."

"None of that matters." Wade grabbed my arm to stop the forward momentum. "Bill and Lilian love you, so don't let Randi get to you."

"I'll try." For some reason, I recalled Logan's expression last evening after his own wife wouldn't even greet the three little boys he'd been taking care of. Logan had looked disgusted with her.

"Okay," I said after taking a deep breath. "I'm going to think positive thoughts, and everything will be fine."

Wade grinned. "There's our little Pollyanna."

I had to laugh. "A positive attitude helps with a job like this one."

"Either that, or bringing a nail gun with you, am I right?" Sean said.

I laughed. "Exactly right."

Wade took off, and I was about to unlock the door to my truck when I heard someone *tap-tap-tapping* across the parking lot. I turned and saw my worst nightmare approaching.

"Well, well, well," Whitney said, her mouth set in a sneer. "Look who's lowering the property values."

I decided to ignore her completely and turned to my truck.

"I don't know if you've been informed yet, but I've received a request to help Arabella and Franco with their renovation project. Which means, I'm in and you're out."

I laughed. "I'm sorry. What were your qualifications again?"

She snarled. "I'm just as qualified as you are."

"Decorating your kid's bedroom doesn't count. Nice try."

"You are hateful."

I chuckled to keep from baring my teeth at her. "Nice talking to you, as always." I quickly unlocked my door and jumped inside. If I gunned the motor a little too hard in hopes of causing her to choke from exhaust fumes, I couldn't help myself.

But once I was driving home in my truck, my anxiety level rose and I gave Lilian a call. "Sorry to bother you," I started.

"You're never a bother," she said. "What's going on?"

"It's silly, but I ran into Whitney, who told me that she was going to be advising Arabella and Franco on their renovation project."

"What?" she shrieked, which warmed my heart. "That will never happen. I'm sorry if she got the wrong idea from Arabella. I'll talk to her."

"Okay. I didn't want to make a big fuss. I was just wondering."

"No fuss, sweetie. I'll take care of it. You have a good evening."

"Thanks. You too."

Was it so wrong to drag Lilian into this fight? No, it wasn't, I decided, and relaxed as I drove.

Two blocks from home, I had a moment of awareness and called Sean. "Sorry if I screwed things up with you and Randi just now. I would never want to put you in her crosshairs."

He chuckled. "You didn't say anything wrong. Besides, she doesn't scare me."

That makes one of us, I thought. "Look, your work is fantastic and Lilian and Bill agree. If Randi tries to mess with you, they'll back you up. And so will I, of course."

"I'm not worried," Sean said. "I really think the office looks awesome."

"I totally agree."

"Thanks, boss."

I turned left onto Apple Street. "Okay, I'm almost home, so listen, good luck tonight. Everything should go smoothly, but if it doesn't, I'll have my cell phone and I'll be right inside the dining room."

"I know," he said, chuckling. "Have a great time tonight with your girl gang."

"And our men," I added.

He laughed. "Of course. Just relax and enjoy your coveted special dinner reservations and don't think about us little people."

I laughed. "Never."

"Good. Stop worrying. Enjoy the dinner."

We ended the call and I pulled into my driveway a minute later.

———————

Since my normal daily uniform was blue jeans, steel-toe boots, and a warm vest, I decided to go completely girlie for our best friends' Christmas dinner. That meant wearing (cue scary music) a dress!

I had worn this little black dress only once, about five years ago for some obscure event I couldn't even remember. I just knew that none of my friends had seen it before. I wanted everything about this night to be special since the reservations were so rare and hard won. And since it had been several months since all of my girlfriends—and our men—had been together.

The dress was a black sheath, which meant that it was rather formfitting, but that was okay because Mac was going to love it.

In fact, his eyes lit up when he saw me walk down the stairs, and that was enough to make me happy. The sleeves were three-quarter length and filmy, with what the designer called an illusion neckline and a beautiful black velvet appliqué design running up one sleeve and across my shoulder.

I had to shake my head. I was a real expert when it came to describing the surface of a roof, but I had no idea how to describe fashion. The bottom line was that the dress was gorgeous and Mac absolutely loved it on me.

I had pulled my thick mop of naturally wavy red hair up and back and held it with a diamond hairclip that Mac had brought back from a recent trip to New York City.

Mac looked insanely handsome and elegant in a dark gray suit with a white shirt and black tie. I had second thoughts about leaving the house, and I could see that he did, too. But we managed to make it out the door and met our friends in the gorgeous lobby of the Cliffs Hotel, where we spent several minutes raving about our beautiful dresses and handsome suits. My girlfriends oohed and aahed at my slinky black dress and sexy black high heels, and I did the same for them. All in all, we were a very impressive group. As my dad would say, we cleaned up well.

These were my oldest and dearest friends, I thought, as we were led to our table by a tuxedoed maître d'. Jane Hennessey and I had been best friends since first grade, when we faced the fact that the two of us were the tallest kids in class—and that included all the boys. Jane eventually grew two inches taller than me and loved to mention it at every opportunity, but despite her great height, I was still taller than many of the boys from school.

Jane had met Niall Rose last year when he moved here to be near his sister, Emily Rose. They had both moved here from Scotland to live and work in Lighthouse Cove.

Emily owned the Scottish Rose Tea Shoppe on the town square and had met and married Gus Peratti, thanks to the odd machinations of a romantic ghost.

Niall was the newest member of our group, but he fit in perfectly with his wonderful sense of humor and his talent as a stonemason. He had his own company but also regularly worked with my crew. He was big and burly and often wore his kilt around town, especially to the pub on Friday nights. Niall was quite possibly the last person Jane's friends would've chosen as a mate for her. But they had clicked and sizzled together, and that was it.

Lizzie and Hal Logan owned the adorable Paper Moon book and paper store on the square. Lizzie was a few years ahead of us in school and used to babysit me and my sister. She and Hal were the only couple of our crowd that had been married for years and had two great kids that I'd known and loved since they were born.

Marigold Starling was another dear friend who owned the Crafts & Quilts shop on the square with her aunt Daisy. Marigold had recently married Raphael Nash, a retired tech billionaire who had moved to town last year and bought a farm in order to raise cows and make the best darned ice cream on the northern coast.

Rounding out the group were my younger sister, Chloe, and her very impressive boyfriend, Chief of Police Eric Jensen. They were engaged to be married, but no date had been set yet. I had a feeling Chloe was waiting for Mac and me to make the first move since I was two years older than her.

We six couples were a family now, and we always had a wonderful time together. I felt so lucky to be a part of this lovely, clever gang of smart women and the cool men who loved us.

The maître d' who showed us to our table looked familiar, and I asked him if he was the one working at the Fun Zone last night.

"That was me," he said quietly as he pulled my chair out for me.

"Balloon animals," I said. "That's awesome."

He smiled crookedly. "When Lilian found out that I had a talent for making balloon animals, I was recruited for the part-time Fun Zone job."

"I'm not going to ask which job you prefer," Mac asked.

The maître d', whose name was Lionel, laughed. "My children would much prefer that I stick with the balloons."

"Any kid would love to have a dad with those skills," Mac said.

As we sat, Lionel placed menus in front of us and pointed out a few of the specials, then left us to peruse the offerings.

I took a moment to look around and take in the impossible beauty and sophistication of the room, with its coffered ceiling, the paneled walls, and the Florentine marble floor tiles. But it was the gorgeous chandelier hanging down from the center of the ceiling that held pride of place, and it was clearly the reason why they called this one the Baccarat Room.

"Wow," I whispered.

"Impressive," Mac said. "But none of it outshines your beauty."

"Oh," I whispered and leaned in to kiss him. "That's good. That's very good."

He grinned. "Thank you. Even though I mean it. You are gorgeous."

I leaned over and kissed him again.

"Eight courses," Marigold said, interrupting the moment. But I didn't really mind. We had all evening to enjoy this lovely room and the wonderful food. "That's a lot of food. Not sure I'll make it through all of them."

"I've heard that they're small servings," I assured her. "And I'll bet the guys will gladly help us if we can't make it through on our own."

"I'll be happy to help ye," Niall said, and we all laughed. He was a big man with a hearty appetite.

"I hope we can meet the delightful Chef Franco tonight," Chloe said.

"Oh yes, definitely," I said brightly.

"He's such a sweetheart," Jane murmured, then dropped her voice even more. "I still can't believe he's married to Arabella, but stranger matches have happened."

"Speaking of," Lizzie said quietly. "You must see Arabella a lot. How's it working out with her and Franco?"

"Apparently very well," I said. "I have it on very good authority that they have quite an active sex life."

Several of my girlfriends perked up at that news, and Lizzie laughed. "You're joking."

"I'm truly not joking," I said. "But that's all by way of saying that they seem to be getting along quite well." I was still trying to keep my voice down. "And even though Arabella treats me like the dog that chased her cat up a tree, I can't really complain because I have almost nothing to do with her. I just hope she's happy, although I really don't think she is."

"Not with a best friend like Whitney," Lizzie said. "She's like a dark cloud that's always threatening to rain. That must get really old."

"And Arabella isn't half as bad as Whitney," Jane said. "She really seems kind of stressed."

"She's definitely not living her best life," I said. "But her husband makes up for it by being the sweetest, most talented down-to-earth guy in the world."

"There's a pattern," Lizzie said. "Why do we know so many couples who follow it?"

Chloe nodded. "Good question. Don't forget Whitney and Tommy. He's a sweetheart and she's the devil made flesh."

Jane frowned. "True enough."

"And there's Randi," I said, my voice dropping to barely a whisper. "How did she end up with such a sweet guy like Logan?"

"I don't know," Lizzie murmured. "Those three women have cornered the market on mean, or not really mean, but just weird in the case of Arabella. And yet they're all married to the sweetest, nicest, most adorable guys possible."

Jane whispered, "I've heard that Whitney never comes over here to the hotel anymore because she doesn't want to hang out with the hired help. Meaning her so-called friends, Randi and Arabella."

"She's still as hateful as ever," I murmured.

Chloe leaned over and whispered, "According to Stephanie, Randi and Logan may not be together much longer."

My eyes grew huge. "What do you know?"

At that moment, I saw Lizzie waving her fingers at me. Then she spoke clearly, "Oh, look! It's time to order cocktails!"

I noticed that Randi and Craig had aligned themselves at opposite ends of our table, preparing to take our drink orders. So there would be no more bad-mouthing Randi or the others. At least for the next few minutes.

I gave Lizzie a thumbs-up to thank her for the heads-up. "That was subtle," I murmured.

"Hey," Lizzie said. "I had to shut you up somehow."

I smirked. "Mission accomplished."

"Do you want a glass of champagne?" Mac asked.

I smiled. "That sounds wonderful."

"We have an excellent champagne tonight and a very special seasonal cocktail," Craig said to the table, and proceeded to explain what it contained.

"Wow, that sounds wonderful," Jane said.

"I had the seasonal cocktail last night," I said. "And it is fabulous. And very pretty, too."

Since I'd had that cocktail the night before, I went with champagne, my perennial favorite, tonight. Mac decided on a local high-end craft beer. He also added several bottles of a wonderful Cabernet Sauvignon to be served with dinner.

I was glad Randi hadn't been the one to take our order, because I'd already received the stink eye once this evening when she first saw me sitting at this table. I wondered if it had something to do with our interaction earlier today in her new sommelier's office. Or was it just Randi being her usual unpleasant self? I had to rub away the instant chill. I was so *done* with her.

Once all the orders had been taken, Craig and Randi moved back to the bar with the promise of a quick turnaround on cocktails.

A few seconds later, Chloe came over to finish her secret news.

"What's going on?" I asked. "What did Stephanie tell you?"

"She's been keeping an eye on Randi, and she thinks she's cheating on Logan."

"Oh no," I said. "What a fool."

When she noticed that Eric was watching us, she scooted back to her chair.

Mac murmured, "Can't wait to hear what you two were talking about."

"Tell you later," I whispered.

Within minutes, our drinks began to arrive at the table. I noticed Joyce was helping Randi deliver the cocktails and wished that the older woman could be a good influence on her. She was always so friendly, very much like her pal Shirley Ann.

I smiled and waved at Joyce and she returned the greeting. Randi disappeared while we took a few more minutes to enjoy our cocktails. One of the waiters began to take orders for soup, salad, and our main course.

"How's your champagne?" Mac asked.

"It's just delicious. I was actually thinking about ordering another glass, but I'd better not."

"You can have my glass, Shannon," Marigold said.

"Really?" I asked.

"Yes. I didn't order it, but somehow it ended up at my place."

"If you're sure," I said sympathetically, thinking she might be slightly under the weather.

She smiled. "Positive." Marigold had been raised Amish back in

Pennsylvania, and during the period known as Rumspringa, when Amish youth are allowed more liberties, Marigold moved out here to live with her aunt Daisy for two years. Then her parents died in a buggy accident, and she decided to stay in Lighthouse Cove with Daisy, who was her only living relative. And of course, now she was happily married to Rafe Nash.

Marigold was deep in conversation with Rafe. Then she nodded and I heard him whisper, "If you think you're ready."

"Yes, I'm ready." She gazed around at the faces of everyone at this table.

"Marigold?" I asked. "What's going on? Are you okay?"

She was beaming now, and Rafe took hold of her hand. "We have an announcement to make."

Lizzie began to squeal and Marigold laughed. "It appears someone might've guessed our big secret."

I gasped, realizing what she was about to say.

"What's wrong?" Mac asked instantly.

To everyone at the table, I simply said, "Rafe and Marigold have an announcement to make."

"Say it quickly before they all start screaming," Rafe murmured in Marigold's ear.

"We're pregnant!" Marigold cried.

And the screaming and laughing and good wishes began.

"I'm so happy for you," I said when I had a chance to get a word in. "How does Aunt Daisy feel about it?"

"She is over the moon," Marigold said. "She insists that she'll be the best babysitter in the world."

"I'm sure she will be." I beamed at Marigold, then glanced all the way around the table. I felt ridiculously happy and lucky to be close to such warm, wonderful friends and to be able to share so many good moments with them. We were all warm and wonderful, that is, unless someone tried to hurt one of us. Then you saw our claws come out, as they had when Whitney's name was mentioned.

"You've got a great group here," Mac said, noticing where my focus had gone.

"We really do." I moved closer and leaned my head against his shoulder. "I love that we were able to get together tonight. It's so nice to see everyone all in one place. It doesn't happen as often anymore."

"Who was able to pull off this reservation tonight?"

"It was Jane. She was tied to her phone for a few hours that day, but she came through."

"I hear it's the toughest reservation in town."

"It's very tough. We got lucky."

"Sure did." He glanced around at the high coffered ceiling and the tall windows. Fairy lights were strung from the beautiful central chandelier to each of the smaller light fixtures hanging from the four corners. "Why haven't we been here before?"

"I guess we could've come here anytime we wanted to. But I've always thought of it as a special holiday experience. It's what we do at Christmastime."

"Yeah, I get that." He glanced around some more, then gazed down the table at all of our friends. Then he smiled at me. "Nice."

"It really is."

"And then there's you." He leaned in and kissed me. "Nice."

"And so are you," I whispered, and rested my forehead against his.

"Should we try to make it to the carousel after dinner?" Lizzie asked the group.

136

"What a great idea," I said.

"Have you been to the Fun Zone yet?" Eric asked.

"Of course," I said proudly.

"She built it," Mac said, his own pride showing through.

"I worked there last night," I said, "and Mac helped me, so we did a little bit of everything. It's really fun. Not just for kids."

"Old-fashioned fun," Mac explained, leaning over to make his point. "It's beautifully designed, with a touch of the old-time big top, plus lots of great games, and an elegant little carousel."

"A little something for everyone," Eric said.

"Exactly," I said.

"We'll have to get over there one of these nights," Chloe said.

"I think you'll all enjoy it," Mac said. "The carousel has a real touch of magic to it. Actually, I'd have to say that everything is magical."

I gave him a grateful look for those lovely words. "Thank you."

He kissed my cheek. "You deserve it." He leaned over. "If you guys are going next week, let us know. We might join you. It's a fun evening."

"Sounds like a plan," Eric said.

Waiters began setting small plates at everyone's place. The first course was traditionally called an amuse-bouche. In French, it literally meant "it amuses the mouth," and it was usually one bite of something wonderful. Since our chef was Italian, tonight that one bite consisted of a thin slice of carpaccio, artistically twisted and seasoned with a dash of lemon juice, salt, pepper, and capers. It was delicious.

This was followed by the soup course, which consisted of a lentil and sausage soup in a clear broth, which was surprisingly delicate, accompanied by a glass of crisp Oregon Pinot Gris.

With the food came more conversation and laughter. In the background was a soft whisper of classical Christmas music, just loud enough to add to the ambience without overwhelming anyone.

As we finished our soup and awaited our next course, the maître d' seated a small group of four at a table nearby. They were beautifully dressed and seemed to appreciate the elegance of the room, which made me happy. We all greeted one another and wished them a happy Christmas.

More tables were seated, and the noise level was starting to grow as drinks were consumed and the laughter grew a bit more boisterous. Much of the conversation at our table was focused around weddings and marriage venues. And now, thanks to Marigold and Rafe's announcement, babies! But there was also a spirited discussion of Mac's latest Jake Slater thriller as well as Lizzie's concerns about her teenaged daughter Marisa discovering high school boys. That was a conversation we could carry on all night long.

The waiters began to clear the soup bowls, and soon after that, the salads were served. They looked absolutely fresh and gorgeous.

Butter lettuce covered in paper-thin red onions and tiny curlicues of toasted Parmesan cheese, which acted as croutons for the salad. We continued to chat and laugh as the servers began clearing the salad plates.

"This salad is fabulous," Jane said. "It's so nice to be able to enjoy a world-class meal and not be responsible for it."

Lizzie laughed. "I've been reading the reviews, Jane. It sounds like you're dining on first-class meals every day at your new restaurant. I'm so proud of you."

I turned to Jane and was about to comment when the lights went out.

"Oh no!" I cried.

"What happened?" Lizzie asked.

And now I realized that it wasn't just the lights in this room, but the lights throughout the hotel that had gone out!

The Baccarat Room was as dark as pitch. I wanted to scream. Instead, I whispered, "I've got to fix this."

I sprang into action, jumped up from my chair, and shouted, "Don't worry, folks. This will only take a minute."

Despite my words, there were several loud shrieks and shouts from the gathered diners. For the most part, though, people were actually pretty chill. I wouldn't blame anyone for shrieking in shock or fear. Even the Christmas lights on the buildings outside were out. It was so dark, I couldn't even see my hand in front of my face.

I grabbed my tiny purse, pulled out my cell phone, and said to Mac, "I'll be right back."

"I'm going with you, babe," Mac said.

"I'll go, too," Eric said, but he took a moment to make another announcement, his voice loud enough to carry throughout the entire dining room. "Ladies and gentlemen, I'm Police Chief Eric Jensen. We'll have the lights back on in a short time, so there's no need to worry. Please stay in your seats so you don't injure yourselves or others."

His voice was calm and reassuring. I could hear a few sighs of relief, and someone commented that Eric's voice was such a comfort to them.

Thank goodness. I pressed my flashlight app, and the spotlight was bright enough to show me the way to the wine cellar door. I banked down the irritation I was feeling that this electrical problem hadn't been fixed last week. I would have to do another quick fix tonight, and then tomorrow I would speak with the electrician. This couldn't happen again!

By now everyone was aiming their flashlight apps every which way and there was more nervous laughter than the formerly fearful moans.

At the cellar door, I said, "Follow me," and reached for the doorknob.

Once again, Eric used his most authoritative police chief voice to assure the diners that everything would be fixed immediately.

I hoped he was right.

I pulled the heavy door open and said, "This way."

"I'm right behind you," Mac said.

"Me too," Eric said.

"Good. I'm taking it slow."

Mac touched my shoulder. "Do you want to remove your fancy shoes?"

"I guess I'd better," I said regretfully, and with Mac giving me a steadying hand, I nudged off my shoes. My beautifully impractical four-inch heels would be hazardous walking down those cellar stairs. I tucked the shoes up against the wall and out of harm's way. When I finished fixing the breaker switch, I'd come back to pick them up.

Mac let the door close behind us and I took a few steps down.

"The stairs going down are wide and spacious," I said, "so we'll be safe as long as we watch where we're stepping. And keep your light on."

"I will, babe," Mac said. "You too."

"I'm right behind you guys," Eric said.

It was a relief to hear him say so.

"Good," Mac said.

I aimed my light around the cavernous space, then took a few more cautious steps down. From what I could see, the stairs were clean and clear of any objects, so I kept walking down, going slowly, and holding on to the railing that ran along the wall.

"What's that?" Mac asked, shining his light on something lying across one of the couches.

"Looks like some blankets," Eric said.

Both men continued to follow me down the steps. I felt a little slippery in my stocking feet, so I kept my hand on the railing and didn't take my eyes off the stairs.

I only had a few more steps to go as I pointed toward the far hallway. "The breaker box is across the room and down that narrow hallway."

Eric said, "Okay. You two appear to have this situation well in hand, so I'm going back to the dining room to check on Chloe, and then I'll hang out at the top of the stairs until the lights come back on. Just shout if you need any help."

"Will do," Mac said.

"Thanks, Eric," I said. "It shouldn't take more than a minute to get everything up and running again."

"Good," Eric said.

I heard his footsteps recede as he walked back up to the dining room.

I made it to the cellar floor and started to cross it, but when I got a better look at the mound of blankets on the couch, I was compelled to check it out. As I got closer, I saw someone's leg and arm sticking out of the pile and figured they had fallen asleep down here.

"Oh, what the heck?" I said. "There's some guy sleeping down here." I glanced up at Mac, who was leaning against the wall, still halfway up the stairs.

"Who is it?" he asked.

"I don't know." I nudged the fellow's leg. "Hello? Are you awake?"

"Hold on, babe." Mac decided to jog down to investigate.

I pointed to the leg sticking out from the blankets. "I think it's a waiter, judging from his outfit." With his leg sticking out, I could see that he wore the black shoes and black pants. And with his arm dangling out, I saw his white shirt. I assumed he must be wearing the formfitting black vest, but I couldn't see it under the blankets. "I nudged him a few times, but he didn't budge."

"He's sleeping on his stomach," Mac said. "So we can't see who he is."

"Maybe he hit his head."

But I thought about it. How could he fall down the stairs, hit his head, and then pile a couple of blankets on top of himself? This was a mystery, but it was probably easily solved.

"Maybe he's drunk," Mac suggested.

"That's more like it," I said, then started to worry. "In case he's sick, I'd better check for a pulse. I fumbled with his wrist for a pulse, but after a minute, I said, "You'd better get Eric down here. He'll do this a lot better than I can."

"Okay." He faced the stairway and shouted, "Hey, Eric. Come here."

The police chief shouted back, "I'm coming," and ran down the steps. "What's wrong?"

"He isn't moving and I can't find his pulse," I said, feeling useless and slightly frantic as I tried to find a pulse. "It's probably my fault.

It's been a long time since I tried to take a pulse, so maybe I'm not doing it right. He's facing the floor, so I can't really get a good hold on his wrist."

Eric quickly took over the situation. "Let's turn him over so he can breathe more easily and you can take his pulse. Mac, give me a hand."

"Thanks, Eric," I said. "You guys go ahead and turn him over. I've got to get the lights back on." I mentally shook my head. I couldn't believe I'd left everyone in the dark all this time. But since the whole world had cell phones these days, it didn't seem to be much of a disaster.

"Good idea," Eric said, then glanced at Mac. "Let's wait for the lights to come on. God only knows what else is buried in this pile."

I cringed at that creepy thought and quickly tiptoed over to the narrow hall and moved down to the breaker boxes. Within seconds, I found the errant breaker and easily switched it back on.

The room lit up and I breathed a huge sigh of relief, although it took me a few long seconds to adjust my eyes to the brightness. I heard shouts and cheers of joy from the main floor as the lights across the dining areas were restored.

"Hallelujah," I murmured, breathing easier. And that's when I caught a whisper of fragrance, and I wondered if I was hallucinating. It was the same scent I'd inhaled in the north cellar. Clove, pine, orange peel. What else? My first thought was that they must be storing Christmas candles down here for the bar.

Another cheer went up from another part of the hotel, and I was struck again by the length of time people had sat in the dark. It was much longer than one minute, and I again felt guilty for leaving everyone trapped in the dark for so long.

But how had it happened? Wade and I had spent hours with the electrician, rewiring all of the kitchen appliances to redistribute the power and prevent this very thing from happening again. So what went wrong?

I'd check in with Bill tomorrow, knowing he'd have plenty to say about this electrical mini fiasco.

I hurried back to Mac and Eric, who were just about to turn the unconscious waiter onto his back to help him breathe.

"On my count," Eric said. "One, two, three."

"This guy hardly weighs anything," Mac said as they turned him over and set him down on the couch.

"Oh God." I sucked in a breath and began to tremble like a leaf on a tree in a windstorm.

"Shannon," Eric shouted to get my attention. "Step back. Get away from him."

"It's not a him," I said, my voice dull. "It's a her. It's Randi. Randi Garrison. Someone slashed her throat."

Chapter Eight

I barely whispered the words. Had I gone into shock? By all rights and under almost any other circumstance, I should've been shrieking in horror. But the shrieks weren't coming.

"I can do chest compressions," I said loudly, and approached Randi, ready to place the heel of my hand on the center of her chest.

"Shannon. Stop," Eric yelled. "It's too late. She's gone."

"How do you know?" I demanded, then realized it was Eric, chief of police. He would probably know if someone was dead.

"It's too late. There's no pulse. And you can see for yourself that she's lost too much blood. I'm sorry."

"Blood," I muttered, then stared at Randi. "Oh my God."

I'd seen dead bodies before. Way too many, to be honest. And I was usually good for a few screams or a good strong shriek, at least. But this time I was well aware that I showed almost no outward emotional reaction at all. I just stared at Randi's face, noting that she was still pretty, although her skin was flaccid and her eyes drooped unnaturally. I was saying those words internally to myself as if I were reporting the weather.

One thing was for sure: Randi would hate to see herself looking like that. The blood that had been seeping from her neck had begun to slow down to nothing. Her white blouse was completely stained red. Her life had simply drained out of her. And I was completely numb.

Staring at the body, I realized that I had just seen her taking drink orders at our table barely a half hour before. She must have been killed just before we got down to the wine cellar. Otherwise, we might've had a chance to save her. But how could we have saved her when her throat had been slashed so viciously? Ugh.

I forced myself to stare at her face. Her skin seemed to be fading to gray as I watched.

It was a disgusting and horrifying sight, but I still couldn't scream. And I couldn't look away.

I was starting to feel sorry for her. I'd never liked the woman. Not at all. But I realized that I could feel sorry for her. It wasn't enough. I should've been devastated by the thought of a young person being found dead right under my nose. I should've been crying, maybe even screeching at the top of my lungs since it was all happening right before my eyes.

But this time it was different.

I wasn't the medical examiner, but I'd seen and heard enough death talk to be pretty sure we'd barely missed running into the killer himself. But wait. Maybe he was still in the cellar. Maybe he was hiding in the closet by the breaker switches.

"Oh God." I refused to feel woozy, but the thought of running into a killer was overwhelming.

"Shannon?"

I sucked in a breath, then blinked as I slowly met Mac's gaze. "I . . . I'm not in shock."

"You sure about that, babe?"

"Yeah. But I do feel a little anxious. I mean, there could be a killer nearby."

"Come here." Mac pulled me into his arms.

"Mac," I whispered. "I'm fine."

"I know, babe."

"I'm just a little frazzled because, you know, the killer could still be down here."

Eric was standing over the body, talking on the phone to his dispatcher, when the wine cellar's secondary doorway, the one that led up to the Garrisons' private kitchen, swung open and slammed against the wall with a bang.

Now I screamed.

Eric's head whipped up to stare at me and Mac as though we could explain what was going on. "What the hell?"

I pointed across the room, where two women stumbled into the wine cellar giggling and holding each other up as if they'd just consumed their third bottle of champagne that evening and were telling each other the funniest damn jokes they'd ever heard.

"Oh! Hey, Chief Jensen!" It was Shirley Ann Johnson, wearing one of her pretty cocktail waitress outfits, which meant that she must've been working tonight. "Fancy meeting you here."

Her best friend, Joyce Brimley from Housekeeping, gaped at Eric. "What's going on here?"

Eric gaped right back, taking in her fluffy purple sweater, black pants, and purple high heels. He quickly covered Randi's body with the blanket.

"Chief Jensen," Joyce said. "Goodness, we certainly didn't expect to see you down here." She turned to me. "And, Shannon. Don't you look pretty? What're you doing here?"

"That's a good question," I muttered.

"More to the point, ladies," Eric said, checking his watch. "What are you two doing down here?"

The chief's sternly worded question snapped the women, including me, to attention. Joyce tried to explain. "Well, gosh, Chief. We're here because Randi lets me keep my bottle of, um, Chardonnay, down here in the wine fridge."

"Does she?"

Shirley Ann jumped in. "She does! She's a good friend. And I come down here all the time, you know, to get a bottle of wine or champagne for a customer. I mean, because that's my job."

"I see."

"Yeah, that's right," Joyce said. "And Randi said it was okay for me to be here since I work in the hotel anyway."

"What's going on, Chief?" Shirley Ann finally asked, since their Chief Jensen sighting was a heck of a lot more rare than seeing the two of them down here.

"I'm sorry to spoil your evening, ladies, but I have to ask you to leave this area." Eric turned to me. "Shannon, would you mind escorting the ladies upstairs, right now."

"Sure, Chief." I moved between the two women and slipped my arms through each of theirs.

"And please stay in the Garrisons' kitchen," Eric added. "Until I can speak to you."

Shirley Ann checked her wristwatch. "I really have to go back to work."

"No," he said bluntly. "I'll speak to your boss."

"Oh," she whispered, taken aback.

Smiling resolutely, I practically dragged the two women toward the stairs while carrying on a weirdly perky conversation. "Sorry about this, but when the chief has a police emergency, we all have to do our part."

"Isn't that the truth?" Joyce murmured.

"Yes," Shirley agreed, but her voice was hesitant. "So I guess we'd better go with Shannon." She continued to look around as if she'd lost something and wanted to double-check. She took one last look at Eric, who was watching every move we made, and then turned and followed me up the stairs.

Naturally, I wondered if she'd seen something she shouldn't have seen. Like for instance, a body under the blanket.

I tried to keep things light as we climbed to the top of the stairs and stepped into the Garrisons' kitchen. The room was empty, and I figured most of the family members had been dispatched to different areas of the hotel to make sure the guests were calm and comfortable now that the lights were back on. And hopefully they were unaware of the disturbing incident in the wine cellar.

"So, Joyce, you're not working tonight?"

"No, I'm not," she said. "I'm just visiting my bestie here." She threw her arm around Shirley Ann.

"And even though the chief said he'd talk to Craig," Shirley Ann said nervously, "I'd really feel better if I could just go back to work."

"I know," Joyce said. "But I'm still glad I got you outside for a carousel ride."

Now Shirley Ann managed to grin. "Oh, me too. That was so much fun."

Joyce took a seat at the kitchen table. "Did you try it yet, Shannon?"

"I did," I said, gazing out the plate glass window at the cliffs. "I really enjoyed it. We played some of the Fun Zone games, too."

I hoped I was making sense, but I couldn't be sure. I was chatting as if I hadn't just seen the body lying in the middle of the wine cellar. Knowing it was the body of a woman I had never liked made me even more wary. I had to hope that Joyce and Shirley Ann hadn't seen anything.

"You guys came down the stairs from up here." It was a statement, not a question, but they answered it anyway.

"That's right," Shirley Ann said. "We'd been out at the Fun Zone, so we came in through the Garrisons' kitchen. Stephanie was in there making tea and she let us go through that way." She glanced around. "Looks like she's gone now."

Joyce smiled fondly. "She's a sweetheart, isn't she?"

"The very best," Shirley Ann said lightly. Then her expression hardened. "Let's stop playing games, Shannon. What's going on around here?"

I was pretty sure my eyes were goggling. "What do you mean?"

Joyce grabbed her friend's arm. "Oh, did you smell it, too? I thought maybe someone got sick down in the wine cellar. Pardon me for saying so, but there's a disturbing odor of bodily fluids down there. Did someone die?"

I stared at both of them in complete disbelief. Not that they were wrong, but how was it that I'd ended up hanging out with these two older women who had both experienced the aftereffects of death?

And I was trying to play dumb. What was the point?

"You know, I've been working in Housekeeping for years," Joyce said, "and sadly, it's just part of the job to enter a hotel room and discover that someone has just died. You can't mistake that smell, sorry to say."

Sadly, I knew what she was talking about.

"You're so right," Shirley Ann said. "I used to go hunting with my daddy and I definitely know what blood smells like, especially when there's a lot of it."

I gazed from one woman to the other. "What are you saying?"

Shirley Ann glared at me. "Are you playing dumb, Shannon?"

As a matter of fact, I am, I thought. But out loud I said, "Why would you ever think that?" I wondered how I'd gotten into this mess in the first place. I needed to get the chief up here because I wasn't prepared to face down these two women and their very specific questions.

"Oh, Shannon." Shirley Ann shook her head. "The fact is, Joyce smelled death right away. And I smelled blood as soon as we walked into the wine cellar. And you're chitchatting away like you've got nothing else on your mind but that silly carousel ride. Now, I'm pretty clear on what happened down there in that wine cellar because I saw the body with my own eyes."

Joyce stared at her friend. "Shirley Ann? What are you saying?"

She patted Joyce's arm. "Sorry, honey, but I know what I saw."

"I don't doubt it," Joyce said, nodding quickly. "I knew I smelled something. But what did you see?"

"I have no idea what you saw," I managed, feeling my stomach churn at having to prevaricate with these women, one of whom had obviously seen Randi's body—or some part of it—down there. "So why don't we go find Chief Jensen, and you can tell him what you saw."

"I think you know what I saw," Shirley Ann said pointedly.

Joyce stomped her foot. "Damn it, Shirley Ann! Tell me! What did you see?"

"Hey," I said, glancing at the empty kitchen table. "Seriously, I'll call Chief Jensen and he can explain it all."

"Now that's a good idea," Shirley Ann said. "Except I already know." She pulled out a chair to rest her feet on. "Oh God, that feels good." She took a few relaxed breaths. "Now, where was I? Oh yeah. So, Joyce, you must've not seen it, but there was a body lying on the couch under that blanket, and I happened to catch a look at one of her shoes."

"You saw her shoes?" Joyce pressed her lips tightly, trying to hold it together.

Shirley Ann clutched Joyce's hand. "Time to be brave, honey."

"Just say it," Joyce whispered.

"I saw a shoe," Shirley Ann said, taking in a breath. "But, honey, it was a chunky, black patent leather Stuart Weitzman Soho loafer."

"No." Joyce gasped. "With the platform lug sole?"

"Yes!"

"Noooo!" Her eyes filled with tears. "Not Randi!"

The two women wrapped themselves around each other and sobbed while I stared at them.

"Why do you think it's Randi?" I finally asked. "Did you see her face?"

Shirley Ann looked at me oddly. "I didn't need to see her face, Shannon, because anyone who knows Randi would recognize those shoes. She loves those lug soles."

Joyce sniffed. "She must've said it a thousand times: 'Lug soles are chunky but classy and comfy.' It was like a"—she had to stop and sniffle—"a poem."

This set them off on another crying jag, and it forced me to think about lug soles. And I had to admit that I'd never even noticed the soles of Randi's shoes. Big mistake, apparently. Even worse, I had originally figured those shoes belonged to a man.

I would bet big money that Chloe and Lizzie and some of my more fashion-forward friends would instantly recognize those shoes.

But I hadn't. And so what? Maybe I lacked awareness when it came to Randi and her patent leather chunky-monkey soles, or whatever they called them. But in my defense, how many of them would recognize an awesome pair of Chippewa Tinsley waterproof steel-toed work boots if they were put to the test? Just sayin'.

"Shannon, sweetie," Shirley Ann said, interrupting my work-boot reverie. "It was nice of Chief Jensen to ask you to watch out for us. And it was very kind of you to try to protect us, but the truth is, Randi is dead. And Joyce and I both have to come to terms with this tragedy." Two tears escaped her eyes and she sniffed. "And another truth is, I have a job to do. I have to go back to the bar and finish my shift. And Joyce promised to keep me company."

"But wait, Shirley Ann," Joyce said. "I agree with Chief Jensen. You shouldn't go back to work under these circumstances."

I reached for both of their hands and gave them a little squeeze. "Joyce is right. I wouldn't normally tell you what to do, but it's been a really weird night. So I'm going to call Chief Jensen and find out what he'd like you to do."

"That's the smart thing to do and it's awfully kind of you, Shannon," Joyce said. "It's true, we've both had a bad shock."

I pulled out my phone and punched in the chief's number. I figured since these two women were aware of what had happened to Randi down in the wine cellar, Eric wouldn't want them chitchatting with any of the other employees.

I ended the call and smiled at Shirley Ann and Joyce. "The chief or one of his people will be right here."

"But what about my job?" Shirley Ann said, and I could see her ratcheting up another crying jag.

"Under the circumstances," I said, "I don't think you should worry about the job. Chief Jensen will take care of things. He'll make sure you don't lose any time."

Joyce patted her friend's knee. "To be honest, I wouldn't be surprised if they shut down the bar for the night."

"You're probably right," Shirley Ann said. "But I still worry. I mean, Craig will be wondering where I've gone. I hate to disappoint him by not showing up."

"It's not your fault," I said. "Chief Jensen said so. And I bet he'll be talking to Craig any minute now anyway."

"I'll bet you're right, Shannon," Joyce said.

We sat in silence for a long moment, then I gave each of their hands another little squeeze. "I know you were good friends with Randi. I'm so sorry for your loss."

"Thanks, sweetie," Shirley Ann said.

We all hugged and Joyce said, "I'm glad you were here for us, Shannon."

"Me too, Joyce."

At that moment, two police cars raced around and came to a screeching, dust-stirring stop in front of the stairs leading up to the Garrisons' kitchen door entrance.

"Ooh, car chase!" Shirley Ann said. She and Joyce ran outside to watch, and I couldn't help but join them. A third car skidded to a stop, and all of Eric's officers jumped out of their cars, grabbed their equipment, and raced up the stairs.

Officer Mindy Payton led the way and grinned when she saw me standing at the top of the stairs. "Hey, Shannon. Merry Christmas."

"Same to you, Mindy." We gave each other hugs. I'd known her for years. "Hope your family's doing well."

"You bet they are. Yours too?"

"Everyone's great."

That's when I noticed that Eric had come upstairs to the family kitchen and waited patiently until Mindy and I were finished greeting each other.

"Officer Payton," he said. "I'm taking you to the butler's pantry, where you can interview Ms. Johnson."

"You bet, Chief," Mindy said, giving him a quick salute. "Hey, Shirley Ann, how are you?"

"I'm doing just fine, Mindy," she said, but she betrayed herself by sniffling.

Eric seemed bemused by the fact that in Lighthouse Cove, everybody knew everyone else. He led Mindy and Shirley Ann out of the kitchen and down the hall to a butler's pantry that I had helped build with my father's crew. It was a beauty.

Meanwhile, Officer Rachel Timmons took a seat at the breakfast table to wait for Eric's return. She had been with the Lighthouse Cove PD for about a year now. Tall, thin, and very pretty, she was always gentle with anyone she had to deal with, and that may or may not have come from her years as an EMT in Oakland, California.

"Ready for the holidays, Rachel?" I asked.

"I sure am," she said. "I've got a few days off to visit my family."

"That sounds like fun." I recalled that she had moved to Lighthouse Cove to be closer to her father in Eureka, about thirty miles north.

"There'll be some fun, but I'll spend most of my time painting my dad's house."

"Oh, wow. I hope you'll have some help."

"I've got four cousins up there who'll be helping us."

"So, a real family affair."

"You got that right."

Joyce finally spoke up. "I've seen you around town, Rachel. I mean, Officer Timmons."

"You look familiar, too," Rachel said. "It's Joyce, isn't it?"

"Yes, ma'am."

Rachel smiled. "Call me Rachel, unless the chief is close by."

Joyce grinned, and within seconds, the two women were carrying on a quiet conversation that included house painting, winter colds, and Joyce's future trip to Miami Beach.

Eric returned to the kitchen and greeted Officer Timmons.

She saluted him and asked, "Where would you like me, Chief?"

He returned her salute. "How about right here, Officer Timmons?"

"Sure."

It was clear that Eric was about to move me out of the kitchen and no longer required my babysitting services. With relief, I took the hint and stood. "I need to go find Mac."

"I saw him near the front lobby just a few minutes ago," Eric said. "He looked ready to hit the road."

I gave him a weak smile. "I'm ready, too. Thanks, Chief."

"You're welcome. And, Shannon, I'll need to talk to you tomorrow. I'm not sure when, but I'll call you."

"Okay."

"Thank you."

"You're welcome." I was pretty sure he was thanking me for hanging out with the ladies tonight. I didn't mind, but now I needed to tell him what they'd told me. I supposed that would be part of what we needed to talk about tomorrow, and I was okay with waiting until then. But my two ladies had sort of blown my mind. Even though they hadn't revealed a killer or anything like that, they just knew a heck of a lot more about Randi than I did, for sure. And they both had experience with dead people! Weird. It was hard to say what little nuggets of information Eric would find interesting, so I'd just have to start at the top and spill.

I stopped at the door and turned to look at him again. Earlier tonight, he'd been enjoying himself at dinner with Chloe and the rest of our group. Now it felt like days had passed since that dinner, and Eric looked as if he'd been working for hours and was ready to drop. But I knew he'd be here late into the night. He had a dead body to deal with downstairs, where his crime scene team was at work. The medical examiner would be awaiting the arrival of Randi's body. Meanwhile, Eric would soon be forcing the management to close down the bar and restaurant so the scene of Randi's vicious murder could be fully investigated.

I was almost out the door when I remembered. "Do you happen to know if Mac has my shoes?"

He nodded.

He was a man of few words, especially when it concerned

something as trivial as my high heels. I didn't mind. I smiled and said, "Thanks."

Since the back hallways were closed off, I had to get to the main lobby by way of the veranda. I hurried along the front of the hotel to the doorway leading into the main lobby. This late at night, the breeze off the Cove was chilly, so by the time I reached the lobby, my feet were wet and I was rubbing the shivers from my arms. Pushing through the elegant double doors, I saw Mac right away, having a quiet conversation with Lilian Garrison, who stood next to a wide table covered in large shopping bags.

"There's my girl," he said, and reached for my hand, pulling me close for a quick kiss.

The carpet was cozy compared to the wood decking, so I rubbed my feet against it to warm up.

"Oh, Shannon, sweetie," Lilian cried. "Are you okay?"

"I'm fine. Eric asked me to hang out with Shirley Ann and Joyce for a while."

"Good lord, are they all right?" Lilian asked.

"They're . . . okay. Except they happened to walk into the wine cellar at just the wrong time. The police were starting to close it off to everyone."

Lilian's hands tightened into fists. "So they saw Randi. I mean, her body. Is that what you're saying?"

"Yes." I didn't need to say more, but I added, "So that's why Eric asked me to hang out with them."

Lilian nodded. "That was good of you."

Would she catch on that the reason I was supposed to hang out with Shirley Ann and Joyce was so that nobody else would hear all the grisly details of what they'd seen in the wine cellar?

Mac leaned in close. "How about if we get out of here so Lilian and Franco and everyone can finish up and go home."

"Good idea." I looked at the bag he was carrying. "You have my shoes. I'm very grateful."

"Do you want to put them on?"

"I guess I'd better," I said, reaching for the bag. "I'll need them to walk to the car."

"I could carry you."

I had to smile. While Mac could easily carry me, I would feel ridiculous. "That's very sweet, but I can walk."

"If you insist." He pulled my shoes out of the bag and held my arm to steady me while I put them on. Luckily, my feet were dry enough and I slipped into the shoes.

"Thank you," I whispered.

"Anytime."

Then Mac gave Lilian a kiss on the cheek. "Thanks for letting me bug you all this time."

"I'm so grateful for your company."

"We'll call tomorrow to see how you're doing," Mac said. "And we're available anytime if you need us for any reason."

Lilian patted his arm. "It's great to have such wonderful friends, isn't it?"

"You got that right," Mac said.

She reached for two logoed Cliffs Hotel shopping bags and handed them to us.

"Oh, Lilian," I said, taking a peek inside the bags. They were filled with individual food containers. "You didn't have to do this for us."

"Oh, yes I did. You all paid a lot of money to dine here tonight, and Bill and I would feel terrible if you didn't get your money's worth. And Franco was beside himself. There was so much delicious food left over in the kitchen that he and his staff insisted on putting these containers together and getting these go-bags filled. So please don't worry. It's making everyone here feel better."

"Well, it smells heavenly," I said. "Thank you. This is fabulous. I hate to admit it, but with everything that was going on downstairs, I forgot all about the dinner. So this is a double treat."

"I didn't forget," Mac said, winking at Lilian. "I've been smelling that incredible pasta Bolognese the whole time I've been standing out here."

The three of us stood smiling at each other for a long moment. Finally I whispered, "I'm so sorry for your loss, Lilian."

"Thank you, Shannon." She sighed. "You're both very sweet. We appreciate your friendship so much."

I kissed her cheek. "We're lucky to have yours, as well. And as Mac said, if you need anything, we're right down the hill. We can be here in five minutes."

"I appreciate that," she said, then suddenly gripped my wrist. "Oh God, Shannon. You've been through this before. Tell me what happens next."

I blinked in surprise. "What do you mean?"

Frantically she waved her hands in the air. "The police are closing down our restaurant and bar and a few of the outside facilities. Our hotel guests will see the warning signs all over the place and start freaking out. How long will the police make us stay closed? Do you know? We're filled to capacity, specifically because people want to enjoy our Christmas offerings."

Lilian had spoken at ninety miles an hour and had to stop and take a deep breath before continuing. "Please don't think I'm being thoughtless and callous about Randi's death. Every minute I'm standing here, I'm mourning the loss of that dynamic, beautiful girl and the gigantic hole her death leaves in this family. And I'm worried that my own darling son is suffering his own pain and guilt, as well."

She paused, seemed to need me to say a few words in response, so I gave it a try. "First of all, you're not to worry about what I may or may not be thinking. My main concern is you and Bill. And since you ask, my experience tells me that the police may keep the wine cellar closed for several days because that's where all the action occurred. But the restaurant and the main bar will probably be open by tomorrow afternoon. That's my best guess. Don't hold me to it."

She smiled and gripped both my hands in hers. "I won't. Thank you, Shannon. You've given me a little bit of hope that despite the heartache we feel inside, our visitors and guests will be free to enjoy our beautiful facilities to their hearts' content."

Mac came around and gave Lilian a hug. "We're going to take off now."

"Thank you, Mac. Please drive safely."

Mac and I left through the double doors, and I started to walk toward the parking lot, but Mac steered me down the stairs to the porte cochere. "You moved the car."

"Yeah. Lilian told me to go ahead and move it since most people had left and there were plenty of spaces. And it would be a shorter walk for you."

"Thank you. And my feet thank you. And many thanks to Lilian. She's an angel."

"Yeah, she is."

Once we were in the car, Mac said, "You might not remember this, either, but inside those bags are certificates for a free dinner anytime in the new year, plus free tickets for the carousel and the Fun Zone."

I rested my head back against the seat. "That's right. I did forget."

Mac drove toward the exit. "Imagine knowing your daughter-in-law was murdered, and you respond by giving away free dinners, carousel rides, and carnival games."

"That's Lilian for you. She's such a generous person. Bill, too."

"They're the best."

We were silent for a few minutes as Mac drove down the hill toward home. In the quiet, my head began to replay the hideous visions of Randi's body under the blanket, her leg sticking out, and then me, mistaking it for a man's leg. I felt so stupid. Maybe it was those clunky shoes she wore. Or maybe I just couldn't fathom a woman like her, beautiful and smart and occasionally vicious, lying dead in the middle of the wine cellar.

And there was all that blood. Who had done it to her? Why? What weapon had they used to kill her? It had to have happened only minutes before we walked into the wine cellar and traipsed down the stairs. Had the killer been responsible for turning out the lights? That had to be what happened. Where had the killer gone? He had to be covered in blood himself.

Or *herself*, I realized.

Whoever killed Randi had left a grisly scene that I wouldn't be able to get out of my head for a long time.

I forced myself to think of something positive. It shouldn't have been easy, but having just spent a few minutes with Lilian, I realized it wasn't that hard to do. Gazing out the window at the night sky, I said, "I've never really thought about it in business terms, but the Garrisons are truly in the business of making people happy."

"I couldn't agree more," Mac said. "Unfortunately, not all of their children seem to be tuned in to the same philosophy."

Another half mile later and I felt tears erupt. "God, I feel so bad for her."

Mac glanced at me for a brief moment. "Are those tears for Lilian or for Randi?"

His question caught me off guard, so I had to think for a minute, then answered carefully. "Lilian, of course. That's who I was thinking of just now and that's who the tears are for. But now that you've asked the question, I have to admit that I'm starting to feel ashamed because I wasn't thinking of Randi at all. Honestly, Mac, I still don't like her."

"Why should you?" he asked. When I turned to look at him, he added, "That probably sounds harsh. But look, you just said that the Garrisons are in the business of making people happy."

"Yes. I believe it."

"Well, you and I both know that Randi never signed on to that positivity mantra."

I nodded glumly. "Isn't that the truth? Ever since I've known her, and that's going back a few decades, she would turn her nose up at me or give me the famous stink eye, or just basically try to make me feel stupid. I can still picture her with Whitney, snickering as I walk by. I used to call them the satanic twosome. And this happened over and over again for years. It's small of me, but deep down inside, I still hate them both for the way they made me feel."

"I hope it doesn't affect you like that anymore."

I smiled. "Oh, it does sometimes. Mostly I just marvel that she can still be the same petty jerk she's always been. From the first day

I met her in high school, she's never changed. It's like her personality has been frozen in amber."

He chuckled. "That's quite a visual." He turned onto Blueberry Lane.

"Yes, it is." I laughed bleakly. "Honestly, though, I feel guilty for even mentioning my feelings about it. Especially about Randi."

"Why?"

I stared at him, not quite believing he would even ask. But since he'd asked, I had to give it to him straight. "Because, Mac. What if all of those hateful feelings of mine were finally able to multiply, solidify, and rise up to cause my enemy's spontaneous death?"

I was glad we'd made it to our driveway because Mac seemed frozen in his seat. He stared sightlessly out the windshield. I wasn't sure he could even speak, so I finally gave him a little elbow poke and said, "Hey, it happens. Am I right?"

That's when he leaned forward and rested his forehead on the steering wheel. I wasn't sure what he was thinking until I saw his shoulders begin to shake.

"Mac?" Was he laughing? Crying? He couldn't be crying, so I decided he was laughing. "Mac."

He lifted his head and I could see he was still laughing. "God, I love you."

"Because I'm sick and twisted?"

"That's definitely a big part of it. But it's more because you have a rare sense of humor combined with a kind and generous heart."

I reached up and gently held his cheek, ridiculously touched. "That's so nice."

He leaned over and kissed me. "Come on. Let's go inside."

Once we were inside the house, we put away all the yummy food we'd brought home and then gave each of the creatures a lot of hugs and some treats. Mac poured me a glass of water and fixed himself a short glass of whiskey.

I sat down at the kitchen table. "I wonder how close Randi actually was to the other family members."

"Anyone in particular or the family in general?" he asked.

"Honestly, I don't think any of them liked her very much. Except Craig. He and Randi worked together, and they seemed to get along pretty well."

Mac sipped his whiskey. "What about Arabella?"

"They're both friendly with Whitney, so you'd think they'd have more in common with each other. But they really don't. Arabella is a delicate flower compared to the velociraptor that was Randi."

"Wow." He chuckled. "Velociraptor. I like it. Okay, what about Stephanie?"

"Stephanie can't stand Randi for a lot of reasons, but mainly because she was certain that Randi was cheating on Logan. That alone was enough for Steph to hate her."

"Hmm," Mac said. "You've got a few motives to kill there." Before I could respond, he asked, "What about Bill and Lilian?"

I frowned. "I don't think they were very happy with her."

"Do you know why?"

"Probably for all the same reasons none of us liked her. She was self-centered, rude, and thoughtless. She had a nasty temper, and she was a liar and a troublemaker. She stirred up trouble everywhere she went. And that must've driven Bill and Lilian bonkers." I gave him a questioning look. "What do you think?"

He shrugged. "I know she could be a real jerk to Logan, which always bugged the heck out of me. And I've never said this to anyone, but I wouldn't be surprised if Bill and Lilian blamed Randi for Logan joining the military."

I had to think about it for a minute. "Mac, doesn't that give them both a motive, too?"

He stared at me in shock, then slowly grinned. "Ruh-ro."

"Excuse me?"

He laughed. "I said, 'Ruh-ro.' The clarion call of the Scooby-Doo gang."

I rolled my eyes, but had to grin. Playing the Scooby-Doo game with Mac was always entertaining, and right then I had to marvel at the many times we'd played it. It wasn't actually a game, but rather a free-wheeling way we'd devised of lining up clues, suspects, and motives. Mac had originally named the game after the cartoon characters who were always getting involved in mysteries and then trying to figure out who, what, where, when, and how.

Of course, to avoid being misunderstood, we'd made it a point to never divulge our game to Chief Jensen.

"We'll play tomorrow," Mac decided.

"Sounds good."

He took a last sip of his drink and set the glass in the sink. "Speaking of tomorrow, that's my usual day to visit Homefront. Would you like to come with me?"

"I'd love to. Logan will be there. We can see how he's doing."

"Exactly my thought," Mac said.

"And we can do some actual good work."

"Another excellent reason to go." He glanced over at me. "Feeling guilty?"

"A little."

"We'll do good works and all will be forgiven."

I smiled. "I really wish it worked that way. It feels like I'm over-drawn at some charitable giving bank."

"Visiting Homefront always makes me feel better. And before we go, we should give Lilian a call or stop by and see if she needs anything."

"Good idea."

I reached over and rubbed his arm. "I know I can go to Homefront anytime I want, but it feels special when you invite me to go with you."

"It's always more fun to go with you."

"Aw, that's so sweet," I said. "Is it because I wear a tool belt when I'm there?"

He wriggled his eyebrows. "Oh, baby."

I laughed, and it felt good. Mac turned off the kitchen light and we walked arm in arm up the stairs.

"I didn't see Logan tonight. Did you?"

He shook his head. "No."

"Do you think he decided not to come home?" I frowned. "He would've called his mom, at least. She would be worried sick for him."

"Eric might've asked him to stay at Homefront until tomorrow," Mac suggested.

That made an odd sort of sense to me. That way, Eric would know where Logan was when he needed to talk to him without having his whole family around. "Let me ask you something unrelated. Do you really think Randi was capable of driving someone to murder?"

"Obviously," Mac answered.

I restrained myself from laughing since we were talking about someone who had been killed. I'd personally wished the woman to hell more than once, but that was different. "I'd have to agree."

"But Logan is not that person."

"I don't think so, either." I frowned. "Mainly because his feelings for Randi seem to have fizzled down to nothing. It probably happened a long time ago." I sighed. "I just hope he called his mother."

He smiled. "Why are you so fixated on him calling his mother?"

"Because Lilian deserves to be treated kindly. She hides it well, but she's in a lot of pain and she'll be frantic until she hears from him."

"That's pretty insightful of you. And I'd say you're right about that."

We gazed at each other for a few more seconds, both of us recognizing that we were exhausted.

"Let's get into bed before we both fall over," he said. "We'll get some answers tomorrow."

Chapter Nine

I sat up in bed, instantly awake. "Was that thunder?"

"No, love," Mac said. He was sitting up in bed, reading a script. "You were having a bad dream."

"A dream." I frowned. I was certain I'd been hearing thunder pounding and seeing flashes of lightning throughout the night. But no thunder, no lightning. I pressed my face against his chest to calm down, but I was still shivering uncontrollably. "It was bad."

"You could sleep another hour or so before it's time to get up."

"I'm driving myself crazy," I admitted, snuggling closer to him. He wrapped his arms around me and pulled me to his side. "Quirky scenarios and strange questions and weird possibilities are spinning around in my mind. I can't stop thinking about it."

"I'll help you," he said quietly. "Just breathe. Slow it all down for a minute."

"Okay." This was better, I thought. Breathing in and out, slowly. Over and over. Curled up next to Mac.

And eventually I fell back to sleep.

When I woke up again, the sun was just rising in the east and casting a soft pink-and-orange glow across the horizon.

Mac had placed a glass of water on my bedside table, so I reached for it and took a couple of sips before returning it to the table.

He was still reading but put the script down and began to rub my back. "Can you tell me what you dreamed about?"

"I guess so." I felt a little foolish; ordinarily, I would never relate my dreams to anyone since I believed that dreams were usually filled with random bits of personal oddities that had little to do with anything but the dreamer's own hang-ups and idiosyncrasies.

But since my dream was connected to Randi's murder, Mac insisted on hearing the details. Still, I wouldn't blame him if he dozed off.

"To begin with," I said after sitting up straight and leaning back against the pillow, "Randi was already dead in the dream. And yet somehow she was yelling at me to turn the lights back on. I was trying to do that, but the breaker box was all cockeyed, like someone had deliberately messed with it, and nothing was where it should've been. The individual breakers didn't even look like breakers, but I could smell them starting to sizzle. I was terrified that the whole box was going to ignite and take down the entire hotel, all the way to the ground. Then suddenly Randi was screaming again and pointing at me as if it were my fault that the breaker box was broken and that she was dead."

I took a breath and continued. "After staring at Randi for a few long seconds, I realized there were literally gobs of blood streaming out of that wide wound across her throat."

"Yuck," Mac said.

"I know, right?" I shivered again. "Sorry my description is so gross. But thanks for letting me tell you all about it."

"Wait. That's it? That's the dream?"

"Yeah. Not much of a plot to the story."

He half laughed and wrapped his arms around me. "It's still better to talk about it than to bury it deep inside."

"I agree."

"I need coffee," he said. "Come on. We can talk about this in the kitchen."

We took a few minutes to make the bed and brush our teeth, and by then, we were both desperate for coffee.

As Mac made coffee, I took care of petting and scratching our little creatures and then feeding them and adding fresh water to their bowls.

At the kitchen table, coffee mug in hand, I gazed at Mac. "So, now I need to know something."

"What?" he said.

"Can you please tell me how Randi died?"

He gave me an odd look. "But you saw her. We were both down in the wine cellar the whole time."

"Right." I closed my eyes for a moment, remembering. "We all saw her down there, and when you and Eric lifted her and turned her over, I saw her throat. It was a bloody gaping wound that made me want to run screaming, but instead I simply stood there, staring, saying nothing. I was practically mute, for God's sake."

I brushed away those feelings of helplessness and guilt. And I wondered, where had the guilt come from? Now that she was dead, what did I do with all that hate I'd felt for her? Had it transformed itself into a boatload of guilt? Maybe. And that was just weird.

"I know she must've died from that gaping wound," I said. "But how did she *get* the gaping wound? What are the details? Does Eric know? Did it happen right there in the wine cellar? Was there a fight? Are the killer's prints somewhere? Did Eric find the knife? Does he have a suspect? Is the killer left- or right-handed?"

"Lot of questions," he said, reaching for my hand and idly playing with my fingers.

"Yeah. So what aren't you telling me?"

"I thought I'd give you another minute to take a few more breaths."

"Okay." So I took a few minutes to breathe, then drank some more coffee. And then I was ready to talk. "Seeing Randi with that gash in her throat was shocking, but someone must've seen the weapon that was used. Unless the killer held on to the knife and walked away with it."

"Eric didn't find a weapon."

My eyes widened. "Are you kidding me?"

"Nope."

"Oh, that's really too bad."

"A bummer for sure."

"Mac, how long have you known me?"

"Long enough to know that you don't shy away from the tough details."

"That's right. So come on, Scooby, give me the scoop."

That startled a laugh out of him and he shook his head helplessly. "I'm serious. He didn't find a weapon."

"Darn it. I really thought you were trying to protect me. Even if I get a little queasy, I always want the details."

Mac grimaced. "I know that about you. You're relentless. But unfortunately, I can't help you."

I blinked a few times, then grimaced. "Shoot. I mean, it would help to have the weapon."

Mac touched my cheeks. "You gonna be okay?"

"Yes. In fact, I'm kind of glad. Not that Randi is dead. But, you know, there have been a few times when the murder weapon was one of my tools, and I really hate that."

I took another minute to recall some of the horrible times my tools had been used to kill someone. It was never easy to accept. I even wondered sometimes if I'd done something to attract a killer to my toolbox. But that was ridiculous. My toolbox did not have magical powers!

"What are you thinking?" Mac asked. He got up and poured us both another cup of coffee, then popped two pieces of sourdough bread into the toaster.

I scowled. "I was selfishly thinking about the fact that my tools have ended up as weapons before. And I really hate having that direct connection to a killer. It means that the killer might've been rifling through my tools. It makes me crazy. And even worse, I hate having anyone on my crew implicated in murder."

"I'm glad you don't have to go through that this time."

"Me too." And then I had the most random thought. "Hmm."

"What are you thinking?"

"Totally random thoughts." I sipped my coffee. "I mean, the murder happened practically in front of us. But there was no murder weapon left behind."

"Right."

"It had to be some kind of knife, obviously. But what kind? And who did it belong to? Or who did they steal it from? The hotel kitchen maybe? Or it could've been taken from one of the dining tables. Have you seen their steak knives? They're formidable."

"That makes it sound premeditated," Mac said. "Unless they have knives down in the wine cellar."

"Right. Randi was arguing with the killer, and he—or she—grabbed the knife that was just sitting there on the counter and slashed her throat."

Mac shrugged. "It could happen. But probably not."

"Probably not," I murmured, and stared at my coffee cup.

"Now what are you thinking?"

I blew out a frustrated breath. "More random thoughts. I was wondering if Sean cleaned my drywall knife and put it back in my toolbox."

"That's pretty random."

"I know." And I hated that I was thinking of Sean in the middle of this conversation about murder.

Mac reached over and rubbed my arm. "You want to call Sean and ask him?"

"I'm sure he took care of it. I always make such a big deal about that kind of stuff."

"You put the fear of God into them."

I chuckled. "Yeah, that's kind of why I do it."

He stood then, and I watched him reach for two plates from the cupboard. Then he buttered the toast, put a piece on each plate, and set them on the table.

"Thanks."

"We need a little sustenance if we're going to talk about this stuff."

"You're right."

"After we finish our toast and coffee, we'll go check your toolbox."

"Yes."

"Because otherwise, it's going to eat at you."

I sighed. "It already is."

———

"It's not here."

"How can you tell?" Mac asked. "You've got five hundred different drywall knives in there."

I scowled. "There aren't more than twenty or so."

"Maybe he put it in one of the other drawers."

"Oh, good thinking." I pulled out the other two drawers, even though I doubted it would be there. Still, I had to check.

I frowned. "Maybe I put it somewhere else and forgot it."

He grabbed my hands in his. "Shannon, you are the most organized person I know. You know where all your tools are at all times. So that means that Sean's the one who didn't put it back after using it."

"But Sean would never—"

"Doesn't mean he killed anyone," Mac hastened to add. "Maybe he wasn't able to finish the job and he left it in the wine cellar office. Or maybe he left it to soak in a bucket somewhere because he knew that if it wasn't pristine when he returned it to you, you would smack him around."

"I wouldn't—"

"Just kidding, babe," he said with a smile. "So, why don't you give him a call? Because otherwise you're going to drive yourself crazy worrying about it."

"I'll drive you crazy, too. Right?"

"I would never say that."

I laughed for the first time all morning.

I ended the call and looked at Mac. "You heard that, right?"

"Yeah." Mac was gently rubbing my shoulders, trying to soothe my worries. "So Sean cleaned the knife and left it in the wine office."

"Right," I said. "Because he still had some more work to do the next day."

"Exactly. Which means that he didn't use it to slice someone's throat."

"He would never do that."

"Of course not," Mac said. "Any chance we can get into the wine office to check that the knife is there?"

"I'm pretty sure the police have sealed off that area until they finish their investigation." Feeling antsy, I took our plates and cups over to the dishwasher and set them on the rack inside.

"You want to call Eric?" Mac asked. "You could ask if he found the drywall knife in the wine office."

"Oh God." I took a deep breath and exhaled. "Guess I'd better."

I found Eric's number and hit call, then waited for him to answer.

"Hey, Shannon," he said.

"Hi, Eric. You said you wanted to talk to me today, and I'm assuming it's about Shirley Ann and Joyce."

"That's right. I'll be speaking with them today, but I wanted to find out if they told you anything or if you overheard them talking about anything in relation to the murder that took place last night?"

"They didn't mention that they saw anything that happened. But they knew immediately that the body under the blankets was Randi. They recognized her shoes."

"Her shoes?"

"Yeah. They're distinctive. Apparently anyone who was friends with Randi knew that she loved those platform lug soles."

"Lug soles," he muttered. "Who knew?"

"Not me," I said. "But while I've got you on the phone, I was wondering if you found my pink drywall knife in the wine office."

"You left a drywall knife in the wine office?"

"No, Sean left it. He was working in there last night and he wasn't able to finish, so he cleaned off the knife and left it there."

"Can you describe the knife?"

"Oh, sure. It's a pink, medium width, six-inch drywall knife."

"Okay, good. I'll give Sean a call."

"Wait," I said quickly. "Why?"

"Shannon," he said, with all the patience he could muster. "I need to confirm what you've just told me with Sean and have it come from him to cover all our bases."

"Yeah, I suppose that makes sense."

"And I don't want you talking to anyone about this. Is that clear?"

"Yeah, it's clear. Except." I glanced at Mac, who grinned unabashedly.

"Except what?" Eric demanded.

"Except that Mac is here and he's listening to this phone call."

I could picture Eric rolling his eyes, but all he said was, "Same goes for Mac."

"Got it, Chief," Mac said cheerfully.

Eric ended the call immediately after that.

"I think that went well," Mac said.

Ten minutes later, the phone rang and I answered immediately. "Hi, Eric."

"Hi. I think I know the answer to this question, but I've got to ask anyway."

"Okay."

"Is your toolbox in your possession at all times when you're working at the Cliffs Hotel?"

"Not always. Sometimes I leave it on the veranda and just take out a couple of the tools I'm going to need instead of carrying the whole thing around with me. It's pretty heavy."

"Yes, I'm aware. Did you happen to notice anyone looking through the toolbox or taking anything out of it?"

"I've been working at the Cliffs Hotel for months, and every day I'm there, my toolbox is in plain sight. Half the time, the top is wide open and at least one shelf is exposed. Anyone who lives or works there has access to it."

"Including your crew members?"

Now I rolled my eyes. "Oh, come on."

"Seriously."

I clenched my teeth. "Yes, including my crew members. Including the entire Garrison family and, frankly, everyone who's ever been to the hotel." I was getting angry, but I was also petrified that he would turn and focus on another one of my guys, and it wasn't fair. My throat was suddenly as dry as dust. But I kept talking anyway. "Look, I don't know if someone used one of my tools to hurt Randi. But I did know Randi. And I really hesitate to say this, but honestly, Eric, she was hateful. Anyone who's ever known her might be capable of killing her. And I'm only slightly exaggerating." I had to take a few breaths and blow them out. "So instead of looking at my crew, I might take a look at a few members of that family if I were you. And while you're at it, I'd look at anyone in the hotel who had to work with her."

He didn't speak for a few long seconds, then said, "Okay. Thank you. Anything else you'd like to add?"

"Yes, darn it." I flopped back in my chair, feeling awful. "I'm really sorry I said that about the family. Most of them are wonderful, so just ignore me, please."

I only just realized that Mac was slowly and softly rubbing my arm as if I were a high-strung pony he was trying to soothe. It was starting to work.

I could picture Eric slowly nodding his head. "We've just started interviewing the family members. Anything else?"

"Yeah, it's about Sean."

"What about him?"

"Sean was one of the only guys on my crew who actually liked Randi. That's why I asked him to supervise construction of her new sommelier office in the cellar."

"He liked her?" Eric said, sounding doubtful.

"Yeah. That's just Sean. He's a contrary guy when it comes to women." I had to smile. "He likes the beautiful, snotty, malicious type."

"You're kidding about this."

"Not really," I insisted. "What can I say? Apparently some guys dig women who can trade insults. Plus she was so gorgeous that plenty of men were willing to put up with some grief to be able to hang around her."

"She was very attractive," Eric said evenly, but Shannon knew for a fact that Eric didn't care for Randi at all. Mainly because she'd been a thorn in Chloe's side for years.

It was too bad that all the beauty in the world ultimately couldn't make up for a crappy personality.

"Yes, she was. So Sean liked her. Thought she was sassy. My crew guys always teased him about it. But I think I've said enough. You should talk to him. I'm just telling you, he would never hurt her. He would never hurt anyone. Never. He's a good guy."

"Shannon, I know Sean," Eric said. "I agree with you."

I blinked. "You do?"

"I do."

"You do," I murmured, and felt my heart lighten. "Okay. Good. I'm glad."

Then he said, "Mac, you still listening?"

"Right here, Chief," Mac said.

"Anything you'd like to add?"

"I pretty much agree with everything Shannon just said." Then he grinned. "And you probably agree, too."

Eric snorted. "No comment."

"Thanks, Eric," I said, sensing he was about to end the call.

"Thanks again for your input," Eric said. "I appreciate it. Now do me a favor and forget we had this conversation."

I smiled. "What conversation was that?"

He chuckled. "Good answer. But just so you know, I will be talking to Sean, so don't get all bent out of shape about it."

"Me?"

Mac laughed.

Eric said, "Sean used a drywall knife and he told me he left it in the wine office. It's not there. So I need to know who or what he might've seen around the time he left for the day."

"Okay," I said, wincing. "Just don't . . ."

"Don't what?" Eric asked. "Flog him? Throw him in the clink? Starve him?"

I wasn't going to smile. "Don't do any of that."

"I'll try to hold myself back."

"Please do."

He chuckled. "See you guys later."

We spent a few hours doing house stuff, and then Mac asked me if I still wanted to go to Homefront with him.

"Yes. I can be ready in about a half hour.'

"Good. I have a short meeting with Logan, and then I thought we'd go out and pull some weeds, clean up the garden."

"I can definitely use a little physical labor," I said. "It'll help me chill out a little."

"Always a good thing," he said.

My cell phone rang and I looked at Mac. "I'd better answer this."

"Go ahead, babe. It could be the Publishers Clearing House Sweepstakes."

"Oh, sure. Wish me luck." I put the call on speaker. "Hey, Lizzie."

"Can you join me for a quick lunch in an hour or so?"

I frowned. Lizzie sounded stressed out, and that hardly ever happened. "Sure. What's up?"

"I'll tell you when I see you."

"Okay."

But then she added, "I didn't realize you know Aurora."

Aurora. The mother of the three little boys. I took a quick look at Mac and had to wonder what this was actually about.

"I've never met Aurora," I admitted. "But I've met her three boys."

"They're little darlings, aren't they?" Lizzie said.

"They're pretty darn cute," I agreed. "So, where are we going for lunch?"

"Emily's," she said.

She was talking about Emily's Tea Shoppe on the town square. "See you there," I said, and ended the call.

"That was quick," Mac commented.

"For Lizzie, that was a world record. She's usually a lot chattier than that, but this time I got nothing. I thought she might be calling about the Christmas party at Jane's."

"You can drop me off at Homefront and go to lunch. Then come back when you're finished. I'll probably be in the garden by then."

"Lizzie only takes a half hour for lunch, so I won't be long."

———————

We left a few minutes later, and soon I was pulling into the Homefront parking lot and stopping to let Mac off. He kissed me before jumping out of the truck.

I drove two miles across town to the town plaza and found a parking place near Emily's Tea Shoppe. As I walked onto the plaza, I ran straight into Lizzie, who had just walked out of Paper Moon, her shop a few stores away.

"Hey, girl," I said, grabbing her arm.

"There you are." She gave me a tight hug and kept her arm wrapped through mine as we walked to the Tea Shoppe.

"You look so festive," I said, gazing at Lizzie's red plaid jacket, matching pants, and red boots. She was self-conscious about her short height and thought that matching her top and pants made her appear taller.

"Thanks. I keep it jolly through the season."

"It's fabulous."

"So how are the Garrisons holding up?" she asked.

I thought of Lilian cheerfully handing out to-go bags after our big dinner. "The only Garrison I've actually seen is Lilian, and she was holding up pretty well."

"I know," Lizzie said. "It was so lovely of her to personally hand out those to-go bags. You'd never know that someone in her family had just been murdered."

"She does have a very generous heart, but I'm pretty sure she wasn't Randi's biggest fan."

"Oh gosh, no way."

"Right?" I paused. "Oh, and Chloe told me that she talked to Stephanie about Randi."

"How's Steph doing?"

"Well, she's trying to act like she's upset about it, but the fact is, according to Chloe, she hated Randi."

"Who could blame her?" Lizzie murmured. "The woman was toxic."

"Totally toxic," I said. "Stephanie told Chloe about this one night when she was out late with her girlfriends."

"Is this what Chloe was telling you at our Christmas dinner?"

I was shocked. "Wait. Could you actually hear her?"

Lizzie gave me a look. "You know I have ears like a bat."

"How could I forget?" I had to take a breath before I could continue the story. "Anyway, when Stephanie got home, Randi's car was gone. Then about an hour later, Steph saw her sneaking into the hotel. So she's pretty certain that Randi has been cheating on Logan all this time, and that was the last straw as far as she was concerned."

"Wow, don't tell Eric that," she said, giggling. "It sounds like a motive to kill."

I had to take another deep breath at that realization. Luckily, the conversation ended when we walked into the Tea Shoppe and saw our friend Emily standing by the front counter. As usual, she looked chic in a fitted black-and-red pantsuit with a bright Santa Claus apron tied at the waist. It might've sounded slightly garish, but on Emily it was simply charming.

We hugged and commiserated about our disastrous Christmas dinner last night.

"That's okay," Emily said. "We can have a pizza party at my house next week."

I laughed. "I was just thinking the same thing. Are you and Gus willing to take on the logistics, Emily?"

"Absolutely," she said with a smile. "If someone will help me."

"I'll help you," Lizzie said. "We can do a phone tree and I'll start it. We just need to discuss the date and time and the food."

"I'll order the food," I said. "Just pizza and salads, right? I'll call Bella Rossa. They deliver. And everyone can bring beer or wine or whatever."

Bella Rossa was a wonderful Italian restaurant owned by my uncle Pete. This was hardly the first time my friends and I had marveled at how great it was to have an uncle with an Italian restaurant right there on the town square. Not to mention his beautiful vineyard and winery just outside of town.

"Let me get you a table," Emily said, and walked us into the charming back room. "Gretchen will be here soon to take your order, and I'll try to get back to visit in just a bit."

Gretchen showed up less than a minute later with a pot of tea and two cups, then took our order.

"I hate to say it, but you look a little harried," Lizzie said.

"I am," I admitted. "I've been working for weeks on the special Christmas Fun Zone that the Garrisons created. And then our crazy dinner took place, followed by, you know, Randi."

Lizzie grimaced. "I heard that you found her."

"Mac and I did."

"I heard she died in the wine cellar."

I blinked. "Jeez, Lizzie. You must have a direct line to Eric's phone."

She shrugged. "You know me. I just hear things."

True. We didn't call her the gossip machine queen for nothing.

I sighed. "It wasn't pretty, that's all I'm going to say."

And I seriously had to wonder if Lizzie had overheard someone talking on the hotel grounds. I didn't notice when she left the dinner last night, but she might've spoken to someone before she left. But who? Shirley Ann had been there, along with Joyce, of course. And Craig, the head bartender, who'd been working all evening. She could've talked to almost anyone else who'd been there, or maybe she'd overheard the dozens of conversations that had been going around all evening after Randi was found.

"Ugh, Shannon," she said. "Poor you."

"I'm doing just fine," I insisted.

"I know you didn't like Randi," Lizzie whispered. "I didn't, either. But now that she's dead, are you suffering pangs of guilt?"

I flashed her an incredulous look. "Good grief. Not at all."

"Don't look at me that way," Lizzie said. "I know you couldn't stand her, but you also tend to have guilt layered upon guilt."

She was right, of course. "Normally, yes," I insisted. "But not in this case. Let's not forget that Randi was the next step up on the Whitney Satanic Scale."

She laughed. "That's a good one. I'd forgotten she was a good friend of Whitney's."

"Yup." I smiled, but I was starting to get fidgety. "Now look, I'm always up for discussing murder and mayhem, but I know you only have a few minutes, and I think you had something else on your mind. Not that I don't love you completely, but I get the feeling you're after some information from me. So what's up?"

"You're right," she said, and took a sip of her tea. "I want to pick your brain."

"Ew."

She laughed. "So, here's the deal. Someone saw you at the Fun Zone the other night with Logan and the three boys."

I was moving from fidgety to confusion. "Lizzie, you're scaring me. Is someone actually reporting my activities to you? It's no big deal. We're all connected through Homefront. Logan and Mac and Eric and others, including the little boys."

"That's not why I'm concerned."

"Okay. What's going on, Lizzie?"

Chapter Ten

At that moment, Gretchen arrived with our sandwiches and salad, exacerbating my impatience. How long was it going to take before we could start talking again? But luckily, Lizzie could read me like a comic book.

"Okay, okay, don't freak," she said as soon as the waitress walked away. "Aurora asked me about you, and I told her."

"Aurora? The boys' mother? How do you know her?"

"It's kind of a long story."

"I'm ready to hear it." I took a big bite of my sandwich and waited for her to talk.

"Oh, all right." She took a good gulp of her tea and began to explain. "Aurora married her husband, David, who was in the air force. She got pregnant, and before David deployed, he suggested that they should move to his family's home in Lighthouse Cove so she would have a support system with the baby coming."

"That makes sense." I felt a little guilty that I wasn't telling her that I'd already heard some of this from Logan. But I confess, I wanted to hear it from Lizzie's point of view.

"Aurora loved David's family, so she readily agreed." Lizzie took a quick sip of tea, then continued. "She's a hairdresser, so as soon as she moved here, she found a good hairdressing job in town. And she was happy despite David's numerous deployments."

"Do I know his parents?"

"Maybe," Lizzie said. "They're the Billinghams. They live just north of Cranberry Circle."

"The name sounds very familiar." And coincidentally, I had worked on a number of homes on Cranberry Circle and nearby streets.

"You probably refurbished their home," Lizzie said.

"I remember. My dad was in charge back then, and we renovated their basement. Turned it into a really cool man cave."

"Nice. So anyway, I had always gone to her hair salon, and when my girl left, I started going to Aurora. One day we started talking about our kids. They're much younger than Taz and Marisa, but we've still gotten together a few times. Her little boys love Taz."

"Of course they do." Lizzie's son, Taz, short for Tasmanian Devil, was the sweetest, smartest boy kid in the world. Her daughter Marisa was a cutie pie, too.

"Her boys are really sweet," I said, "so she must be a nice woman."

"She's the most awesome woman I know. I mean, besides you."

I laughed. "Oh yeah, good save." But then I sobered. "I know that she's sick."

"Seriously," Lizzie said after taking another bite of her chicken salad sandwich. "It's so sad. She's beautiful, talented, a wonderful mother, and a good friend. And now she's sick and she can't work, so she couldn't pay for her apartment anymore. Thank God they were able to get the whole family into Homefront."

"That was lucky."

"It was more than luck," Lizzie said. "It was Logan."

I frowned at her. "But Logan only just started working for Homefront."

"Yes, but Logan and Aurora have known each other for years before that. More than friends, really. He's such a sweetheart."

"He really is."

"So anyway, all her friends are trying to visit as often as we can and do her laundry and cook for her and drive her to doctors' appointments. We try to keep her happy and healthy and aware of all the latest news. And we all take turns finding fun stuff to do with the boys."

It wasn't like Lizzie to simply breeze over the fact that Logan and Aurora had been friends for years. There was more to this story, but I wasn't sure I'd get it all from Lizzie. She sounded exceptionally protective of Aurora.

"She's lucky to have such good friends," I said.

"She makes it easy," Lizzie said. "So anyway, when someone told Aurora that they saw you with Logan and the boys at the Fun Zone, I thought I'd better ask you what was going on."

"Um, why?"

"Because we watch out for the boys."

"I get that. But what did you want to know?"

She held up her hand. "Here's the deal. Aurora said that the boys and Logan were there, and that you and Mac joined them."

"So far, that's true."

"Well, and then Randi joined your group and met the boys. So I wanted to know if she said anything to the boys or to Logan about Aurora. You know how Randi can be. She used to say horrible things to Logan in front of anyone who was standing there. She was such a you-know-what."

"She didn't say a word to the boys. In fact, Logan introduced the boys to her, and she didn't even acknowledge them."

"Oh, she's horrible!" She instantly covered her mouth. "I shouldn't have said that. I mean, she's dead and all. But my God, what's wrong with her? Did the boys notice? Did they say anything?"

"No, they didn't notice she was being rude. In fact, the youngest boy stared at her and told her she was pretty."

Lizzie pressed her hands to her heart. "That's so sweet. And she still didn't say anything?"

"No. But seriously, I don't think the boys even noticed, because it was really loud and they were all distracted by the games and the carousel.

"I hope that's true."

"I'm sure it is."

"She was always such a beyotch," Lizzie muttered. "Again, I shouldn't speak ill of the dead, but she still manages to burn my butt."

"I hear that." Something occurred to me. "Lizzie, I have to ask you something."

"Okay."

"The way you're talking about Aurora and Logan, I need to ask if they're having an affair." I held up my hand. "Not that it's any of my business, but Randi might've thought so, and she might've said something to someone."

"Someone like Whitney, for instance?"

"Exactly." It was good to have friends who'd known me since

kindergarten and knew all the ugly details of my life. Mainly, my connection to Whitney. Lizzie had seen me though the worst days of Whitney and it was weird but nice to have someone who knew me so well.

"Shannon," Lizzie said. "There's no way Aurora would get involved with Logan as long as he was married."

I nodded. "I would say the same for Logan. There's no way he would ever cheat on his wife."

Lizzie shrugged. "But just in case someone approaches Logan or one of the little boys claiming it happened?"

"There are people in this world who would do that," I said. "The aforementioned Whitney, for instance. It would be a lie, but she wouldn't care about that."

"So forewarned is forearmed, right?"

"You got it."

She raised her teacup in a toast. "Here's to Aurora's good health and happiness."

"I'll drink to that," I said, taking a sip of tea. "And maybe you'll introduce me to her one of these days."

"Oh! I'll try to set that up. I know she'd love to meet you, but it's always a little iffy because she gets sick so easily with all the chemotherapy."

"Her boys must be frightened to death."

"They put up such a brave front."

"They're good boys."

We both reached for our sandwiches and took bites.

"I'm so worried for her," Lizzie said after she'd taken a sip of her tea. "It's only stage two, but that's like saying it's only World War Three. It could turn into anything. Cancer sucks, any way you look at it."

"Do you see her much?" I asked.

"I try to get over there two or three times a week."

"So how did she meet Logan?" I asked.

"Oh, this is a sweet story," she said. "Aurora told me that they met at some summer camp when they were about ten years old. He proposed to her and she said yes. Then summer camp was over and they both went back home. And didn't see each other for years afterward."

"Oh no! I'm already invested in their love story."

"I know. Isn't that cute?" she took a quick sip of tea. "So they hadn't seen each other in years, and Aurora ended up meeting a nice guy from Lighthouse Cove who was in the air force. So I told you this part. She moved here to be close to his family and have a support system for the boys."

I shook my head. "So she moved here and then her husband was killed in Afghanistan?"

"Yes."

"That is tragic."

"Absolutely. But then she and Logan ran into each other and they tried to renew their friendship. But now he was married to Randi so like I said before, nothing was going to happen between them. And now Randi is gone."

"Yeah. So what happens now?"

"Well, now she's got to concentrate on getting well and taking care of herself. She has two more chemo sessions and then they wait and see."

"That's just awful. Those boys must be so frightened at the thought of losing her."

"They are, and some days Aurora is so weak that they cry because they think she's dying. And that's why it's so nice that Logan is watching out for her and the kids."

"I can imagine. He's such a good guy."

"He really is."

I wrapped my hands around the teacup for warmth. "I'm so glad we built a couple of those larger houses to accommodate people like her and the boys."

We both took bites of our sandwiches and thought about the sad situation.

"Do you think she'll ever get together with Logan?" I asked.

"I know there's a spark there, but I hate the thought of them having to base their future happiness on Randi's death."

"Yeah, that's creepy."

"I know," she said. "But I think the spark was ready to ignite anyway."

"I'll bet you're right." I checked my wristwatch. "I should get going, but I would really love to meet Aurora sometime."

"I can introduce you. Although, if you go to Homefront regularly and you're already close to Logan, you might want to meet her through him."

"Maybe so. Plus, he's good friends with Mac."

"Oh, that works out well. But if the situation arises when I'm around, I'll be sure to introduce you."

"Thanks, sweetie." I pulled my wallet out of my purse. "I promised Mac I wouldn't keep him waiting too long."

"Oh, I left Hal to run the store, although we've got some great Christmas help, so he should be okay for another few minutes."

We both stood and pushed our chairs back.

"Let me know what I can do to help with the Christmas party, take two."

"Oh, that's cute. That's what we'll call it."

We walked to the front counter and paid our bill, then walked down the square until I turned to find my car.

All the way back to Homefront, I thought about Aurora and her sad predicament. I did the math, and based on the timing Lizzie mentioned, Aurora's husband would've been dead for almost six years. Which meant that their youngest boy, Hudson, had never met his father. And that was another blow to poor Aurora and her boys.

I was going to talk to Mac when I got back and see if we could do something to help them.

———

I parked in the Homefront lot and sent a text to Mac. **Where RU?**

A minute later he responded, **Come to the garden. XOXO.**

As I walked to the garden at the far end of the property, I made a mental list of things I needed to take care of at Homefront. The first thing was to check up on my handywomen and see if they were keeping up with their skills. I had taught several classes last year on carpentry and building basics, focusing on women. The goal here was to get people, especially women, into good-paying jobs doing work that not everyone could do, as carpenters, construction workers, roofers, masons, and other careers in the building industry. We'd been pretty successful so far. I was ridiculously proud of the fact that twelve of my graduates had found some decent jobs in the construction field.

Homefront had been offering job training from the very first day.

It was actually part of its mandate. Mac had taught a few writing classes, and others offered everything from typing to truck driving. There were computer classes, bartending, and other various hospitality jobs.

The only training class more popular than my construction skills class was cooking. The food industry was always looking for trained cooks, and even if you weren't seeking a job, you could still learn a few cooking tricks that might come in handy.

As I walked past the community center, I was assailed by the wonderful scents emanating from the kitchen.

At that moment, Logan walked out the main door and straight toward me. "Hey, you," he said, grabbed me in a hug, and held on for a long moment.

"How are you doing, Logan?" I asked.

He exhaled slowly. "I'm really not sure."

"I'm so sorry," I said.

"Yeah, me too," he said. "It's horribly sad, and it was a particularly vicious crime. She shouldn't have died that way."

"If there's anything we can do," I said, "please just say the word."

"Thank you." He glanced around, then said, "Are you looking for Mac?"

"Yes. He said he was out in the garden."

"That's where I saw him a few minutes ago. I'll walk with you."

"Good." I checked the sky and assured myself that it wasn't going to rain anytime soon. Then I wasn't sure what to say, but I settled on, "How are your parents doing?"

"They're having a hard time, mainly because the police have shut down the restaurant and bar for another day, and this is such a busy time for us."

"I'm sorry to hear that."

"God, I just realized that sounds so callous," he said. "Randi is dead, and all they care about is business. It's not true. They're very upset. But they're managing to hold up under horrible circumstances. They met with staff to try to lift their spirits and keep them from worrying that there's a mad killer on the loose. I feel terrible, but I call them almost every hour, and they've strongly suggested that I should stay here at Homefront for another few days."

"That's not a bad idea," I said. "I might drive by and see your parents tomorrow. I'm not sure what I can do, but I'd like to give my condolences.

"They would love to see you, Shannon."

"I just don't want to add to their burden."

He wrapped his arm around me. "That could never happen. They love you."

I reached over and touched his hand. "The feeling is mutual. And let me just say it again. I'm so sorry."

"Yeah. It's pretty damned awful." He dragged both hands through his hair and blew out a heavy breath. "And beyond the fact that my wife was murdered, I have to confess that I was just about to file for a divorce."

I felt my eyes widen. "Oh no."

"Yeah. I'm sure you and Mac both caught the negative vibes that had been suffocating us for the past few years."

"I don't know about negative vibes, but I never thought she was very nice to you."

"Thank you, Shannon, and I must agree, she was not." Logan shook his head and he lowered his voice. "We were so incompatible. Had been for years. At this point, we were barely speaking to each other. And forget about love or sex or anything like that. We just existed in the same general space, and not happily. It's why I stayed away so often. Of course, the military helped me out there."

"I hear you," I said, unable to come up with any kind of helpful comment.

"I could've been assigned to a military base closer to home, and I know Mom and Dad would've loved that. But the thought of having to deal with Randi on an ongoing basis was just too much. Call me a coward, but she was so freaking negative and so wrapped up in her own ego, I couldn't face that day to day."

"I'm so sorry." I kept repeating those words, when what I should've been saying was, *I totally agree with you.*

"Yeah, thanks. Anyway, I was going to tell Mom and Dad about the divorce after the holidays. I didn't want to bum them out during the season."

"Did Randi want the divorce?" I asked.

He gaped at me and finally let out a short laugh. "It figures you'd ask that question, Shannon."

"Why? What do you mean?"

"I mean, because you seem to have a real grasp of human nature. You had to have guessed that Randi didn't want a divorce."

I felt my eyes widening. "But why was she so . . . ?"

"So nasty?" he suggested. "So mean? Spiteful? Malicious?"

"Well, yeah," I said. "But come on. You guys had been married for years, and I figured there had to be something about her that you fell in love with. She was a beautiful girl."

"Maybe in the beginning," he said. "But it had been a long time since I felt anything for her. And truly, she felt the same way."

"She did? Are you sure?"

"Trust me. She was miserable."

"Why didn't she leave?"

"You want the truth?"

"Of course."

He smirked without humor. "She didn't want to lose her primo sommelier job at the best hotel and restaurant in Northern California. There was no way she was going to give that up, and she figured as soon as we filed for divorce, my parents would kick her out on her ass."

"Would they?" I asked, not quite believing we were having this conversation.

"Oh, absolutely. They were just as fed up with her as I was. My mother, especially." He shook his head in disgust. "But as long as we were married, they were willing to keep her on salary. Even though she caused all kinds of havoc among the staff and even the customers." He had to take a breath. "What really pissed me off was that a few years ago, she managed to convince Mom and Dad that I would be absolutely furious if they ever tried to fire her."

"And they believed her?"

He scowled. "Of course. She can be pretty convincing when she wants to be. And that's when she talked them into paying for her sommelier course."

"That's not cheap," I said.

"No, and it takes a few years to complete the entire course, so naturally she took advantage by cutting back on her real duties in order to play the hoity-toity wine connoisseur."

"Your poor parents. They probably felt they were doing exactly what you wanted them to do. And all the while feeling so guilt-ridden, knowing they wanted to get rid of her but believing you'd be upset if they did."

"Exactly," Logan said. "Randi was nothing if not manipulative."

No kidding, I thought but didn't say. "Did you know she was doing this?"

"No. Stephanie finally told me, just last week."

"Stephanie," I murmured. "Of course."

"Why do you say it like that?" Logan wondered.

"Because Stephanie pays attention. She follows the money, plus she got all the smarts, but she's still really nice." I winced. "That was rude. Sorry. You're really smart, too."

Logan laughed out loud. "I like to think I'm nice, too. And that I got a modicum of those smarts."

"You absolutely did," I insisted, feeling my cheeks redden. "And you're nice, of course."

"Thanks," he said, still grinning. After a moment, he lost the smile. "But poor Arabella. She's totally out of luck. She sold her soul to Whitney Reid years ago, and it seemed to leave her without much brainpower or thoughtfulness."

I pressed my hand to my chest. "It hurts my heart to hear you say that about your younger sister, even if it's true. I'm convinced she can always make a comeback. But she'll need your help to wean her away from Whitney. Your help and Stephanie's."

And I couldn't believe I was saying such things. But Logan obviously agreed. It was frankly mind-blowing.

"We're all aware that we've lost Arabella to that awful woman." He gazed at me and winced in pain. "And I just now remembered that you and Arabella used to be best friends."

"True." I smiled. "We were, until Whitney moved to town."

"How did you manage to avoid Whitney's clutches yourself?" he asked.

I chuckled mirthlessly. "She and I were never going to be friends. At the risk of sounding completely overwrought, Whitney very quickly decided that the thing she wanted most in life was my boyfriend Tommy. And she was determined to do whatever she had to do to destroy me."

Logan stared at me. "That's right. She went after Tommy."

"Yeah." I shrugged. "She manipulated him into sleeping with her and getting her pregnant." I grinned. "Okay, let's admit that he didn't put up much of a protest. So once she conquered the guy, she moved on to my girlfriends, starting with Arabella. She manipulated her by telling lies about me."

"Wow."

"More recently, she even used Mac to try and hurt me," I said.

Logan gaped. "Swear to God?"

"Swear to God. You should ask Mac about that. She actually flew to New York to try and catch him outside of his agent's office, where she pulled a big fat lie out of her little bag of evil tricks."

Logan's eyes widened. "Okay. Wow, that's . . . evil."

"She is that. She's brown-recluse-spider evil when it comes to poisonous."

"Wow. And poor Tommy got screwed," Logan said.

"Oh no, no, wait." I held up both hands. "I have to keep it real. Don't feel sorry for Tommy. He's perfectly happy and content with his beautiful wife and three darling girls."

"He does seem pretty happy."

I had to shrug. "He's just a seriously happy guy."

"But my poor sister." Logan frowned. "She doesn't seem very happy at all."

"She's not," I said. "But now that you're back home, maybe you can help her find her way back to the light."

Logan chuckled. "Back to the light, huh? Not sure that's possible."

"If anyone can do it, you can," I said. "Because you're really smart and really nice, and she looks up to you. And I'm glad you're back in town for good."

He laughed. "Nice try, Shannon."

"But I mean it."

Logan looked at me for a long moment. "Yeah, I think you do."

"Of course I do," I said. "I'm sorry if I ever gave you any doubts about that."

He nodded. I noticed Mac standing by the fence as we approached, and I waved.

"So, if you really want to help your sister," I said, "I'm all in. But she won't want to hear anything from me because I'm too much of an enemy of Whitney."

His expression turned cloudy. "So, what can I do? I really want her back in the fold."

"Talk to Stephanie," I urged. "She's brilliant and she's female, which means that she's automatically got a whole different perspective from you. Together the two of you might be able to find a way out of this situation."

"You're a good person, Shannon."

And, again inexplicably, I laughed. "Thanks, Logan."

Then he glanced at Mac. "Hey, buddy. Just had an enlightening chat with your lady here."

"It happens all the time," Mac said, and stretched over the fence to kiss me.

I was distracted for a moment, then recalled where I was and brought Mac up to speed on my conversation with Logan. "We were talking about Whitney and Arabella."

Mac nodded and his expression turned serious. "Your sister will need some help to escape the manipulator."

Logan took a deep breath. "Maybe I really can help."

"I know you can," I said.

Mac sighed. "I'm a firm believer that people don't have the right to manipulate others. Unfortunately, those manipulators are everywhere, and they naturally prey on susceptible people who aren't strong enough or savvy enough to fight back. My books are filled with both kinds of people. It makes for a really wild ball game."

Logan laughed and I nodded in agreement. But in that moment I realized that many of the most manipulative people who inhabited Mac's amazing novels were the same ones who died a terrible death in the end. And I was suddenly overcome with chills as I thought of Randi, the queen of the manipulators, who had also suffered a horrible death.

Chapter Eleven

"You still feel like doing some yard work?" Mac asked when I joined him in the garden.

I glanced at the sky. It was clear and cold, and the sun was another hour from setting. "I'd love to work off some of this annoyance I'm still feeling about Randi."

I walked up the short incline and around the fence to join Mac in the garden.

"Oh, look, there's Oliver," I said, pointing to the men who were walking up the incline toward us.

"And Bill Garrison, too," Mac added, obviously surprised. "Were they mysteriously transported away from the Cliffs over to Homefront?"

I laughed. "Maybe." There was definitely a connection between the two locations, because Oliver was Logan's oldest friend from the time they'd started restoring the old gardens and orchards at the

Cliffs Hotel. And now they were both hanging out at Homefront, along with Logan's dad.

Oliver was the gorgeous miracle man who made flowers sing and trees smile. And from what I'd seen by the steps of the hotel the other morning, he made Stephanie smile, too.

"Hi, guys," I said.

Bill and Oliver waved. They joined us on the far end of the vegetable garden, where they began rooting out weeds.

"Hey, you two," Oliver said. "I thought I'd try to get Bill out to the garden for a workout."

"Looks like we weren't the only ones with that bright idea," Bill said.

"No, you weren't," Mac said.

I smiled. "That was our plan, too."

There were more tools leaning against the fence, along with several pairs of gardening gloves, so I grabbed a hoe and began digging at the weeds growing around the edges of the vegetable garden.

Bill grabbed a pair of gloves and began to yank at a tough weed that seemed to be pulling back. "Oliver insists that all this physical labor will take my mind off any unproductive thoughts that pop into my head."

"It really works," Oliver said. "I rarely have a single thought when I'm working in the garden."

We all laughed.

"That can't be true," I said.

"You're right, Shannon," Bill said. "I can verify that Oliver is one of the most thoughtful men I've ever known." He glanced at me. "He's the first person I sought out when I heard about Randi. His words were very helpful."

None of us spoke for a moment, almost as if we'd planned a brief tribute.

"That's kind of you to say, Bill," Oliver said, breaking the silence. "But admit it. You're just sucking up to me so I'll agree to plant that avocado orchard you want."

I appreciated that he was teasing Bill, getting him to smile. He was carrying a heavy emotional load today.

But wait, an avocado orchard? Sign me up!

"That sounds awesome," I said. "Everyone loves avocados."

"See?" Bill said. "It's a good idea. And nobody is pushing for it harder than Stephanie. Avocados are fantastic in a hundred different ways, according to her. In the kitchen and the dining room. And in the spa."

"The spa, really?" I asked. "Are people rubbing avocado oil on their faces?"

"You're close," Oliver said. "The oil is used for moisturizing and to prevent inflammation. It's an antioxidant, and it increases collagen production. But the fruit itself can be mashed up to use as a facial mask. Works wonders."

"If I'm going to mash up avocado," Mac said, "I'm going to make guacamole."

"That works for me," Bill said.

"The oil makes a really good salad dressing, too," I said.

"I'm getting the full sales pitch," Oliver said, laughing. "Did you plan this, Bill?"

"I've already been getting the pitch from Stephanie," Bill said. "My girl knows her stuff."

"She sure does," Oliver said. And I tried to remember if he always sounded so wistful when he spoke of her.

But wait a minute. Oliver and Stephanie? I'd seen them on the steps that one time, and they had looked awfully friendly. I had felt a definite attraction between them. But still. Stephanie had been married to Craig, the bartender, for almost six years. But Oliver had been Logan's friend since grade school, and he'd been working at the hotel for years. He was practically a member of the family. Had Stephanie ever had her eye on him before Craig came along and lured her away? Or maybe Oliver had been the one to be lured away by another woman. I had to laugh at myself for caring. But it was more fun to think about these nice people than murder and mayhem, right? And that reminded me. I had to call Chloe. This was just the sort of fascinating puzzle that she would love to help me solve. Especially because her best friend, Stephanie, was a key to the solution.

We worked for another half hour before quitting. The sun was still high in the sky, but it was getting chilly.

"I've got one hour to get to our meeting," Bill said, checking his watch. "Lilian thought it would be a good idea to spend the evening with all the kids. Sort of hunker down and be together."

"That'll be nice," I said, not quite believing it.

"Yeah, we'll see," Bill said. And it sounded like he didn't quite believe it, either. "Anyway, I'd better get home and take a shower first, scrape off this layer of dirt that somehow got all over me."

Oliver laughed. "I've got to go, too."

"It was really fun working with you," I said.

"Yeah, this was great," Mac added.

"I'd be glad to show you around the Cliffs' gardens sometime," he said. "We're doing some amazing work with sustainable gardening and water conservation. All sorts of good stuff."

"I would love to see what you're doing," I said, glancing at Mac.

Mac agreed. "Yeah, we'd really dig that, Oliver. Thanks."

He and Bill took off, and we watched them jog down the slight incline toward the parking lot. Mac and I stacked our tools inside the small utility shed, and I threw our pile of weeds into the trash can that was set aside for vegetation of all kinds.

As we put stuff away, Mac asked, "Is the Fun Zone open tonight?"

"No. It's closed for two nights because of Randi's death. It'll open back up the day after tomorrow. Tonight will be just family, and tomorrow evening a memorial."

"So, a two-day memorial?"

I shrugged. "Apparently, Lilian and Bill took a vote among the kids and that's what they decided."

I could read his expression as easily as if he'd spoken the words: *That's cold.*

Five minutes later we headed down the hill to the parking lot.

Mac stretched his arms and rolled his shoulders. "My shoulder is a bit tweaked, but that'll go away. I feel a whole lot better for having done the work."

"Me too. My brain's doing better, too. I'm not feeling quite so bummed out."

We held hands walking down the hill toward the parking lot. With every row of tiny homes we passed, I felt happier. And then I realized why. "Did you notice?" I asked, marveling. "Every single owner of every tiny home has put up Christmas lights. It's so adorable."

Mac was staring, just like I was. "It's so cool."

There were decorations on the windows and the doors. One house even had a miniature sleigh and little reindeer on its roof. I could see through some of the windows that most of the houses had a Christmas tree with decorations and tiny lights shimmering.

"It makes me happy to see it," I said. "I wonder if everyone just happened to decorate, or if they took a vote of some kind."

"However they decided, it looks spectacular," Mac said. "Like a tiny Christmas village. And this is our first Christmas at Homefront. All of Lighthouse Cove should check this out."

I stared at Mac for a long moment. "That's a great idea."

At the community center, Mac started for the car, but I stopped him. "Wait. I need to find Logan for a minute."

"Okay, let's see if he's still in his office."

We walked into the community center, and I wasn't surprised to see Logan sitting in the cafeteria with a group of vets, eating a sandwich and drinking apple cider.

"Hey, you're still here," Logan said, pushing away from the table.

"And so are you," I said. "I'm glad we found you. We want to talk to you for another minute."

"Do we need to use my office?"

I glanced around. "Maybe just a little corner table?"

"You got it." He led the way to a table in the far corner. "How's this?"

"Perfect." As we sat, I explained, "I didn't really need privacy, but I had an idea, and I thought I'd run it by you before anyone else."

"You want some cider or hot chocolate? Or cookies?"

"No thanks," I said, although it all sounded delicious.

"So, what's your idea?" Logan asked.

"You might've already thought of it, but I figured it wouldn't hurt to mention it."

"Okay." He grinned. "You seem nervous. Spit it out."

"I don't know why. It's a great idea."

"Spill it, Shannon," Mac said.

"Okay." I took a breath. "I think you should open up Homefront to the whole town so everyone can see the lights on all the houses. I mean, have you noticed that every single house is decorated? It's so charming. And it's really meaningful that this is the first Christmas for everyone here."

His eyes narrowed. "I hadn't noticed, but I should've. So, exactly what do you mean by opening it up?"

"Look." I pointed up the hill. "Invite the public. Maybe for just two or three nights, or a long weekend. And give it three hours each night. People can park down here and then walk up and down the streets and enjoy the decorations, then maybe stop at the community center and have cider or coffee or hot chocolate and cookies. And they can find out more about the programs you offer. Get them interested in the community. You know?" I was starting to wonder if I was the only one who loved this idea.

"Yeah, I know," Logan murmured.

"Oh, wait," I said, thinking on my feet. "You'll absolutely have to check with all of the residents to make sure they're willing to keep the lights on for a few hours each night. And hopefully, they don't mind having people walk by and stare at their houses." I frowned. "That may be a problem. But then, it's only for two or three nights."

"We might be able to work around that," Logan said cautiously. "Offer a free dinner to each resident. Or maybe a food basket. It's almost Christmas, after all. And we have many generous donors who are always willing to help out, which is wonderful."

"If you think that'll work," I said, "it'll be great. Because I have to tell you, as we walked past each street, I felt happier and lighter. I just think it's remarkable that every single house in here is decorated. That's the kind of spirit you don't see every day."

"That's really great to hear, Shannon."

"I don't know if that was part of a plan, but every single one has some doodads on it. Some have more than others, for sure. But everyone made an effort to be festive. And I think most people in our town would love to see that."

"Hmm," he said. "Maybe."

"People love to look at beautifully decorated homes at Christmas, and they love to honor our veterans. This does both for everyone. It's very inspiring."

"True enough."

"We could even vote for the best decorations or have a raffle if you wanted to give a prize. For the most elaborate or the funniest or the silliest. Or the most inspiring. Or not. I might be going too far." I shrugged. "But everyone here made an effort to raise their spirits, and that counts for something. Besides, it would be fun. You might make some money for the center itself. Charge a fee for cookies and drinks. The money could go to the Homefront community or maybe another charity. Whatever." I took a breath. "Sorry. I get caught up sometimes."

As I stopped talking, I realized that Logan was simply staring at me as if I might be crazy. "Well, anyway, it was just an idea." I looked at Mac, feeling ridiculous. "We'd better go."

"Hold on there," Logan said, grabbing my arm to keep me in my chair. "You kind of blew me away for a minute. But, Shannon, that's an amazing idea. It would be fun for most people and, yeah, it could be a charitable event. It would bring our people out of their houses, and it would bring the outside community in to us."

"Exactly."

"I have a question," Logan said.

"Okay."

"How would you feel about making it happen?"

"Me?"

He laughed. "Yeah, you. You're organized and you're a natural leader and you've got great ideas. And I believe you personally know everyone in town."

"Well, so do you."

He laughed. "Yeah, but I've got this job here." He swept his hand across to indicate the whole of Homefront.

"We all have jobs," I said, wondering how I would fit this into my own schedule. "But okay, okay." I thought about it for a minute. It wasn't that outlandish a suggestion. "I could call my friend Palmer at the *Lighthouse Standard* and ask him to write a couple of stories and maybe do a little free advertising. I mean, we're pretty close to Christmas, so it's not like we'd have to take the next six months to set it up. It's like, right now."

"It would be great to have the support of the town newspaper," Logan said. "Really helps to let people know that it's going on. People are always looking for something fun to do with the family. This is something they would enjoy for an hour or two in the early evening. And you're right that it would make people feel good."

"You absolutely must make sure the vets are willing to open up the village for two or three nights." I thought of the date and almost fainted. "Wow, it's only two weeks until Christmas." I had to take a deep breath to center myself. "Okay, we can do this. We'll need flyers. I can print a bunch to hand out to the stores on the town square. I'll get Lizzie to take charge there. She'll make them look festive and inviting. Seriously, it shouldn't be too challenging. What do you think?"

Logan grinned. "I think we'll be talking very soon. And every day for the next two weeks."

As we walked away, I turned back around. "You'll need a couple of volunteers to make cookies and serve hot cider."

"I'm on it," Logan said, laughing.

I stared at Mac. "What have I done?"

He laughed and grabbed me in a hug. "You are a good person. A bit of a sucker, but a really good person."

"I'm crazy, aren't I?"

He laughed. "Yes, but you'll do a great job, and it really won't be that insane. Like Logan said, you know everybody in town. And it's only for two days sometime during the next two weeks. You know who to call for whatever you need. And you've got all your friends on the plaza to post about it. It's a really great idea."

I stared at him. "Really?"

"Of course. And it's a cause that's near and dear to our own hearts."

I nodded. "That was the best thing you could've said."

He grinned. "Hey, I'm a writer. It comes naturally."

I chuckled at that. We made our way toward the front door, but before we could get out, we were suddenly surrounded by three little creatures in monkey costumes.

"Hey, hi! Hi!" the smallest monkey said. "'Member me?"

I stared down at the little guy wearing a very elaborate monkey suit. It even had wings, just like his brothers'. They were so cute!

"Are you a flying monkey?" I asked.

"Yeah! Yeah!"

"Hudson," his older brother whined. "We gotta go."

"Oh, okay, okay." He looked at me. "That's my brother Finn."

I turned and waved. "Hi again, Finn."

"Hi. We gotta go."

"Okay," I said. "Where are you going?"

"Hudson!" his big brother Rowan scolded. "We gotta go."

"I can't tell you now," Hudson whispered. "But maybe tomorrow."

"Okay," I said. "Maybe we'll see you tomorrow."

"Yeah! Yeah!"

"Okay. Bye, Hudson," I said with a wave. "Bye, Finn. Bye, Rowan."

"Goodbye," Rowan said very crossly as they traipsed out the door to the parking lot.

"They're so cute," I said.

"Wonder what's up with the monkey suits," Mac said.

"Something for a Christmas play, maybe?"

"Maybe." Mac started the car, and we drove slowly out of the community center parking lot.

The next day, Mac drove with me to the Cliffs Hotel to check on Lilian. I just felt like she could use some TLC, and Mac was always a good person to bring along.

We found her in the wine cellar, of all places, going through inventory. That would've been Randi's job, so now somebody had to do it, and Lilian probably thought she would be the best person to take it on until they could hire someone new.

"Hey, Lilian," Mac said.

"We thought we'd come by," I said. "See if there's anything we can do for you."

"Ah, you guys are the best." She blew her bangs away from her forehead. The rest of her long blond hair was pulled back in a ponytail

213

that made her look like a teenager. "Well, as you can see, our cleaning crew really did a great number on this room." She patted Mac on the back. "Thanks for that recommendation, by the way. Those guys did an amazing job."

Mac glanced around. "Yeah, I can tell."

"What guys?" I asked, glancing from Lilian to Mac.

"Crime scene cleaners," he murmured to me.

I felt my eyes bug out. I'd used that service myself, more than once. I frowned at Lilian. "I'm so sorry you're having to go through this."

"Thank you, sweetie."

"We came by to see if there was anything we could do for you."

"I don't think so. Right now I can't even think straight. Last night we all decided to keep the memorial service very informal. It mainly consists of each of us standing up and saying how we feel. Like a little speech. What am I supposed to say?"

"Maybe Mac can help. He's a writer."

Lilian smiled at Mac, who tried to look as though he'd be thrilled to memorialize Randi. "Don't worry, Mac," she said. "I'm not going to ask you to do that."

"I wouldn't mind a bit," Mac said graciously. "And look, sometimes it helps to have someone outside the family give you a few thoughts to help move your brain along."

She chuckled. "That would be so incredibly helpful, Mac. Honestly, my mind is a blank."

"That's understandable," Mac said. "You just need some prompts. I'll email you a few ideas."

"I feel ridiculous, but I'm eternally grateful. Thank you." She heaved a sigh. "It doesn't help to hear Logan confess that he'd been

214

planning to divorce the woman before all of this happened. Can you believe it?"

"Well, to be honest, yes, I believe it," I said. Especially since Logan had told me this yesterday, but I wasn't going to mention that to Lilian, ever. "They didn't seem very happy."

"See?" She shook her head. "Even you saw what was obvious to everyone except me." She waved that thought away. "Oh, I knew she gave him a lot of trouble, but I chose not to look too closely."

"Why should you?" I said. "You've always seen the best in everyone. And he's your oldest son and very dear to you. You didn't want to see him hurting."

"That's very sweet." She dabbed at the tears in her eyes. "Bill always called Randi our problem child. She could certainly be a problem, even if she wasn't a child. And not *our* child, either." Lilian shook her head. "That's probably harsh. I don't even know what else to say. I'm sure you've heard all of this before."

"Some of it," I admitted. "But it's still a sad time, and we're here to help with anything you need."

"Thank you."

Bill walked in just then.

"Oh, darling," Lilian said. "I'm glad you're here."

"I'm glad *you're* here," he said, and kissed her. Then he looked at us. "And I'm glad you guys are here, too. What's going on?"

"I actually had a question to ask you," I said.

"Okay," Bill said. "Want to sit down?"

"Sure." I glanced around and noticed that the couch wasn't the same one that had been here the night Randi died. Smart of them to get rid of that one immediately. We all sat down on the new sofa, and Bill said, "So, what's up?"

"It's not a big deal," I admitted. "I mean, I'd already heard that you were going to shut down the Fun Zone for one more night. But I wanted to double-check, make sure that's written in stone, because I'd like to pass the word along to my crew to either send them out on some other jobs or keep them scheduled right here with the Fun Zone responsibilities."

"Of course," he said, and pulled Lilian closer to him.

"Tonight, and that's it," Lilian said insistently. "Written in stone. We want to get everything up and running again and get people out here to enjoy life and each other."

Bill nodded. "Lil and I took a vote last night, and I've got to tell you, our kids are a great group. They're forward-thinking and they're upbeat. They want to keep doing the dinners and the carousel and the Fun Zone and all that good stuff. Well, most of them do, anyway. As usual, we've got one person who wants to shut it all down."

"One person?"

"Yeah."

"Are they upset about Randi's death, or is it something else?"

Bill glanced at Lilian, who shrugged. "No, strangely enough, it has very little to do with Randi. It has to do with their own paranoia that we're spending all of their inheritance on Christmas silliness and giving away too much food at the dinners and too many prizes at the carnival games."

"Oh, wow." I winced. "Have you gone over the expenses with your kids?"

Lilian looked puzzled. "No."

"Oh." I gave Mac a quick glance. "They might benefit from having that knowledge. Especially if the numbers are good."

Bill nodded. "The numbers are very good. But we've never really gone over the finances with the kids, especially for the Christmas events. You know, the dinners and the special treats, like the train and the carousel. We just know that we make a boatload of money every year. People love our Christmas surprises."

Mac sat forward. "Maybe you should give your kids a clearer understanding of things, because right now, they might think you're driving them into the poorhouse."

"That's exactly what they think," Lilian said. "But they should trust us to do the right thing. Honestly, we make so much money at Christmas it's almost scandalous."

I smiled. "That's wonderful."

"I guess we really should share the news with the kids. I mean, we do go over everything with Stephanie because she's officially the CEO. But she's like a vault. You tell her something, and she doesn't whisper a word of it to anybody. Even her own husband." Bill shook his head. "Maybe they should all be told. It's not like they're kids anymore."

"They're my age," I said.

"I've always thought you were very mature for your age," Bill said. "You helped your father with his business for many years. You made some sacrifices at a young age and took on responsibilities. I just can't see my kids doing that sort of thing."

"They're not exactly givers," Lilian said. "It's our fault."

"Well, don't blame yourselves completely. After all, you've started to give them more responsibility, like the renovation that we'll all be doing on the north tower building. Most of them seem really excited about it, and I think they are going to come up with great ideas."

"That's so nice to hear," Lilian said.

"But as Mac mentioned," I said, "they really should start to be included in business matters. It helps to know what's really going on. That way they'll be happier when you give them even more responsibility."

"And that's how you can turn this problem around," Mac said. "Include them in financial meetings. It'll open their eyes to a whole new way of looking at things."

"That's right," I said. "Sharing information with them will give them a view of the real world they don't really have right now."

Bill looked from Mac to me. "How'd you get so smart?"

I laughed. "I don't think I had a choice. My mother was dying, and Chloe was having such a hard time in school. Dad buried himself in work, so I just had to take charge, I guess."

Lilian frowned. "I'm a little concerned about sharing information with some of the kids."

"Well, that's a problem," I admitted. "But your kids are pretty smart. They'll get it. And it's not a bad thing to give them enough space to screw up and learn their own lessons."

Bill gave Lilian's shoulder a little squeeze. "We talk about doing that all the time, and I guess it's time to start."

Lilian frowned. "This year we're giving a big lump sum to Santa Steve's charity, and we haven't even mentioned it to the kids."

"Why not?" I asked.

"Don't you think they would support you?" Mac wondered.

"Most of them would," Lilian said. "But there have always been one or two who balk at the thought of giving money away."

"It's just my opinion," Mac said, "but I think you should say something. Most of your kids, if not all, would be immensely proud to know how successful you are and what you're planning to donate this year."

I grinned. "And you might remind them that most donations are tax deductible."

Bill looked at Lilian. "What do you think?"

"I want to hear more of what you two think," Lilian said, pointing to Mac and me.

"Okay," I said. "Well, when it comes to finances, it just seems to work better when everyone is aware of where the money's going. Then they can take ownership of the activities and the food and the charitable event, or whatever else you've got going on."

"I suppose it's a good idea," Bill agreed. "For so many years, the kids were too young. And then when they got older, we wanted to do exactly that. But from the time the kids got married, we always had one or two troublemakers who we just couldn't trust with our bottom line."

"That's an entirely different problem," Mac said. "But there's a way to deal with that."

"How?"

"You talk to each person individually and make it clear that this is a confidential discussion and you'd prefer they not share it with anyone else."

"Oh." Lilian sighed, shaking her head. "You know they'll all talk amongst themselves."

"Some of them will," Mac admitted. "But some won't. They'll take your words to heart because that's the grown-up way to work in business."

"I like that," Lilian said.

"Also," I said, "you've got someone in your family who's had to deal with those kinds of problems, and he might be the one you can turn to for help."

Lilian frowned. "Who are you talking about?"

"Logan," Mac said. "He's running a corporation now, dealing with different individuals with their own ideas and problems. He was hired because he's proven to be someone who can deal with trouble-makers and oddballs and every personality known to man. He really knows what he's doing in that regard. You might think about taking him into your confidence and getting some ideas from him."

Lilian was crying now, but I could tell they were happy tears. "I'm so proud of Logan. It's so wonderful to hear you say it."

"And if you want to start talking about finances with your kids, you might talk to a financial adviser who can help with the conversations. Especially when you've got a troublemaker on board."

Bill paused for a moment, then said, "Strangely enough, one of the troublemakers is gone now."

"Oh." I blinked. "Oh, wow." I glanced up at Mac.

"That's . . . enlightening," Mac murmured.

"Yeah, isn't it?" His smile was tinged with sadness. "Guess I should've kept my mouth shut, but we were ready to pull our hair out over the whole situation."

"I get that," Mac said. "But look. We're not here to tell you how to run your business. We just hope you'll keep things running as well as you've always done."

"Especially the carousel," I said. "I love that thing."

"And the train," Mac added.

Bill grinned. "The train will always be here. And we've decided to keep the carousel, too. In fact, we really think the whole Fun

Zone is a perfect long-range attraction for the hotel. So that'll stay, too. But to return to your original question, we've decided to close it just through tonight so that everyone can take some time and attend the memorial service we've planned. Then we'll bring it all back online."

"That's great news," I said.

Bill chuckled. "We think so, too." He stood and stretched, then reached down and pulled Lilian up from the couch. "Let's try to round up the kids and enlighten them."

"I'm game if you are," she said.

"Be prepared for some negative comments at first," I said. "Maybe at your next meeting, you can invite your financial adviser."

"I'm ready for the negative comments," Bill said, and glanced at Lilian. "We should talk to Stephanie before we meet with everyone. Maybe she can talk Craig down off the wall."

Mac stood and shook Bill's hand. "Good luck, Bill."

We walked upstairs and wandered out to the veranda. I turned to Mac. "Obviously, Randi was a problem for them."

"That's what we thought all along," he said. "But then, she was a problem in so many ways."

"I wonder who the other problem child is," I said. "I thought maybe Arabella because she's so wrapped up with Whitney. But who knows?"

He frowned. "Bill just mentioned Craig."

"I heard that," I said. "I know he complains sometimes, but I didn't really see him as a troublemaker."

"I'm going to take a guess," Mac said, leaning on the railing. "I think Craig must've really lost it when he found out about Randi. Those two had been really close for a couple of years. They both worked in the bar, so there were plenty of long hours and lots of time to chat and complain and gossip."

"That's a good point," I said. We stood and stared out at the horizon for a long minute. "It's so pretty out here."

"I was just thinking the same thing, and then I had a radical thought."

I turned and gazed at him. "Good heavens. Radical?"

"I might be slightly exaggerating."

"No way."

He laughed. "What do you say we go to the bar and have a refreshing afternoon cocktail?"

"The bar?" I laughed. "Very radical!"

"Well?"

"I'd love to. Except I don't think you really want a cocktail. I think you want to pump Craig for information."

"I wouldn't exactly put it that way."

I chuckled. "No, I guess not. So what is your real reason for stepping into the bar? Are we going to explore the depths of Stephanie's marriage now?"

He looked at me. "That would be rude, wouldn't it?"

"Yes," I said. "Maybe we should call Chloe and ask her. She and Stephanie are very close friends."

"So close that she might not actually give us any information?"

"That would never happen," I said, smiling. "Not with Chloe."

"But we're here now."

"True enough."

Mac grabbed my hand and led the way into the bar. We waved at Craig, who was standing at the bar wiping glasses. We took a small table along the window facing the cove.

We sat in silence for a long moment. "Have we reentered the realm of Scooby-Doo?"

"Yes," Mac said. "Take two."

Making lists of suspects and villains and possible motives and all sorts of things like that was fun, sort of, as long as we weren't being arrested for meddling in police business.

"I don't have a notebook with me," I said. I had always been the one to write out a list. It helped me keep things straight in my mind.

Mac pulled out his phone. "I'll use the Notes app on my phone."

"Good thinking."

"So, we have a victim," Mac said. "Randi. Wife of Logan."

"Sister-in-law to Stephanie and Arabella. And then there's Craig and Franco. Brothers-in-law."

"And daughter-in-law to Bill and Lilian."

Mac typed quickly on his Notes app.

"All of those in-laws belong on our list of suspects."

"I would have to agree," he said. "Now, do you think one of them actually killed her?"

"That's usually the way it goes with murder. Someone close to the victim is the killer."

"Yeah. It almost always comes down to that."

"Which is a really sad thing to admit, but it's true."

"Okay. So let's talk about these suspects."

"Wait," I said. "I think we should add some of the people around the hotel who knew her well. For instance, she was friendly with Shirley Ann and Joyce."

"I know Shirley Ann," he said. "And I think I know who Joyce is. They're good friends, right?"

"Yes, very good friends."

"Good to know," Mac said. "So, does Whitney belong on this list?"

My mouth fell open. "How could I ever forget her? She should always be on our Scooby-Doo suspect list."

Mac grinned as he typed Whitney onto the list. "Would you say that Whitney was friends with Randi?"

I had to think about it because it was a tricky situation. "I know they're friends, but I don't see them together very often."

"How come?"

"It's just a theory, but the two of them are both such strong personalities that they would probably repel each other half the time."

"Interesting," Mac mused.

"Also, Whitney would hate to hang out with Randi too often because Randi is so gorgeous. I'm not sure Whitney could stand the competition."

"That's fascinating," Mac said. "And I happen to agree with you. I could see the two of them causing havoc wherever they went and ending up in a vicious fight to the death."

I stared at him. "Wow. I don't even want to consider that creepy scenario."

Mac laughed.

"Arabella was probably closer to Randi in terms of going shopping or having a glass of wine and gossiping. But I don't think anyone liked Randi very much, and that includes Arabella."

"But we know Arabella and Whitney are close. Some of these women," Mac said, "I picture them lighting candles and chanting to Grand Diva Wizardess Whitney. Even if they don't see her every day."

"That's sick, but close enough," I said. "And I'm not sure *wizardess* is acceptable as a replacement for the word *witch*, but whatever."

"I'll look it up, and we can discuss it at our next meeting," Mac said with a short laugh.

"I've already added it to the agenda," I said.

Mac was still chuckling when Craig walked over to our table. "Hi, you two." He wasn't smiling and his usually ebullient charm was gone. He looked sad.

"Hi, Craig," I said, reaching to touch his arm sympathetically. "How are you doing?"

"Not so great," he admitted.

"Do you really have to work today?" Mac asked. "This seems like a good day to take some time, walk along the beach, stare at the ocean. I'm really sorry for your loss."

"Thanks, man," he said. "But, yeah, I'd rather be here than wallowing in my room, you know?"

"I get that," Mac said.

Craig sighed deeply. "Well, what can I get you?"

"I would love that holiday drink you made before, with vodka and white cranberry juice."

"Randi named it the Winter White Cosmo," he said.

"Pretty name," I said.

"Yeah," he whispered. I could see his eyes filling with tears, so I reached up and squeezed his arm.

"Do you want me to call someone to take over the bar for you?" I said quietly.

"No," he said forcefully. And sniffed back the tears. "But thank you. Don't worry. I'll keep it together. We worked together for a long time, so forgive me if I have these little moments."

"Of course."

"I'd still rather be here."

"I hear you," I said.

"I'll have two fingers of scotch," Mac said.

"We have the eighteen-year-old Glenmorangie."

"Perfect. Thanks."

He walked back to the bar, and Mac and I stared at each other.

"He's suffering," Mac said.

"He really is," I agreed. "Much more than Logan or Lilian or any of them."

"They were really good friends, I guess."

"Yeah. After all this time working together, it's hitting him hard."

"I'm going to call Chloe when we get home. Maybe she talked to Stephanie today."

"It would certainly help with our Scooby-Doo assignment."

I rolled my eyes and sipped my drink.

We were both quiet for a minute, thinking things through. Finally I said, "I would say that Randi's best friend was actually Craig."

"I think you're right. They basically did everything together, in terms of working, anyway."

I took another sip of my very tasty cocktail, then leaned closer to Mac and whispered, "I'm worried about Stephanie. She's going to be working like a crazy woman, and I know she loves it, but it doesn't feel like she's got much support."

Mac sipped his scotch. "From her spouse, you mean. Yeah, I agree. I think her strongest support will come from her parents and her closest friends."

"Okay," I said, keeping my voice low. "I'll give Chloe a call. She's probably her closest buddy in town."

"Good."

I leaned closer. "Do you think the other Garrison spouses have good support?" I thought about it. "Franco is a dear. He loves Arabella, and by the way, I've never even seen him interact with Randi."

"But Arabella is besties with Whitney."

"Yeah, I really wonder how that works out."

I shook my head. "Don't ask me. I have enough trouble trying to figure out how Tommy puts up with Whitney."

"Yeah, similar personalities," Mac said. "Weird."

"Maybe people say these sorts of things about you and me."

"Probably," Mac said. "They say things like, 'What does Shannon see in that scruffy outsider Mac?'"

We grinned at each other as we sipped our drinks and stared out the window for a long quiet moment.

Mac frowned. "Still playing the Scooby-Doo game?"

"I don't know. This time it's not so much fun."

"Not so much," he agreed.

"I think I've got even more reasons to call Chloe. We have to talk."

"You'll tape the conversation, right?"

I laughed. "No, but I have a good memory. I'll tell you everything."

Chapter Twelve

Mac had to work, so I stopped by to see my sister. We sat together in her adorable kitchen at a wooden table for two that she'd found at an estate sale soon after she moved in with Eric. Chloe hated to hear me ask questions about Stephanie, but she was more than willing to talk about her friend's husband, Craig.

"You won't tell anyone, will you?"

"Of course not," I said. "I'm just concerned about Stephanie because it seems like Craig was very close to Randi, and when we saw him in the bar this afternoon, he was trying to hold back the tears."

"Oh, for goodness' sake," she said, disgusted. "He's such a jerk. Stephanie is the best person in the world. She's beautiful, smart, clever, kind, and so savvy about business. Much more than Craig will ever be. And yet, he was always fawning over Randi in the bar. Thank goodness Stephanie rarely walks in there, but Eric and I have been there in the past, and though Craig is perfectly nice, he's kind of a lummox. He never has anything really intelligent or funny to say. With customers, he'll talk about sports and maybe the very biggest headlines. But when we're out together, he mainly whines about everything."

"You guys all go out together?" I asked.

"Only once and never again," she admitted. "Eric has very little patience for some people."

"Especially if they whine."

"That's right," she said. "Most of his whining has to do with Steph's parents and the way they run the business. In my opinion, he's so incredibly lucky to be a part of that family, and all he does is moan and groan about it. He thinks he would run it so much better than they ever could."

I snorted a laugh. "Oh, because they're doing so badly?"

"I know, right? That place is absolutely gorgeous, and it's all because of Bill and Lilian."

"But he does run the bar," I said.

"It's a really good bar, but he's not the world's greatest bartender," Chloe said. "Even though he thinks he is. And believe me, Stephanie goes over every one of his checks and bar tabs the very next day."

"Ooh." I winced. "That's rather revealing."

"It sure is," Chloe said. "It's a good thing the place is computerized, because he is always making mistakes, adding incorrectly or writing down the wrong product."

"That can't be a good thing for the business."

"It's not, but Stephanie covers for him. And of course, he would never thank her, but she saves his butt on a daily basis."

"She's amazing," I said. "Wait. She seriously covers for him?"

"She does," Chloe agreed. "She's like a business guru. She could probably run the whole place, because she's made it her goal to know everything about every aspect of the business. The hotel, the restaurant, and the bar. The spa, every internal department, the tours, all the extras. She is a genius."

"Wow. Good thing Logan moved to Homefront."

"I know you're joking, but it's true. Stephanie was determined to do the best job ever, no matter where she ended up. She would've done it in any position her parents asked her to take on."

"She's pretty awesome," I said. "So, what's the attraction to Craig?"

"Well, you have to admit, he's very handsome," Chloe said.

I smiled. "Oh, he's a stud, definitely."

"And for a while, Stephanie was trying to get over some other guy, so Craig came along at just the right time. They hit it off and got married. Maybe a little too soon."

"Another guy?" I asked. "Was it Oliver?"

"Oh my God, I never said that!" Chloe looked ready to panic. "You did not hear me say that."

"It's okay," I said. "Don't worry. Oliver's great."

"But you can't tell anyone!"

"Why not?"

"Because Craig is a little too jealous of Oliver. And, well, same goes for anyone else she's ever dated. He's that guy."

"Really? Because he doesn't seem like the jealous type."

"He hides it well in public, but he especially hates Oliver."

"Because she was involved with him right before he came along?"

"Exactly. So swear to me that you won't tell a soul."

"I swear." But I chuckled as I said it.

"It's not funny."

"That laugh was just between you and me. I'll never say a word to anyone at the Cliffs."

She exhaled, sounding exhausted. "Okay."

"Stop worrying," I said.

"It's just that Stephanie gets a little paranoid about the subject."

"But what about Craig's friendship with Randi?"

"We don't talk about that."

"Oh dear." That didn't sound very equitable. "Why not?"

"She's brought it up to Craig before, just teasing, you know? And he gets angry. I mean, really angry, like she's accused him of treason or something."

"Sounds like he's protesting too much."

"Exactly."

As I drove home, I had to wonder if I was getting the whole picture. Was Craig really the jealous type? Was Stephanie jealous of Randi? When I thought about it, Stephanie would make the perfect suspect for Randi's murder. She had told Chloe that Craig was the jealous one, and I believed it. But was that the whole picture? Her husband was very close to Randi, and let's face it, the woman was gorgeous. Not only that, but she was kind of a predator. She would go after a guy if she was attracted to him and not care who she might be hurting. No wife I know would enjoy having Randi as her husband's constant companion at work.

Stephanie had just climbed up to the number one suspect spot.

My phone rang the next morning while Mac and I were having breakfast. I was surprised to see Eric's name listed. "Hi, Eric."

"Hi. Wanted to let you know that your head carpenter has an alibi for the other night. He hadn't been high on my list, but he's no longer a suspect."

"Oh, that's great! Thank you." I didn't want to ask what Sean's alibi was. I'd get that information from Sean himself. "Thank you so much for calling. I really appreciate it."

"You're welcome." We ended the call and I fell back in my chair. "Whew."

"What happened?" Mac asked.

I gave him the news and he gave me a high five. "That's great news. Give my regards to Sean."

"I will." I had to take a deep breath. "I'm so relieved."

"I know, babe." He went back to staring at his computer.

"Are you working?"

"Yeah. I've really got to hunker down and finish this book." Mac took a sip of coffee. "I want to turn it in before Christmas."

"I'm sorry I've been such a distraction lately," I said.

He laughed. "No, you're not—sorry, I mean. But as far as distractions go, yes, you are. The very best kind." He leaned over and kissed me. "I've been enjoying myself way too much lately, so now I've got to get back into business mode."

"Me too," I admitted. "I'll be leaving you alone for part of the day. I'm going to call Sean and congratulate him. Then I want to see if he'll rummage through the north cellar with me. He's always so good at picking through old stuff and finding gems."

"Sounds like fun."

I laughed. "Only to a select few, including me and Sean."

———

I picked up Sean, and we headed for the Cliffs. He was excited to check out the north cellar, especially the gargoyles. The very idea of all those creepy figures gave me chills, but I was hoping to get another look at the burl wood desk in the cellar. If Lilian agreed to sell it to me, Sean would help me get it into my truck.

I parked the truck near the Garrisons' kitchen door. "I'm going to ask Lilian to come with us to rummage through the cellar."

"That would be great," Sean said. "She must know everything that's down there and most of its history, too."

"Yeah. I hope she's not too busy."

We climbed out of the truck, walked up the steps to the kitchen, and knocked.

"Good morning, you two," Lilian said. "What are you up to today?"

"We are here to try and lure you to take a quick trip with us through the north cellar."

She stared at both of us and her smile burst through. "Oh my God, you've saved my life."

"Really?" I looked at Sean. "I wonder what she was actually planning to do today."

"Something involving fire walkers?" Sean said.

"Or maybe carving something out of peanut butter?"

Lilian burst out laughing and I joined her. "It wasn't going to be nearly as fun as that sounds," she said. "Thank you so much for coming by. I'll just go get my vest and be down in a minute."

We waited in the kitchen. Lilian was halfway up the stairs when she shouted, "There are still some donuts left on the table. Help yourself. And there's coffee. I think it's fresh."

Sean was grinning. "I really like this place."

I laughed. "Yeah. Me too."

We walked down the lane to the north cellar, and on the way, I slowly broached the subject of buying the burl wood desk with Lilian.

"Do you ever sell any of the items in the cellar?"

"Only very occasionally. My vague plan from years ago was to have an annual sale and get rid of a lot of things, but as you can see, that plan hasn't worked out so far. But that's my excuse for keeping so much stuff in here. Someday we will sell it all. Because really, what will we ever do with all those sheets? They're used and they're not in bad shape. But still, I can't use them in the hotel rooms."

"No," I murmured. "When I first saw them, I thought of using them for drop cloths. But nobody would need that many."

"Shannon, that's a great idea. Feel free to take whatever you want from here."

"I, um, did see something that I really love. I would be happy to buy it from you."

"Really? I'm dying to know what it is."

"I'll show you when we get inside."

Lilian pulled the key from her pocket. She slipped it into the lock and it turned effortlessly.

I looked at Sean. "The first time I came to this door, it kind of blew me away. Can you see why?"

"Yeah." He ran his hand along the edge of the wood door and fiddled with the lock and key. "The door itself is ancient. Well, at least two or three hundred years old, anyway. But those hinges are shiny and new. And obviously, the lock mechanism is either new or completely refurbished."

"Right," I said. "It was a little mystery that was quickly solved, thank goodness."

"When we first decided to refurbish this building," Lilian began, "we took care of all those little details that can slow things down. I knew we wouldn't start work until after the New Year, but I was anxious to go through the rooms as soon as possible to see what our biggest obstacles would be."

"That's really smart," Sean said.

Lilian smiled. "Thank you. It was my idea."

"Brilliant," I said.

"Once we get inside, I'm going to want to hear all about the gargoyles," Sean admitted.

Lilian's laugh was a happy trill. "Oh, I love my gargoyles."

I shuddered. *That makes two of you,* I thought. *Just leave me out of it.*

The door opened easily and Sean commented, "You really cleaned that lock mechanism well."

"We were so pleased when it opened so smoothly the first time," Lilian said, and pushed the door open. "It barely made a sound, it was so clean."

"That's nice," Sean whispered.

"The light is somewhere along this wall," Lilian said.

"I think it's right about here," I said, remembering from the last time I was here. I found the switch and turned it on.

I stepped aside to let Lilian pass me, then I followed. Sean came last.

"Wow," he said. "That vaulted ceiling is fabulous. And it's a lot higher than you'd expect. What is it? About nine feet?"

"Something like that," she said. "Bill's ancestors were very tall."

"Cool." He continued to look around in every direction. "You know, this would make a really awesome pub."

"You nailed it!" Lilian exclaimed. "That's exactly what we're planning to do with this space."

"Oh, that's cool," he said. "It's going to be fantastic."

"You're right," I said. "It's the perfect size and location." And suddenly I smelled the Christmas scent again. The cloves were stronger this time, and I wondered again where it had come from.

"Can you two smell that Christmasy scent?" I asked. "I smell cloves and a little waft of orange peel."

"Come on," Sean said. "You're hallucinating."

"I'm not."

"Shannon," Lilian said, changing the subject, "show me the piece you were talking about."

"Okay." I aimed the light from my phone at the far wall. "It's right over there. It's a beautiful burl cylinder desk that I know Mac would love. I'd love to buy it for him."

She started to chuckle. "I'm sorry to laugh, but I was just talking to Bill about that very piece last week. I bought it twenty years ago, and he never liked it. Said it was weird."

"You're kidding," I said. "It's beautiful and unique."

"I think so, too," she said. "But trust me, we'll never use it, so I would be thrilled to give it to you."

I felt lightheaded. "It must've cost you plenty, so I'm happy to pay whatever you'd like for it."

She smiled. "You're so sweet. Tell me, what do you think it's worth?"

Now I was starting to worry. I had no idea how much it was

worth! "Um, okay. A thousand dollars?" I knew it was worth more than that, but it was a good place to start.

"Oh, don't be silly." She waved her hands. "It can't be worth more than four hundred dollars."

"No way," I said.

"Yes. Four hundred, and I won't take a penny more."

"But, Lilian, it's worth—"

"No, Shannon. First of all, Bill doesn't care for it, so we'll never use it inside the hotel. I have a fondness for it, but only because my father was a burl man."

"A burl man," Sean said with a grin. "I like it."

She smiled. "Me too."

I laughed. "I'm hoping Mac will turn out to be a burl man, too, so I would love to have it for four hundred dollars."

"Oh, yay!" Lilian gave a little cheer. "That's wonderful. I feel good about giving it to someone who will love it as much as I do."

"I promise I will." I hugged her. "Thank you. You're just the best in the world."

"And so are you, sweetie."

"Okay, where are those gargoyles?" Sean said, changing the mood. "Let's get hunting."

We all laughed.

"When we leave, I'll bring my truck around, and Sean will help me carry it out of here."

"Perfect," she said.

"Thank you again."

Lilian gave me another hug. "I'm happy it's found a new home."

Sean put his hand on her arm. "You're a really good person, Lilian."

"Thank you, Sean."

It was true, and this was a special moment, so I waited a beat before I spoke. "Let's check out the next room. That's where the gargoyles live."

"Can't wait to see those little critters," Sean said, and stepped into the next room.

I stayed back in the main room to avoid the curse of the gargoyles.

"Ew," he said. "Can you smell that?"

"Is it that Christmas smell?" I asked, still standing in the front room. "It's like someone used a bunch of pine and cloves and herbs to freshen the rooms."

"Well, it's not working, but whatever," Sean said. Then he let out a little scream and shouted, "Gargoyles!"

Lilian and I both laughed.

"Jeez, Sean," I said. "You're such a goon."

"I know." He grinned. "This is amazing. There must be a hundred of them. They're everywhere."

"Don't you love it?" Lilian said, "I've been collecting them for years from all over the place."

I busily studied a pretty set of green etched parfait glasses and resisted whistling as if I were walking through a graveyard. Anything was better than staring down a few dozen freakish gargoyles.

"Man!" Sean said, holding up two of the odd creatures. "What are you going to do with all of these amazing little monsters?"

"I thought we could mount them on the corners of the roofs and maybe over some of the doorways. They were popular during Victorian times, so they would fit right in, but I'll have to discuss it with Bill and the kids. Not everyone is a fan."

"Don't listen to them," Sean said. "These are fantastic."

"I'll bring you to the meeting," Lilian said, "in order to convince the skeptics."

Sean grinned. "I'll be glad to share my valued opinion." He stepped farther into the room to look at more gargoyles. "Hey, I think I just smelled what you're talking about, Shannon."

"Really?"

"It was just a waft of something. It's gone now."

"I'm glad you can smell it, because the first time I came in here, I could smell it in little pockets here and there."

Lilian looked around. "I can definitely smell it. Maybe because I grew up with that scent in my house, and it was not pleasant."

"What's the scent?" Sean asked.

"It's bay rum. My uncle used to wear it, and he was mean."

"Oh no," I said. "That's not a fun memory."

"So, who around here uses bay rum aftershave?" Sean asked.

"I don't know anyone who wears it," Lilian said. "If I did, I'd probably force him to take a shower and never wear it again."

"So, what's it doing smelling up this cellar?"

Lilian laughed. "Hell if I know."

Sean wandered from the old couch to the dining table to the steamer trunk, looking at all the treasures. When he found more gargoyles, he started giggling.

"Sean," I said with a laugh, "you sound ridiculous."

"But this is so cool. Look at these. Where did you get them all?"

"Oh, they're not recent purchases. I think some of Bill's relatives brought them back from different parts of Europe. They could've been removed from an old church or something."

"They're amazing."

"I appreciate that you appreciate them," Lilian said. "Shannon, do you not like them?"

"They kind of creep me out, but I realize there can be historical significance to some of them, so I'll keep an open mind."

"Don't keep your mind open too long," Sean said. "Gargoyles will feast on your brain."

"Oh, that's disgusting!" But I laughed. I couldn't help it. "You're crazy."

"Come on, that was funny."

"Yes, it was funny." Then I clapped my hands like a disciplinarian. "Now back to work."

He just grinned and kept looking around.

"You could have an exhibit with all this etched glass," I said. "There's probably a glass catalog with information about these pieces. They're so pretty."

"Hmm," Lilian said. "That's not a bad idea. A display or an exhibit of glassware would be interesting. I know they're worth a lot." She shrugged. "Another reason why they're still here."

"There a door here?" Sean asked, running his hand along the frame. "Is this a closet or something?"

"I think so," Lilian said. "I've never been inside. It's a little creepy, I'll admit."

"There's something stuck in the door," he said.

I took a look at what he was talking about. There were a couple of layers of lace, and they were indeed stuck in the door. I stared for a long moment, then shouted, "Get that door open."

"I'm smelling that foul odor again," Sean said. "It's pretty bad."

"I don't care. Someone's stuck inside that room."

"Oh no!" Sean shouted. He ran his hand along the edge of the door and tried to pry it open. Finally it sprang open and we all jumped back.

I held my shirt over my nose to keep from smelling the unpleasant odor.

"Oh, what is it?" Lilian demanded, but she couldn't stay to find out. She looked like she was about to faint and ran outside.

"I have to make sure she's okay." Sean didn't hesitate and followed Lilian outside.

I watched them both go, then turned to peer inside and caught the top half of a cocktail waitress uniform. It looked like a low-cut tuxedo shirt with a black bow tie around the neck. The shirt was tucked into black satin shorts.

"No!" I squeezed my eyes shut, but I could still see it. "Call the police!"

I opened my eyes and managed to stumble toward the cellar door. In seconds I was outside. Sean and Lilian stood right there, staring at each other as I slammed the door shut and fell back against the stone wall.

How could this be happening again? "It's . . . it's Shirley Ann Johnson. She's dead."

———

Lilian was sitting on the low wall across the lane, sipping on a cup of water. One of the EMTs had checked her out first thing, thank goodness, because she had fainted dead away from the news that Shirley Ann was gone.

"Sean," I whispered, "how did she get in there?"

"I don't know. But I'm glad you had the wherewithal to tell me to call the police."

Sadly, that was something I was really good at. Sean had made the phone call, and the police were here within five minutes. The EMTs were barely a minute behind them.

Eric approached me. "Are you okay?"

"I'm fine. Just really bummed. She was such a super lady."

"I know," he said. "I wanted to let you know that the weapon that killed Randi Garrison was found with Shirley Ann's body."

"Oh no. Can you tell me what it was?"

"Yes, although I'd like you to keep it quiet until their killer is found."

"I can do it." I took a deep breath and let it out. "What was the murder weapon?"

"It was your pink drywall knife," he said solemnly.

"Oh God. The same knife killed them both?"

"No, it killed Randi."

"What about Shirley Ann?"

He took a deep breath and exhaled, then said, "She was strangled."

"Someone strangled her? Oh my God."

"I'm sorry."

"Yeah. Me too."

He gave me a hug, and I said, "Thanks for letting me know."

"Like you said, Shirley Ann was a super lady."

Not just super, I thought, but sweet and cheerful and always up for a good time. And it just wasn't fair, damn it. It just wasn't fair.

The area around the entrance to the north cellar was a traffic jam of police and ambulances and people running around every which way. The lane had been cordoned off with yellow police tape, but it didn't keep the hotel guests and various townspeople from getting as close as they could to the scene, such as it was.

What would people say? I sighed, picturing the headline: **Another Dead Body Found at the Cliffs Hotel**.

But it was a lot worse than that. It was the body of Shirley Ann Johnson, a lovely person, a funny, clever woman who didn't deserve to die. And her body hadn't deserved to be shoved inside that cramped room in the north cellar. It was just wrong and disgusting and mean, and I really hated that it had happened again.

I couldn't explain it. Who would kill Shirley Ann? She was beloved by so many people, especially her best friend, Joyce. *She never met a stranger,* people said. God, even Randi liked her, I thought. I was being uncharitable to think of that, but it was true. Everyone loved Shirley Ann.

So who would kill her? And who killed Randi?

For two days, the town was buzzing with the news of another murder. Even the newspaper put out a special edition to let people know that Shirley Ann Johnson had died. They had nothing but good things to say about her and had gone through the trouble to hunt down dozens of townspeople to get their opinions.

Sadly, unlike with Randi, there were tremendous outpourings of love and sympathy and many memorial services being arranged in Shirley Ann's honor. Even Lilian and Bill seemed more upset by Shirley Ann's death than their own daughter-in-law's, although they tried not to show it. Shirley Ann had been a loyal employee of the Cliffs Hotel and restaurant for well over twenty years, and most of the town had a warm, happy relationship with her.

For Shirley Ann, they closed the Fun Zone and stopped the carousel. They spent two days arranging memorial services for her, and in the end, Joyce begged them to turn the carousel on again because Shirley Ann had loved riding it.

Chief Eric had no more clue as to who had killed Shirley Ann than he had with Randi. The difference between the two women was that everyone loved Shirley Ann, but very few people had loved Randi. We had all managed to get through the very private ceremony for Randi, and then the following week, they had a lovely service in the hotel followed by a wonderful meal made by Franco to commemorate Shirley Ann. Everyone who could possibly be there attended. It was truly memorable.

It was also a big horrible mystery. Mac and I couldn't begin to play it out the way we always did. It would take days before we could even face the list of suspects. Who in the world would be cruel enough to murder that poor, vital, beloved woman? And we had to ask ourselves: Since Shirley Ann had been killed only days after Randi's death, were the two murders connected?

Chapter Thirteen

To work through my sadness for Shirley Ann, I spent several days at Homefront working in the garden and teaching a new carpentry skills class.

Our "First Christmas at Homefront" event was already up and running, and it seemed like the entire town was excited to come by and see the sweetly decorated tiny homes. We kept it going for two hours each night, and there was never a lull. The happy visitors would walk up and down the streets to see the homes, then stop in at the community center to enjoy hot chocolate or hot cider and cookies and maybe donate a few dollars for what I had decided to call the Christmas fund.

Logan agreed that the vets would vote for the most worthy recipient of any charity money that was collected. I suggested that the money be kept for the residents of Homefront because, why not? Logan still insisted on taking a vote, but I knew that he agreed with me.

It felt like everyone in town was coming to see the tiny homes all decorated and spruced up for Christmas. Logan and I were hard at work, continuing to get the word out to the community that it was lovely fun to stroll up and down the lanes and see the adorable tiny homes decorated for Christmas. I was pleased that Logan was beginning to think that it might be a nice way to make a little extra money for charity and for Homefront every Christmas from now on. The local newspaper had pulled out all the stops and placed a full-page feel-good story on the front page. It was a pretty great way to advertise.

Despite the horrible discoveries of Shirley Ann and Randi, it was actually uplifting to realize that our simple idea had contributed in some small way to bringing the Christmas spirit back into people's hearts.

Now that the police were being kept busy with the murders at the Cliffs Hotel, the local porch pirates seemed to have upped their game. Of course, it was getting closer to Christmas, so some people were feeling a bit desperate.

There were cases of robbery being reported every night. Eric had already caught one group but was forced to call in reinforcements from the neighboring towns when the thefts didn't stop. He warned the local delivery services to take extra care when delivering packages. Some of the wealthier neighborhoods were considering hiring their own private security services.

Eric couldn't say he approved one way or the other. He would've loved to hire a whole platoon of temporary Christmas workers to add to the security of the neighborhoods. But that was out of his control.

One porch pirate group indiscriminately took whatever they found and pawned it at a well-known shop in the next town over.

And then there was a group that seemed as if they were carefully curating their ill-gotten goods. They would return to the scene of the crime and leave the packages that didn't suit them. It was the oddest Christmas that Eric had ever experienced.

Back at the Cliffs Hotel, Mac and I and our small family, including my dad and his girlfriend, Belinda; Chloe and Eric; and Mac's delightful niece Callie, who was in college now and growing up way too fast, enjoyed a wonderful holiday dinner with no interruptions and perfect lighting this time. If only they could've pulled it off that way the other time. I tried not to think about it, but it was never far from my mind.

At one point during our dinner, after the salad had been served, I noticed Joyce in the bar with a few work friends, and I popped over to say hello. Joyce stood and gave me a warm hug and wished me a merry Christmas.

"Same to you, Joyce," I said. "How are you doing?"

"I'm just okay, but I've got to tell you, Shannon. I miss my bestie."

I gave her another hug. "Of course you do. I think we all miss her."

"I even took a part-time job downtown to make some extra money and keep my mind off thinking about Shirley Ann every minute."

I squeezed her hand in sympathy. "That's a lot of hours you must be working," I said. "What are you doing?"

"Same thing. Barmaid. It's easy for me, and this is the best time of year to take advantage of the extra jobs out there. I'm determined to get to Miami and make Shirley Ann's dream a reality. And meet a millionaire of my own, too, of course."

I smiled and gave her one more hug. "Good for you."

Her eyes welled up as she talked about Shirley Ann. "My friend died too soon. She had so much more life to live."

"Yes, she did," I agreed. "And I wish we could find out who hurt her."

Craig approached our little group with a small tray of cocktails ordered from the bar. "Merry Christmas," he said, and set the tray down on their table. They all said hello, and he flashed a smile that didn't quite meet his eyes. He had to still be mourning his pal Randi, I thought. And he'd worked with Shirley Ann, too. He'd taken the brunt of those two murders.

"How are you doing, Craig?" I asked.

"I have my good days and my bad days," he said philosophically. "Thank God for Stephanie," he added. "She's my rock."

"She's the best," I said, and patted his sleeve. "If there's anything we can do, please let us know."

"Thanks." He nodded to the rest of our party and walked back to the bar.

"Well, I'd better get back to my own family dinner," I said to Joyce. "So I'll say good night and Merry Christmas."

"Merry Christmas, Shannon."

As I was walking away, Joyce scooted from the table and ran into the hallway where the restrooms were located.

I decided I'd better make a stop at the ladies' room myself before returning to the table. I caught Mac's glance and waved. He waved back, so I knew he'd seen me.

In the ladies' room, Joyce was sitting in front of a mirror crying. It broke my heart.

I sat down next to her and gave her a hug. "I know you miss Shirley Ann so much."

"I do," she said. "We were such good friends, and I know I'll never have a better friend than her. It's not as if I don't have other friends, but Shirley Ann was the best. And I'll never find anyone who'll move to Miami with me."

"I'm so sorry."

"But that's not why I'm crying," she said.

I frowned at her. "Why are you crying? What's going on?"

She pulled out a small shopping bag and showed it to me.

"Right after I finished my shift this afternoon, Lilian asked me if I wouldn't mind cleaning out Shirley Ann's locker.

"How did you feel about that?" I asked.

"Oh, I didn't mind at all. I was honored to do this one last thing for my girlfriend and for the Cliffs. Lilian has always been nothing but kind to me, so truly, I was happy to do it. But I just checked the things in the bag, and in the pocket of one of the little aprons she wore, you know, the one that goes with her waitress outfit?"

"I remember."

"Well, I found this threatening note in Shirley Ann's tip pocket, and it was clipped to a roll of hundred-dollar bills."

"What?" I tried not to shout. But good grief, it sounded like something out of a gangster film. I took a breath. "Do you want me to get Mac?"

"That would be great." Her gaze darted around. "I'd better stay in here, because I don't want anyone to see me."

A minute later, Mac followed me into the ladies' room.

"Wait," he said. "I can't go in there. You're kidding, right?"

"Just come in and lock the door," I said.

He locked it, then followed me over to talk to Joyce.

"Hey, Joyce," he said kindly. "What's going on?"

She handed me the piece of notepaper, and I read it, then passed it to Mac.

I know what you did, and I'm ready to make a deal.

"Whoa," Mac said. "Do you know how much money is here?"

"It's two thousand dollars," Joyce said. "And that's Shirley Ann's handwriting."

"And somebody gave her all this money?" Mac asked.

"Shirley Ann wrote the note, but I don't know who she gave it to. She never told me about any of this. If I knew, I'd probably know who killed her."

"And you might've gotten killed yourself," Mac said firmly.

Joyce started wringing her hands.

I reached for one of them to help calm her down. "You don't want to get involved with whoever that person is."

"That's right, Joyce," Mac agreed. "Whoever killed Shirley Ann isn't fooling around."

Joyce took a heavy breath. "I think Shirley Ann knew who killed Randi. I think she wrote this note to try and get the person to give her more money."

Mac and I exchanged glances, and he said, "You may be right."

I wondered who Shirley Ann might've been blackmailing. And I would bet that she probably hadn't considered it blackmailing. She probably just thought she could make some extra money for her move to Miami.

"She's been so nervous lately," Joyce confessed. "She wasn't herself. But I also know that she didn't have a bad bone in her body. She must've done this as much for me as for herself. I feel like I owe it to her to find out who did this."

Mac sat forward. "I'll bet the person who received this note from Shirley Ann was feeling pretty desperate herself. Or himself. They were probably going crazy, worrying that Shirley Ann would point them out to the police one of these days."

"That's what I'm afraid of. That's why they killed her."

I had no doubt that Joyce was right.

"Why did she do this?" Joyce wondered, and I saw her eyes tear up. "We told each other everything. Why didn't she tell me what was going on?"

Mac planted both elbows on his knees and leaned forward. "She probably didn't want you to get hurt, in case this guy came after her."

"I think you're right, Mac," she said. "Honestly, she was the best friend ever."

The next morning I stopped by Chloe's house for coffee and a strategy discussion regarding the holidays. Where would we spend Christmas morning? Who was cooking Christmas dinner?

"What's Eric working on this morning?" I asked as I took my first gulp of Chloe's deliciously rich coffee from her new coffeemaker with its built-in grinder and espresso attachment.

She made a face. "He's been crabby since last night."

"Why?"

"He got called to a house where some packages had been delivered, and shortly after that, they were stolen."

"Oh no," I said. "Porch pirates."

"You know," she said, "I lived in Los Angeles for over ten years, and I never even heard of that term until that thing with Randi and the wine. But now I guess it's the latest thing."

"I guess so." I sipped my coffee. "So, what's happening with Eric's case?"

"There were three robbers, and they took some stuff off one porch. But the homeowner saw them and went running after them."

"Did he catch them?" I wondered.

"That's why Eric was especially annoyed. Because he thinks the thieves were just kids. The homeowner husband went running after them, but his wife pulled him back. She thought they were too cute to get arrested."

"Oh no. Eric must've had a fit."

She rolled her eyes. "You got that right."

"Did the guy yell at his wife? I mean, these kids just tried to steal their stuff."

"The thing is, the kids got about a block away and dropped the stuff and kept running."

"The homeowners got their stuff back. So why is Eric angry?"

"Because he wanted those owners to hold on to the kids until he got there. He was concerned that they might be involved in a bunch of other thefts around town."

"I hope he catches them."

"He will," Chloe said. "He's already caught six thieves in two other porch pirate rings, and now they're all in jail."

"Well, that's great news." I took another sip of coffee. "So, what about those kids who dropped their stuff and kept running? Did the victims describe them?"

"Yeah," Chloe said. "Three kids wearing monkey costumes."

I almost swallowed my tongue, then choked and coughed for a full minute.

"Are you okay?" Chloe pounded on my back. "Do you need some water?"

I coughed once more, then took a few deep breaths. "No water. I'm okay. So, say that again."

"About the three little kids in monkey costumes?" She grinned. "It does sound kind of cute."

"Yeah, they're cute all right." I buried my face in my hands.

"What's wrong with you?" she demanded.

I looked up and sighed. "We know these little boys. They live at Homefront with their mom, who's undergoing chemotherapy. Logan is very good friends with her, and he's sort of helping with the kids. In fact, the whole community is probably watching out for them."

"Hmm. Maybe you should make a phone call."

"I guess I'd better. Right now, I kind of wish we were drinking wine instead of coffee."

"You need a little liquid courage? It's kind of early." She grinned. "Maybe you want me to call Eric?"

"Very funny." But I was hesitant to make the call. "I think I'll call Mac first."

"There you go, champ," Chloe said, laughing. "Make *him* call Eric." Then she whispered, "Chicken."

"I am okay with being called a chicken! But I'm calling Mac because we both saw the boys in the monkey costumes. So, yeah, I want him to come with me when we meet Eric at Homefront." I started to press Mac's number.

"This is getting good," she said. "He loves Homefront, so it might help him chill out a bit."

"We all love that place."

When Mac answered the phone, I explained what was happening. A minute later, I finished the call and smiled at Chloe.

"First, Mac's going to call Eric and tell him to meet us at Homefront. Then he's coming by here to pick me up. Then we'll go to Homefront, where we'll introduce Eric to the possible culprits."

Chloe fluffed her hair. "When Mac comes by to pick you up I think I'll go with you."

"Why?"

"Because I want to see those cute little boys."

"How do you know they're cute? Maybe they're three little hooligans."

"Hooligans can be cute," she said. "But you were the one who told me they were cute."

"They are. But Eric might swoop down and arrest them instead."

She gasped. "First of all, Eric doesn't swoop. And second, there's no way he would arrest three adorable little boys!"

"But they stole from those people."

"But they realized it was wrong, so they dropped the stuff and kept running."

"They were being chased, so they probably dropped the goods so they couldn't be blamed."

"Which makes them smart little hooligans."

I chuckled. "They are pretty smart. I wonder if they meant to drop the stuff."

She narrowed her eyes. "Well, maybe they did."

"Yeah. Maybe they changed their minds." I patted my chest. "I have a feeling they had a change of heart."

"Oh, that's so sweet." Chloe was clearly turning this into a heartwarming melodrama of her own. And I was right there with her. I hoped we weren't making a mistake.

I sighed. "Guess we'll find out."

She put our coffee mugs in the sink. "Do you think they'll wear their monkey suits for me?"

I rolled my eyes. "For you, absolutely."

———————

At Homefront, we explained the situation to Logan, and after a few minutes of consideration, he decided that the best place to arrange this meeting was outside at the picnic tables. The boys could play on the swings until Eric got here, and maybe that would lower the freakout level. I wasn't sure who'd be doing the freaking out. The boys? Their mother? Eric? Me?

Only time would tell.

Logan jogged toward one of the biggest of the tiny houses on the last block. These were the latest homes to be built, and they were larger family houses, although they were still quite small. They had a loft that would sleep two children, plus two hide-a-beds that tucked back into the walls during the day. There was an extra closet, a study area, and a slightly larger bathroom and kitchen than the regular tiny homes.

It would suit this family for the short term. Logan had said that Aurora was grateful to be living there because, since she was the wife of a deceased veteran, not only was there no rent to pay, but she and the boys could dine in the cafeteria for free every day if they wanted to.

Chloe and I took turns pushing the boys on the swings. Mac was talking to Parks, another friend we'd met when we first started building the houses last year. Parks had been badly injured back then, and we were all glad that he had made it through that vicious attack. He was friendly to everyone, including Aurora, who walked slowly over to the swings, holding Logan's arm. She gave Parks a soft hug, and all three of her boys jumped off the swings and hovered around her.

Logan introduced us to Aurora and I shook hands with her. She was a beautiful woman, despite looking very thin and pale.

"You're Lizzie's friend," she said after shaking my hand.

"She used to be our babysitter," I said, making her smile.

Chloe joined us as we sat on the nearest bench, and I introduced them to each other.

"You're sisters," Aurora said. "Isn't it wonderful to see how we all connect together?"

"Yes," I said. "Lizzie told me that you knew Logan many years ago."

She gazed across the yard and focused in on Logan, who was talking to Mac while we all waited for Eric.

"He's such a great guy," I continued.

"He's been a wonderful friend to me and my boys," she said quietly.

"Your boys are delightful," I said.

She laughed lightly. "They're my three angels, although some days I don't think heaven would agree."

"Did you happen to make those flying monkey costumes?" I asked.

"Yes. They saw *The Wizard of Oz* a few months ago and they were frantic to be flying monkeys for Halloween. I looked into buying the costumes, but they're outrageously expensive, so I made them. I used to sew most of my clothes, so it wasn't much of a hardship."

"You did a beautiful job."

"Thank you." She glanced at her boys and smiled ruefully. "Knowing my little guys, they're going to want to be something even more outrageous next year."

Logan came over and sat next to Aurora, and I stood and joined Mac. A minute later Eric strode up the hill and walked into the park.

Chloe gave him a hug and introduced him to Aurora. They talked for a minute, and then Aurora called the boys over to sit down.

Eric explained to everyone what happened last night with the homeowners, and Aurora looked at her boys with as stern a look as she was capable of giving.

"But, Mommy," Rowan said. "We didn't steal nothing."

"But it sounds like you wanted to."

"No, Mommy," Hudson said. "The box was too small, so we left it there and ran away."

"The box was too small?" Eric asked.

I was pretty sure everyone was just as stymied as Eric.

"It was too small to fit a bathrobe," Hudson explained.

Rowan slapped his hand against his own forehead in disgust.

"Hudson," Finn cried. "You gave away the secret!"

"Oh." The little one frowned, then he brightened. "But she doesn't know it's a blue bathrobe."

Chloe and I both laughed, and Aurora shook her head, trying not to smile.

"Boys," she said sternly, "you know it's not right to steal, even if you end up putting it back. If Chief Jensen wants to arrest you, what do you think I should do about that?"

"You should bail us out," Rowan said.

Now Eric was fighting to hide his smile.

"I'm sorry, but they're just too cute," Chloe whispered, then added, "How can we make this all better for everyone?"

Eric took a deep breath and exhaled slowly. "I have one very important question for you boys."

"Yes, sir," Finn murmured, sounding funereal.

"I'd like to know how many times you took things from other people."

All three boys looked shocked and frightened. They turned and looked at each other and shook their heads.

"But we never did," Hudson said.

"It was only that one time," Finn insisted. "And it didn't work."

"Honest, Chief Jensen," Rowan added. "We did it that one time, and we had to give stuff back, so we didn't try it again." He scowled. "Next year we'll need another plan."

The other two boys nodded in agreement.

Eric continued. "Okay, boys. I know that the owners were willing to let you off with a warning. But I'm in charge, and I think you need an extra penalty besides the warning."

"What's a penalty?" Hudson asked.

"It's like a spanking," Finn explained.

"We don't spank in our house," Aurora said softly. "But if Chief Jensen thinks that level of punishment is warranted, we should discuss it."

"What sort of punishment do you give the boys instead of spanking?" Eric asked.

"We have to write letters," Finn said contemptuously, rolling his eyes. "It's worse than a spanking."

"It sucks," said Rowan, scowling.

"Rowan," Aurora said.

"Sorry, Mommy," Rowan whispered.

"I don't like spankings," Hudson said.

"Nobody's going to spank you," Aurora murmured, and tucked her youngest boy under her arm.

I kept going from laughter to tears with these little boys and their mother. I just wanted to hug them all, including Aurora.

Eric gazed at the three boys, then turned to Rowan. "What do you think your punishment should be?"

"I think you should make us drive around in your car for a week. Or maybe a month. We could work the siren!"

"Can we see your gun?" Hudson asked.

"Hudson, no," his mother said.

"Didn't think so," Hudson grumbled.

"You boys are not grasping the seriousness of this situation," Aurora said, her voice getting stronger. "You were going to steal something, and you know that's not a thing that nice people do. So what shall we do instead?"

"We could bring those people a present," Finn said.

Aurora looked at Eric. "What do you think of that idea, Chief Jensen?"

Eric appeared to be considering this idea very carefully. "That might work, Finn. What do you have in mind for a present?"

Finn stared into space, then held up his finger in answer. "We could bring them dinner."

Aurora blinked. "Oh." She gazed at Logan, then turned to Eric. "What do you think, Chief Jensen? Do you think the homeowners would accept as reparations a dinner cooked by my boys?"

Eric was clearly trying not to smile. "I personally would accept that as compensation for their troubles, but I won't speak for the

Wickers. They're waiting for me to signal them to join us. Let me ask them if that's acceptable."

While we waited, I asked Finn, "Do you cook?"

He nodded briskly. "I can make toast. And my brothers can cook, too. And I can make bacon if Mommy helps," Finn added.

"I'm a good cook," Rowan said. "But Hudson cooks the best. He can make scrambled eggs. And they are good."

Rowan's enthusiasm for his brother's cooking skills was so sweet. When I looked at Hudson, I could see the tips of his little ears turning pink, but he was smiling and nodding.

I glanced at Mac, and he was beaming from ear to ear. Clearly he was enjoying this charming scene.

Eric joined Mr. and Mrs. Wicker and they walked the rest of the way to our group. When then got here, Mrs. Wicker took a seat on one of the benches. Mr. Wicker remained standing. "I understand that you have a way to pay back your debt."

"Yes, sir," Rowan said. "I'm sorry."

"Me too," Hudson said. "I'm sorry."

"So am I," Finn added.

"Your apology is accepted," Mr. Wicker said. "Now, I hear you boys can cook."

"Yes, we can," Rowan said. "Hudson cooks the best. He makes scrambled eggs."

"Does he?" Mr. Wicker said.

Mrs. Wicker looked at her husband. "That's one of our favorite things."

"Since you make scrambled eggs," Mr. Wicker said, "would you mind if I add my special homemade toast and jam to our menu?"

"You make homemade toast?"

"I make bread," he said. "Homemade bread. And it is delicious, especially when I toast it."

Hudson had to think about this. "And you make jam, too?"

He nodded. "Yes, jam, too, starting with the best fruit we find for the week. This week it's strawberry. Does that suit your menu?"

His eyes widened. "I like strawberry jam."

"I do, too."

Hudson looked as if he were about to jump up and down, then remembered his place. "Is that okay, Mommy?"

Aurora smiled. "I think it sounds delicious."

Hudson didn't say anything, just nodded enthusiastically.

Aurora turned to Mr. Wicker. "Strawberry jam is a particular favorite in our home. Thank you, Mr. Wicker."

"Yes, thank you, Mr. Wicker," Hudson said politely and then asked, "Do you like bacon?"

"Bacon is one of my favorites."

Hudson beamed. "Mine too. Can we have bacon, Mommy?"

"Of course, sweetheart," Aurora said, running her fingers gently through Hudson's hair. "We want to make this a very special breakfast—or dinner—for Mr. and Mrs. Wicker. Do you know why?"

Hudson looked at his mom for support, then turned to Logan, who gave a quick nod. Finally he stared directly at Mr. Wicker. "Because we were going to steal from you, but then we didn't."

"That's right, darling," Aurora said. "And we want to make sure that this breakfast is up to the standards Mr. and Mrs. Wicker expect every day."

Mr. Wicker sat down on the nearest bench. "Hudson, can you come and sit with me for a minute?" He patted the empty bench next to him.

"Okay." Hudson walked over and sat down next to Mr. Wicker.

Eric took that moment to join Chloe on the bench. She squeezed his hand and he held on to hers.

Hudson looked up at Mr. Wicker and smiled at the man, and my heart almost broke. I could hear several people sniffling, and one of them was Chloe. And one of them was me. Mac moved closer and put his arm around me.

"So tell me, Hudson," Mr. Wicker asked. "What color were you hoping your mother's bathrobe would be?"

"I wanted to find a blue robe to match her eyes."

I glanced at Mr. Wicker and even his eyes looked a little damp.

I had to wipe my eyes and I wasn't the only one. If Aurora didn't find a lovely blue bathrobe under the tree on Christmas morning, I would eat my power drill.

Chloe used a tissue to blot the tears from her eyes.

I leaned closer and whispered, "I think we just experienced our own little version of a Christmas miracle."

Chapter Fourteen

Two days before Christmas, Lilian called to invite us to an impromptu cocktail party at the Cliffs Hotel bar. I pushed the speaker button so Mac could hear.

"We have no more Christmas dinners to be served, and we've shut down the Fun Zone for the weekend. And even though the hotel is packed, we're setting aside a section of the bar for our special friends." Then she chuckled lightly. "Somehow, our list of special friends keeps growing. But you're on the list and it'll be fun. Santa Steve will be here, and you'll see plenty of other friends as well. And please feel free to invite others if you'd like."

"It sounds lovely," I said. "We'll be there." And I would bet my Christmas candy that Santa Steve would show up in his full Santa regalia.

"Oh," she said, "and it's casual. No killer heels, please. Be comfortable."

"That sounds even better."

"But I've been dying to wear my killer heels," Mac cried, and we all laughed.

We mentioned the invitation to my dad and Belinda and Uncle Pete, who all politely declined. "I really want to chill out right here and then walk to the pier," Dad said.

"That sounds wonderful," Belinda agreed.

Pete grinned. "I've got a date with a lovely lady I've known for years, so you all go out and enjoy yourselves, and so will I."

Mac texted Callie, who thanked us for the invitation but said she was getting together at the pub with some Lighthouse Cove friends she'd known ever since her uncle Mac moved here.

Then I called Chloe, who quickly informed me that she and Eric were invited as well.

"That's perfect," I said. "We'll see you there."

The first person we ran into was Lilian, who wore a long skirt and a sleeveless denim shirt with Birkenstocks. "So you weren't kidding about the killer heels," I said with a laugh.

"I'm totally casual tonight," she said. "And so is Bill. I can't speak for the kids, but I warned them." She laughed and rolled her eyes. "Like they would listen to me about wardrobe choices. Anyway, please come in, order a drink, and relax."

We did as we were told and went to the bar. "The usual?" Craig asked jovially.

"Can't go wrong with scotch," Mac said.

"And I'll have the Winter White Cosmo," I said.

He grinned, obviously in a better state of mind than he'd been for the last few days. "Coming right up. And if you want another drink, just wave. I've got a couple of extra bartenders coming in a few minutes."

"Great," I said. "Thanks, Craig."

"There you are."

I turned and found Chloe standing in front of me, with Eric holding her hand.

"Hello, you two," I said, giving each of them a hug. "Merry Christmas."

Mac grabbed our drinks when Craig delivered them and we stepped aside so that Eric and others could order. Then we found a table and pulled up a couple of extra chairs so we could enjoy ourselves.

I looked up and saw Logan walk in with Aurora, and I thought they looked perfect together. She looked lovely, if a little pale still. I knew they weren't officially a couple, but I had a feeling it wouldn't be long before they made that announcement.

I whispered to Mac, "I wonder how nervous Aurora is to be surrounded by Logan's family."

Mac, meanwhile, had been observing the same thing. "Lilian and Bill both look thrilled to see Logan, and they seem curious about Aurora. Stephanie is grinning from ear to ear, and I'm wondering if that means that she has already secretly met Aurora and maybe the little boys."

"Oh, that would be nice."

"Oliver just walked in and Stephanie looks gobsmacked."

Gobsmacked was one of Mac's favorite words, and he tried to use it once in every book he wrote.

"Can you see why?" I asked.

"Yes. Because I'm pretty sure she's crazy about Oliver. But nobody can know that since her husband is standing behind the bar. Oh, Oliver is standing at the bar with Bill Garrison, so that's interesting."

"Something tells that there will be some changing partners in the New Year."

"That's fascinating." I touched Mac's hand. "You're doing a fine play-by-play, but I really need to turn around to see everyone's faces."

"No problem." Mac gallantly stood and scooted my chair around to give me a better view of the action.

I stretched up and kissed him. "Thank you."

"And this is interesting," Mac said, still watching the action.

I took a sip of my cocktail. "What? Who's here? Now I have to face the other way?"

Mac laughed. "No, it's just Craig. He's trying not to look as apoplectic as he feels."

"Why do you think he's freaking out?"

"Because he just now noticed that Oliver has joined Bill at the bar, and they're having a jolly old time. As if they're old friends."

"Why would Craig care?" I held up my hand. "Wait. I just remembered. He's jealous of Oliver, so if Oliver is laughing with Bill, that's enough to make Craig crazy."

"Exactly," Mac said with a grin.

"Oh dear." I didn't have the best feeling about this situation. I glanced around. "Where's Stephanie now?"

Mac leaned in close. "At the far end of the bar. Can you see her talking to Chloe? Standing next to the chief of police?"

"I see her." I frowned. "And I'm really glad Eric is nearby."

"Just in case Craig has any homicidal thoughts about doing away with Oliver?"

"Exactly. Or Stephanie."

Mac gave me a funny look. "You're really nervous."

"I'm getting a bad vibe."

"About what?" he asked.

"I don't know, but Joyce just walked in, and she does not look happy."

"Okay." Mac rubbed my shoulder. "Thanks for the rundown. Let's just chill out for a minute. Do you want another cocktail?"

I stared at my empty drink. I hadn't realized I'd drunk the whole thing. "Yes, I'd like the same, please."

Mac held up his hand to signal Craig.

Craig sauntered over to our table. "Two more of the same?" he asked. His tone was not quite as cheerful as it had been a little while ago, although he was attentive.

"Yes, please. Oh, Craig," I added, "what is this garnish you use? It's like a combination Christmas herbal spice thing?"

"I call it the Cliffs Bay Rum."

"Bay rum. That's an aftershave, isn't it?"

He chuckled. "Yeah. My dad used to wear it all the time, and I did, too, until Stephanie told me she didn't like it. I guess it made her sick or something. Whatever." He rolled his eyes. "But I still wear it sometimes when I'm at work. Because *some people* like it."

I smiled. "You mean, some women like it."

He grinned. "You get me."

"I do." I smiled. "You know, I've been down in the north cellar a few times, and I keep smelling a similar scent to this one. A little bit of clove, some orange peel, nutmeg. Do you know what that's all about?"

His eyes grew wide and he swallowed a few times, then he turned and went back to the bar.

"Was that a no?" I whispered at his back.

He ignored me, of course. But as I watched his face turn redder and his movements grow more erratic, I realized I'd hit the mark. The man had to be guilty as sin.

"Oh crap," I muttered.

"What just happened?" Mac asked.

"I just figured out who Shirley Ann's killer is."

He wrapped his arm around me. "What are you talking about?"

"But wait. If he killed Shirley Ann, he must've killed Randi, too."

"Sweetheart," Mac said, staring into my face. "You're talking to yourself. What happened?"

"It's Craig."

"What about Craig?"

"He killed Shirley Ann." I gave him the briefest recap of my conversation.

"I'm not sure that means he killed her."

"Trust me. As soon as I mentioned the north cellar and that Christmasy clove aroma, he freaked, then quickly turned and went back to the bar. And I just looked at him again, and he's staring at me like he wants to throttle me." I suddenly couldn't help but touch my neck defensively.

Mac turned to watch Craig, who immediately turned and checked his glassware, grabbed a bar towel, and began cleaning a highball glass.

Ugh, I thought, rolling my eyes. He was suddenly Mr. Innocent.

"I'll get Eric and we'll have a talk with Craig."

"It might not help."

But Mac left to find Eric, and as soon as he was out of the room,

I watched Craig leave the bar and head straight for me. His face was mottled and his teeth were clenched. His hands were tightly gripped. He was already out of control. It didn't take much.

"Who do you think you are?" he demanded. "Sticking your nose into everybody's business."

"Calm down, Craig."

"Randi was right about you," he said.

I was instantly on guard, planting my feet firmly on the floor. I would either run or strike back if he attacked me.

Craig's eyes had glazed over, as if he'd gone to another place and time in his mind.

Taking a chance, I asked, "Did you hurt her?"

"She was such a pain in the neck." But he said it fondly.

"But you loved her," I whispered.

"We planned to move away from here."

"That would've been a good idea," I said.

"She was ready to go, and then Lilian came up with that hare-brained idea."

"The renovation project? She was going to pay the winner a lot of money."

"Yeah."

He seemed to be dreaming and I wasn't about to wake him up.

"Did she want to move away with you?"

"Yeah. Until she realized that she could make more money staying here and winning that stupid contest."

"But then you could leave after she won the money."

He looked at me then, and I could tell that he was no longer dreaming. His expression had turned ugly.

"She told me she would have to work with Logan to win that money. And I heard it in her voice. She was never going to leave this hellhole. And it just made me so mad."

"You could've moved after the contest was over."

"No!" he insisted. "I was tired of waiting for her to make up her damn mind."

He was half out of his mind, I thought. But he was still dangerous. I took a step back.

"What did you do, Craig?"

His grin was pure evil. "We were in her office in the wine cellar. I was so mad. She stormed out, I grabbed the nearest thing I could find to hurt her, and I whipped it across her throat." He stared at his hands. Was he seeing all the blood?

He must've grabbed the drywall knife that Sean had left in her new office.

"What did you do then?"

He blew out a heavy breath. "I moved her to the couch and covered her in blankets. I wanted her to be comfortable. She was so beautiful, but she made me so angry."

The music was loud and the crowd was cheerful, but I saw Stephanie a few feet away, staring at Craig. Mac had come back into the room and looked ready to grab him.

How many people had heard Craig's confession?

Craig stirred as if he'd just awakened. He looked at me, confused and disoriented.

"You okay?" I asked.

His eyes changed again, and he snarled as he grabbed me and shouted to the crowd, "I'll kill her!"

Mac was poised to attack, but before he could make a move, Joyce

let out a jungle shriek and jumped on Craig's back! "You killed Shirley Ann! I'll kill you!"

"Get off me!" Craig shouted.

Joyce wrapped her arms around his neck and squeezed. "How
does that feel, you creep?"

His face turned even redder and he tried to cough.

Stephanie stood in front of Craig, looking remarkably calm, but
I could tell she was seething mad. She didn't make a move to
help him.

Craig tried bucking Joyce off him, but she was stuck like a burr
to his back.

"Admit it!" Joyce shouted. "You killed Shirley Ann."

"So what if I did?" he said, his voice raspy from her choke hold.
"She was just a stupid cocktail waitress. But she saw us. I had to shut
her up."

"Just a stupid cocktail waitress?" Joyce screamed at him. "She
could shake a margarita better than you could ever do. And she had
style. All you've got is a weak chin."

He tried to buck her off again.

"The only reason you have your job," Joyce continued, "is because
you married the boss's daughter. And she's a thousand times better
than you'll ever be."

All the anger seemed to drain out of Joyce, and she began to slide
off Craig's back. I moved to grab her, but Lilian beat me to it. She
eased Joyce off Craig, wrapped an arm around her, and pushed her
over to a safe spot.

Craig had forgotten all about me as he stared daggers at Stephanie.

I watched Mac and Eric move in to grab Craig's arms.

"You idiot," Stephanie said.

"I've had it with your crap!" he shouted, trying to pull away from Mac and Eric. "You tried to ruin my life."

"How did I do that?" she asked.

"Don't play dumb with me. You and your mother concocted that whole renovation charade and offered that cash prize, all so that Randi would stay with Logan to win the money."

"I can't help it if your girlfriend was a money-grubbing husband-stealing slut! She wrapped you around her little finger and made you dance to her tune every time. You're pathetic."

"And you're a cold witch," he countered, but there wasn't much fury in his words. He was still coughing from Joyce's choke hold.

"Did you think I wouldn't know that you and Randi-Dandy were running off to the cellar every night as if nobody was watching?"

Somehow he managed to free his arm from Mac's grip and back-handed her once. Everyone gasped. There were screams and shouts as others saw what had happened. Stephanie looked shocked for just a brief moment, then she smacked him across the face so hard that every single person in the room could surely feel the sting.

Mac started to confront Craig, but then Oliver rushed forward and punched Craig once, and he went down.

"Back away!" Eric shouted in his awesomely authoritative way, and the crowd moved like the Red Sea to let Eric get through to Craig. Oliver was holding Stephanie, which must have infuriated Craig, but I didn't care. I looked around for Joyce, but she was safe on the sidelines with Lilian and Bill. They sat on either side of her and held her hand. It seemed to calm all three of them.

Before I knew what was happening, Mac had me in his arms.

"Damn it," he whispered. "Can't leave you alone for a minute."

"Yeah, sorry about that." I could hear my voice shaking and had to take a deep breath. "I'm glad you made it back."

"I saw your confrontation with Craig. You calmed him down enough to extract a confession from him."

"I think he was unbalanced. He kept going in and out of reality. But I knew he would attack me at some point, and I was ready for him."

"I wanted to kill him when he grabbed you, but I wasn't close enough," he said. "Luckily, we've got a few heroes surrounding us."

"Right. Who knew?"

Eric had called for backup, and several of his officers were streaming into the bar.

Craig was up on his feet, screaming at Oliver now, but a couple of Eric's men were holding him back. Stephanie was trying to convince Oliver to let her go so she could kick Craig in all the right places. Bill and Lilian approached Craig and demanded to know what he was up to.

"Ask your daughter. She seems to know everything. The only thing she doesn't know is how to satisfy a man."

Bill surprised everyone by punching Craig so hard he collapsed. "That's for my little girl, you jerk."

Stephanie started laughing so hard that she had to sit down. "Thanks, Dad. I owe you one."

Now half the bar was laughing while the other was itching for a fight.

Eric and three officers moved in just in time to save Craig from the crowd. They picked him up off the floor and carried him out of the hotel.

Joyce had moved a little closer to the action and pounded her fist against the palm of her hand. "Darn. I wanted to hit him for Shirley Ann."

I smiled. "You choked him pretty good."

"Shirley Ann knew it was Craig who killed Randi," Joyce said. "If only she'd told us."

Stephanie heard and shook her head. "What a loser."

Joyce gasped and turned around. "Oh, I'm sorry, Stephanie. I didn't realize you were close enough to hear that."

"Don't feel sorry for me," she insisted in a clear voice, then turned and faced the crowd. "Don't anyone feel sorry for me. I'm rid of that creep, and I'll never have to spend another minute with him again."

I turned to Mac and whispered, "Now that's what I call a happy ending."

"Well put." He laughed out loud, then pulled me in for a kiss. "Merry Christmas, sweetheart."

"Merry Christmas to you, too."

Stephanie grabbed Lilian and Bill and hugged them tightly. "Thank you, Mom and Dad."

Lilian sniffled and I knew she was crying a little. "We love you, honey."

"I love you, too. Merry Christmas."

I had to laugh. All of these people, including me, had been in mortal combat a few minutes ago. Now we were wishing everyone a merry Christmas.

Mac caught my gaze and started laughing, too.

Lilian came and hugged us, then said, "There's something in your truck, Shannon."

"There is?" I frowned, wondering. "What is it?"

"I think it's a Christmas present for Mac."

"Oh! Thank you for remembering! With all the craziness, I completely forgot!"

"Well, I didn't," she said, and hugged us both. "You've been such good friends to us. I hope you enjoy it and have a very happy holiday.

"Same to you, Lilian."

"What was that all about?" Mac asked.

"You'll know when you see what's in my truck."

"I can't wait." And he kissed me again.

But suddenly, we were all distracted as Arabella came forward and wrapped her arms around Stephanie.

"Oh," Lilian whispered. "My girls."

"I hope you're not too badly hurt." Arabella gave her sister a soft kiss on the cheek where Craig had smacked her. "He doesn't deserve you."

Stephanie sniffled. "Thank you, sweetie."

And then Arabella shocked me even more when she turned to me and said, "Merry Christmas, Shannon."

I blinked a few times and nodded. "Merry Christmas to you, too, Arabella."

Franco came forward and took Arabella's hand and kissed it. Then they walked out of the bar.

"Wow," I whispered.

Mac took my hand. "Are you okay?"

"I thought I was. But Craig being carted away to jail wasn't as big a shock as Arabella's words. Did you hear her?"

Mac smiled. "Yeah. Christmas miracles keep piling up."

"I think I'm going to cry."

"You can cry all you want. You'll never be anything but a super-hero in my eyes."

"Oh." I sighed with pleasure at his words.

Someone took my hand, and I turned to see Santa Claus!

"Merry Christmas, Shannon. Merry Christmas, Mac."

"Merry Christmas, Santa Steve," we both said.

"Ho ho ho! Merry Christmas to all!" he shouted, and then made his way through the crowd, wishing each person happy times and good wishes.

"Well, that does it." My tears welled up and began to fall. "Superhero, huh?"

"Believe it," he murmured.

That's when Chloe moved in and gave me a hug. "Lots of little miracles happening these days."

"Yeah," I said, sniffling. "Mac just said the same thing."

"Well, here's another one," she said, and held out her hand to show me the most beautiful diamond ring I'd ever seen.

"Oh my God, it's gorgeous. Is that my Christmas present? You shouldn't have."

She was laughing as she slapped my arm, and I gave her a big hug. "It's beautiful, Sis. I love you and I'm so happy for you."

"I'm happy, too."

There were more hugs and the tears kept coming.

I found Eric standing nearby and hugged him, too.

Mac came up behind me and pulled me into his arms for another tight hug. "Have I told you lately that I love you?" he said.

I kissed him. "Not for at least six minutes."

He grinned. "Well, I do. You are the love of my life."

I pressed my forehead to his. "And you're mine."

We stood like that for another few seconds, and then he said, "Quite a Christmas, eh?"

Looking around at a scene that could've been horrific but was turning out to be so much better than I could've ever dreamed of, I had to laugh.

"Quite," I said, and kissed him.

ACKNOWLEDGMENTS

As always, I am grateful to work with so many wonderfully talented and dedicated people, especially:

My ultrafantastic executive editor, Michelle Vega, along with the outstanding team at Berkley who always makes me and my books look brilliant and beautiful;

My superagent, Christina Hogrebe, and everyone at Jane Rotrosen Agency;

My true miracle-worker assistant, Jenel Looney;

My ingenious plot besties, Jenn McKinlay and Paige Shelton;

And finally, my handsome and clever husband, Don, who is always there to guide me through the treacherous world of drywall knives, grommets, and Christmas cocktails. Love you always!